Eadric
~and the~
Wolves

A Novel of the Danish
Conquest of England

David K. Mullaly

This is a work of fiction. Although it reflects very limited available information about certain historical people and events, it is primarily a product of the author's imagination, and should be viewed as such.

This novel is dedicated to Mardell, my wonderful wife, partner, and friend, who has put up with more of my Viking obsessions than I had any right to expect from her.

Introduction

This novel looks at the period before and just after the Danish Conquest of England involving Sweyn Forkbeard and his son Cnut, primarily through the perspective of Eadric of Mercia. The man rose from obscurity to become both a powerful political leader under the English king Aethelred II, and an important military ally of Cnut as well.

If one takes at face value the cumulative portrait of the man based on the accusations of a series of Church chroniclers, Eadric was a corrupt, evil official who stole land from the Church for personal gain, and an immoral animal responsible for multiple murders. Plus, he committed treason on a grand scale. In 2005 he was selected by the BBC History Magazine as the worst Briton of the 11th century. This portrait is very different.

The novel includes the major events that historians believe happened during the life of this controversial individual. However, I have added a good bit to the story and Eadric's role in these events, just as the hit musical *Hamilton* has blended actual history and magical creativity. Think of this as a written docudrama, trying to fill in a few of the huge gaps in our knowledge about the medieval past and the real people who lived during that time.

This narrative reconstruction is at least as plausible as the accounts from Church historians at the time, almost all of whom lived a century or more after Eadric's death, and who had a very large ax to grind. The *Comment On The History* at the end of the narrative discusses some of the issues in greater detail.

Southern England
at 1000 A.D

Important Note: The Map Appendix at the end of the book provides four detailed maps giving a clear visual explanation of events during the time period 1012-1016 in England, when the Viking Conquest of that country took place.

The maps were drawn by the late Reginald Piggott, and provided by the Department of Anglo-Saxon, Norse, and Celtic of the University of Cambridge. I am grateful to that department and the University for the high resolution images provided for my use.

Chapter One
October 18, 1016

The battle was approaching like a dark and violent storm, and all the soldiers could do was wait for it. They were standing around in small groups, but any conversations were brief, and men avoided the subject of combat. That it was a sunny, crisp autumn morning went unnoticed. The army was on a large, broad hill, men scattered amidst a forest of mighty ash trees standing leafless and silent. There were dramatic views in all directions, including the quiet settlement at Walden south of there, and Assandun immediately to the east.

The soldiers had marched for some days from their homes in Mercia, and they were neither rested nor combat ready. Most of them, leaning on their spears or sitting on their small round shields, seemed like they were about to collapse from fatigue. In fact, a few of them looked asleep on their feet. Many who weren't exhausted were bored.

Some men were sharpening their weapons, although the edges were already like razors. A few appeared to be praying. There were small circles of soldiers competing to see who could spin a seax in the air the most times before having the blade stick in the ground. For some, searching for fleas in their beards and hair was preferable to just standing there. One man seemed to be puzzling over some marked pieces of bone, trying to predict what would happen that day.

They were waiting to assemble for their final orders, anticipating a battle that day against a large Viking army led by Cnut, whose father Sweyn Forkbeard had briefly been king of all

England. For some of the soldiers, very little was known about Cnut, except that his armies had been involved in several battles over much of southern England. For others, it was a confusing situation. They had actually fought alongside the Vikings earlier in the year, and now they were being told to see the same allies as enemies, and their enemies as allies.

A warrior whose status was apparent from his silver-inlaid sword hilt and scabbard and the chain mail covering his upper body looked around at the nearby soldiers, shook his head, and grinned. He glanced over at a similarly dressed man who was gazing at the sky, lost in his thoughts. "My lord Eadric, these men look about as happy to be here as you do. Perhaps you could tell some of them a joke?"

He expected the sort of friendly and clever reaction that was typical of his leader's relationship with him, but he was clearly in no mood for a humorous exchange, and didn't immediately reply.

Eadric, a handsome man with quick blue eyes and long blond hair tied behind, always seemed to carry the burdens of his office as though they were nothing at all, but today was different. He hesitated for some moments, considering whether he should respond at all. Then he spoke quietly, so only his deputy could hear him.

"None of us want to be here, Wenric. Even Edmund Ironside really doesn't want me--or us--to be here. He only accepted another alliance with me because he needed to. He does not trust me any more than I trust him, but without the warriors from Mercia he will likely lose this fight, and probably the crown. And he knows it."

He smiled, muttered to himself "and little else," and gazed at the large number of soldiers scattered on the tree-covered hill. Most of these men were not trained warriors. They came in all sizes and shapes, and they wore nothing that suggested that they were members of the same army. They were part of the Mercian fyrd: farmers, craftsmen and tradesmen who were obligated to arm themselves when their ealdorman called on them to gather and fight for him.

In truth, many of them were angry about being at

Assandun that day. They had personally known neighbors and relatives whose houses and steads had been robbed and burned by the king's forces some months ago, and they had no desire to have anything to do with Edmund Ironside, let alone fight for him. However, all of these men had sworn an oath to serve their ealdorman, the crops had already been harvested, and they had no choice but to march with him to Essex. There they would fight next to some of the same men who had recently ravaged large areas of western Mercia.

Eadric walked a little apart from where many of his men had gathered, and looked down the hill and to the west, where a large open area would be the likely battlefield. He knew that Edmund would send for him shortly, and give him his battle orders. He would play the part that he needed to play, and say nothing about his actual intentions. However, he was certain, after he left Edmund's tent, that he would surely remember the oath he made to a murdered friend long ago, a commitment that he was finally in a position to honor. And he would remember someone he had loved and lost.

He smiled once again. Things had worked out exactly as he had hoped they would after he'd left Cnut's service some weeks earlier. If he truly wanted an opportunity to alter the course of the war between the English and the Vikings, it lay there before him like a feast before a hungry man. He was ready.

Chapter Two
Watching The River

Mortal danger entered Eadric's small world in the woodlands of Mercia early in his life. He was in his eighth year, and his experiences up until then had been blissfully uneventful. He had been too young to remember the death of his mother, and there seemed little to fear in the surrounding forests except for the occasional wild boar or wolf.

He was a well-formed boy with pale blond hair and bright, active blue eyes, very different from the brown hair and brown eyes of all six brothers and a sister who filled their large timber-built home with so much noise. A suspicious man might have guessed that a clever Dane had slipped in through the back door and shared some pleasure with Eadric's mother, but she had never done anything that would have aroused suspicions. His father Aethelric, a prosperous thegn who was frequently away from home on what he called "the king's business," never treated Eadric as anything but his legitimate son.

His aunt Brytha, a surly woman with few teeth, was in charge of the household when the father was gone, and she was clearly happiest when the youngest children were outside, doing whatever it was that children did when they weren't supervised. She didn't know, and she didn't care to know. She watched and scolded the thralls who cooked and cleaned, and that was all she felt any obligation to do.

Eadric loved the freedom that his aunt's indifference provided. He made friends with every free born child close to his age within walking distance of his home, and explored every inch of the other farms and steads surrounding his own. He and his brother Brihtric and several other children would walk all the way to the river, and wait for hours to catch fish on their hooked lines. They sometimes captured frogs and set up races to see whose favorite won the prize, which was being set free. The losing frogs weren't so lucky: the evening meal was particularly tasty after those races.

In the spring of 997, a large fleet of Viking ships from Denmark sailed around the southwestern tip of England, passing Cornwall and Devon, and entered the wide mouth of the Severn River, where raiders began to attack settlements, churches, and monasteries in both English and Welsh lands. Towns were burned, people murdered, and plunder seized. Word was quickly sent to Worcestre, the only fortified town or burh on the Severn, and then on to thegns further up the river in the north of Mercia. Nobody knew where the Viking raiders would go next.

A neighboring thegn personally conveyed the alarming news to Eadric's father, who waited until the rest of the family assembled for the evening meal before addressing the situation with all of his children.

Aethelric didn't mince words. "Pay attention now. I have something that I need to share with all of you, but I don't want any of you to panic. Don't let fear rule you--I am looking at you, pretty Goda. We have a dangerous situation at the south end of the Severn River. There are two dozen or possibly more Viking ships filled with raiders attacking area settlements there, and we don't know their intentions. They could easily come up the river as far as Shrewsbury within a short time, so we are in danger. What should we do? I need your suggestions or ideas. Now is the time to make plans."

Each child glanced at the faces of the others, looking for guidance, but none of them spoke.

"I'm directing this at you, Aethelwine, Aelfric, and Beohtric, my three oldest sons. You've each passed your twelfth birthday and are now adults, and thegns like me. You need to have a role in defending our lands and our workers. The rest of you should pay attention to our discussion here, because all of you boys will some day become thegns as well, and will need to respond to dangers of your own. Plus, it may save your lives, and the virtue of your sister Goda, should the Vikings ever come up the river in force."

He was determined to get his children to take part in dealing with the crisis, and not simply to depend on him for all of the answers. The younger ones looked anxious, with his daughter almost in tears, and even the older sons were reluctant to offer anything useful.

Aethelwine, the oldest son, knew he should be the first to speak. "Father, what can we do to respond to this danger? Are we on our own, or are there others we can turn to for help?" He was stroking his chin, perhaps hoping to stimulate the growth of a beard, which had thus far failed to appear in any form.

"That's a good beginning, two questions worth asking! I can't answer them yet, but you and your two brothers are going to ride with me to Worcestre right away to find out what the authorities are prepared to do."

"Father, what can the rest of us do while you are gone? What can we do to help?" Everyone looked over at Eadric, a little surprised to see that he was the next to speak, although they shouldn't have been. They had seen him becoming more assertive every day.

"I was hoping someone would ask that. We'll probably be away no more than two days. We should be able to learn without any delay how the authorities in that town plan to respond. Before our return, I need you boys to visit every stead within walking distance and warn them of the peril that might be coming up the river. Tell them to arm themselves."

"The two older boys, who know how to ride, should go farther afield and warn others, including those who live around the settlement. Eadric, I put you in charge of talking to every free man who works on this estate. They must find something suitable as a weapon to defend themselves if it comes to that. Goda, help your aunt to assist the thralls in making bread and drying out some meat in case we need to move to a safer place, or flee into the woods."

Aelfric, the tallest of the boys, had a nagging concern. "Father, can we count on the Danes living nearby as allies, or are they likely to side with the Vikings?"

The father took a deep breath. "Well, we need to know who our friends and enemies are. Although we cannot be certain, I suspect that they will be in danger as much as we will be. Viking raiders will take plunder from them just as they will from us. Those of you visiting our neighbors to warn them should be certain that you include all the Danes. If trouble comes, we will need armed support from them as well."

After Aethelric rode away with the three oldest sons, the situation felt much darker and more ominous for the children left behind. Instead of their father's knowing hand and his calm demeanor, they were left with their aunt Brytha, who was as worried as the youngest child, and even less interested in contributing to their efforts. They felt like they were on their own, and worried about whether they could live up to their father's expectations. There was no talking at the evening meal, and nobody seemed to have much of an appetite. Getting to sleep later wasn't easy for any of them.

However, early the next morning, Goda began her day by directing the kitchen thralls to help her make some bread with rye grain left over from the last harvest, grinding it in a hand-mill, and baking small thin loaves in the baking oven near the great hall. She went through with her aunt the stock of dried and salted meat still remaining in the larder, and they both concluded that they had enough for an emergency. More animals could be slaughtered on short notice if the need arose.

The four boys awoke to their sister already hard at work. Eadric, who had the closest relationship with his sister, told his brothers that her efforts were making them look bad, and their embarrassment drove any lingering fear out of their minds.

The two boys old enough to ride, Alchred and Aethelweard, saddled horses and went in opposite directions to alert every thegn and free man outside of easy walking distance about the danger downriver. Aethelmar started walking to nearby steads to raise the alarm, and Eadric visited the home of every free man on their estate.

Unlike his brothers, Eadric had a way of talking with the men and women who worked for his family which told them that he was respectful of them and their efforts, despite their humbler

13

station, so he was a welcome visitor to their homes. He smiled when a mother showed him her baby, and he always laughed at the jokes of the men, even when he didn't completely understand them. His father was beloved because of his casual generosity, but Eadric was the favorite child among the people who labored for the family.

By the time the weary men returned from Worcestre somewhat less than two days later, everything the father had asked of his other children had been done. Although they expected him to be pleased, they could tell that he was in a black mood, which was a rarity for him. He and his older sons put off any discussion until the evening meal of fish and rye bread was finished.

After everyone was done eating, and a few candles were lit, Aethelric put his elbows on the board, rested his head on his hands, and began. "Our long trip was worth taking, because we got important information, but we were told that we can look for no help from anyone but ourselves."

"We were brought to see Ealdwulf, the bishop of Worcestre, a very pious man, and he was sympathetic to our concerns, but he refused to do anything against the Vikings if they come north. He is determined to defend the town and its church behind its fortifications, and nothing more. Curse the priest for his damnable caution!"

Alchred spoke up. "Did he give you a reason?"

"Of course. He explained that over one hundred years ago, King Alfred set up a series of fortifications called burhs, which were scattered around Wessex to protect key towns from the great Viking armies that were rampaging throughout southern England. Worcestre was one of those burhs. So the bishop intends to do nothing to stop any Vikings going up the Severn past the walls of the burh at Worcestre, and we have to try to defend ourselves."

"Sadly, he is ignoring what has changed: things are not as they used to be. There are no massive Viking armies threatening to take over the whole country; the survival of England is not in question. So there is no need to set up islands of safety in a sea of invaders. These are bands of raiders, not conquerors, but I'm sure the bishop looks to the past for guidance, and I also suspect that protecting his precious church in Worcestre is a priority for him."

Aethelwine then remembered something else about the meeting. "The bishop did inform us that if the Vikings did come north, we were welcome to come to the town--of course bringing food and supplies for ourselves--and avail ourselves of its protection. However, as our father pointed out to him, if the raiders did sail in our direction, by the time we found out and could travel towards Worcestre, they would probably already be past the burh and able to prevent us from getting there. The bishop offered to pray for us." The boy shook his head.

Everyone sitting around the board was silent, and the flickering candles provided a soft glow around them in the now dark interior of the great hall. The night seemed all around them, and Aethelric knew he had to say something reassuring to his children. "Enough about this for now. I want you all to try to sleep tonight. Tomorrow we will plan how we are going to protect ourselves from these savages, and we will use our wits to stay safe."

After a very long night and a quick morning meal, Aethelric explained to his children what he decided they needed to do, having thought about it long into the evening.

"Aethelwine, I would ask you to ride south along the river, and find a stead not far from the Severn and above Worcestre. Whoever the thegn might be, beg him to set up a daytime watch on the river, and to ring his alarm bell if even a single Viking ship is sighted. Every estate is required by the king to have an alarm bell. If he needs some silver for that responsibility, we would be willing to help. Assuming that he agrees, find other steads near the river north of there and ask that they ring their own bells if an alarm is sounded downriver from them."

"I am going to take Brihtric and Aelfric along with me to meet other thegns in the north of Mercia and organize locations where fighters will assemble if Viking trouble comes. Individual thegns cannot defend themselves successfully by themselves. We need to work together to deal with a large raiding party."

Aethelric met quickly with a number of estate owners, and everyone along the river was warned. All of the steads along the river as far north as Shrewsbury were ready to ring their bells if an alarm was sounded downriver. For several weeks, much of Mercia was alert for approaching Vikings, and many people didn't sleep well.

Eadric had the same dream over and over. He saw himself sitting at the board having a quiet meal with his family, and feeling warm and secure in their presence. Suddenly, the door was thrown open and big wild-eyed men covered in hair and animal skins rushed in and started hacking at his brothers with huge axes. One of them grabbed his sister and she began to scream.

He got up from the board and tried to run away from the horror of these savages, but his legs wouldn't move. He was frozen, standing in place, watching as blood flew everywhere and everyone else was being cut down. Finally, one of the attackers spotted him and very slowly walked towards him with his axe held high. As he got closer Eadric could see his rotting teeth, his yellow eyes and filthy beard. The attacker swung his bloody axe back, let out a terrifying inhuman sound, and began to bring it forward for the killing blow. Then the dream suddenly ended, and he awoke with his body sweating and shivering.

His brothers and sister shared stories of similar nightmares, even the older boys who were thought to be adults. The youngest boy refused to tell anyone else that he had wet his bedding more than once. He hadn't experienced that problem since he was a baby. Goda, a gentle girl with long brown hair, began to keep a sharpened seax blade next to her at night, despite Eadric's reassurances.

"Listen Da--his nickname for her--nothing is going to happen to you. I will watch to make sure you are safe. Besides, you are too young to tempt the lust of any raider. And we'll run like the wind if someone comes."

Terror was in the air, and everyone was weary from the constant unknown. In fact, stories circulated of two pregnant women living near the settlement who were so frightened that they miscarried and lost their babies.

Finally, after weeks of this torment, Aethelric received

word from a friend in Wessex that the Vikings had begun moving to the south, attacking settlements and monasteries along the coasts of Devon and Cornwall, and unlikely to sail up the Severn in the near future. People were still being robbed and murdered, but it wasn't them.

At the evening meal, when Aethelric told his family that the danger had passed, they shared some ale and quietly celebrated.

Eadric leaned over to Goda. "You should put that blade away in your coffer. I've been worried that you might cut yourself while you're asleep. Just remember where you put it, in case the danger returns."

She smiled and spoke in a low whisper. "Do you know that right now I am taller than you, and probably stronger than you are? I might be better able to take care of you."

He pretended to look sad. "Of course. But I'd like to keep believing that I am your protector, so don't destroy that story for me. I will grow into the job if Brihtric or Aelfric doesn't kill me first."

He did become her protector, dealing occasionally with boys who didn't treat her with the respect that Eadric thought she deserved. And he continued to be her watchful guardian until some years later when she met and married a friendly and decent thegn from across the river, and she died during childbirth.

The people of Mercia were finally able to relax their vigilance and readiness to defend themselves, and life nearly returned to normal. However, they now shared a common experience with other English men and women who lived near any water that could carry Viking ships to their homes. Every settlement or home near the sea was vulnerable, as well as anywhere near a river that ran to the sea. They knew that a surprise attack was always possible, but they couldn't live their lives in the constant fear that it might happen.

Chapter Three
First Battles

Children cannot resist trying to imitate adults. Whenever Eadric and a group of boys gathered together during pleasant weather, they walked to a nearby meadow to play. During the late spring and summer, the field was covered with tall grasses under a sea of tiny golden flowers, only marred by small areas that were trampled by friendly warfare.

The boys always divided themselves into two evenly matched warrior bands, and role-played English and Vikings. Although a few of the boys living close by dressed a little differently from the others, and they pronounced some words in unexpected ways, their Danish identities had no bearing on who played the Vikings and who played the English.

They would take out the round wicker play shields that Eadric's household thralls had woven for them, distribute the thin blunt sticks that they brought to serve as swords for the occasion, and form two shield walls, playing at combat primarily for the fun of it. However, it also represented early training, since they might as adults find themselves in a real battle.

First, each line would hurl insults at the other. Eadric had been told adult warriors always did that before combat began, so he insisted that each side should follow that tradition.

Eadric always began the exchange. "Your mother is a troll!"

On the other side of the shield wall, perhaps the son of a silversmith would reply. "Your father humps sheep at night!"

Then maybe a boy who stood next to Eadric, and whose father worked on the family estate might shout out, "Your sisters roll in dung, and no one will marry them!"

Then a taller boy from the other side might yell out, "Your women thralls are more manly than you!"

And then one more slur from Eadric's side, "Why are you so afraid, you coward?"

At some point, they would begin to push against the other shield wall, take wild overhead swings with their sticks, and some would try to poke legs below their wicker shields.

Nobody was seriously injured during these battles, nothing more than a scuffed knee, a split lip from an over-zealous "sword" swing, or at worst a bloody nose. Eadric found himself becoming comfortable leading whatever shield wall he joined, even though he was never the biggest or strongest member of the group. He was effective as an organizer, and most of the others boys were comfortable following his lead. Even his older sibling Brihtric listened to him.

One late spring day, two brothers, who were sons of a leather tanner who had recently brought his family to the settlement, joined the usual soldiers in the group. They were standing in the wide meadow where they held their regular war games, and the new boys introduced themselves as Leofric and Leofhelm. Both looked and acted like they'd be willing to begin an argument for no good reason, and each stood a half head taller than Eadric and most of the other boys.

Both unfortunately smelled faintly of urine, a necessary part of their father's tanning business. However, the other boys were grateful for some new combatants, so they welcomed the brothers despite the odor and the attitudes. Everyone suspected that they could add some intensity to the shield walls.

As usual, Eadric began to divide the boys into two groups. Right after he placed one of the brothers in a different army from the other, both started yelling. Leofric was the louder of the two. "What are you doing, you dwarf? We don't fight on opposite sides. Who said you could tell us what to do?"

Eadric started to explain to Leofric that he was trying to create equal sides, and separating the brothers would make that goal easier because they were two of the largest boys—when the other brother came up behind him and knocked him down with a hard forearm to the head. Eadric was momentarily stunned, but before he could begin to get to his feet, another boy walked in front of him, and stood there facing Leofhelm.

He had a slight smile on his face, but his eyes were as cold as his words. "You don't want to do that again, you son of a turd." Leofhelm started to say something defiant and the other boy grabbed his right hand and squeezed it very tightly. "Be very careful with your words right now. Do you want to work with your left hand for the rest of your life?"

Eadric spoke while still sitting on the ground. "Let them go. No harm done. I'll be fine."

The boy released the hand of the tanner's son. The two brothers looked at each other and then at him, and they slowly backed away from the group without saying another word. Combat was obviously over for the day, and most of the warriors returned home.

The other boy helped Eadric to his feet and introduced himself. "I'm Thorunn, son of Thorunn, and my family and I live not far from your estate. Are you sure you're able to walk without falling down?"

He was at least as tall as either of the tanner brothers, and definitely stouter. Until now, Eadric had never exchanged more than a few words with him, but they had been both opponents and allies on their shield walls and, given how well the boy had fought, Eadric very much preferred being an ally. He was obviously a Dane, and that difference interested Eadric, who had never had any real contact with one. Plus, he had the same light blond hair, and Eadric was happy to find somebody who looked more like him.

He knew that there weren't many Danes in the area. He also suspected that many of them were pagans, not Christians like everyone he knew. However, he sometimes wondered about his own beliefs. His father only took them to the small church at Wenlock Priory when he was at home, which was infrequent, and they seldom said a prayer before eating, except when he was there. Whenever they attended mass, the priest was always telling unbelievable stories about a Saint Milburga and her miracles, and Eadric wanted nothing to do with that church.

After considering how the Dane had acted and handled

himself, Eadric decided that he and Thorunn were meant to be friends, and it seemed that Thorunn had concluded the same thing. They walked back together to Eadric's home stead, and shared a meal of cold beef, beans, and hard bread with his brothers and sister. Of course, that was over the quiet objections of his aunt, complaining about having yet another mouth to feed. Thorunn indicated that he had never eaten beef before, so it was a treat for him. Afterwards, the two made plans to go fishing at the river.

On the way to the river the next morning, Thorunn showed Eadric the modest bow-sided house that the Dane and his family called home. Eadric had never seen a building quite like this one. It was narrow at each end, and then got wider in the middle, where the door was. It almost looked like the hull of a large boat that had been turned upside down. Eadric met his father, also called Thorunn, and his mother and two sisters.

When the boys approached the dwelling, the father strode out to meet them like he was on an important mission. A big man with a thick red beard and a hearty laugh, he shook the English boy's hand, hustled him and his son into the small hall in the middle of the home and, once inside, called to his wife: "Ilsith, see if we still have some of that nice ale that we enjoyed last evening, and bring some of it at half-strength for the two boys."

His blond-haired wife, putting on a sweet smile, was ready for him and his orders. "I don't believe that there is a thrall ready to do your bidding here, but you could certainly buy one the next time you're down the river to Ireland selling your sorry excuse for fine cloth. Then you can order her about if you'd like."

All the while that she was speaking, she was fetching the ale and finding some water to mix with it, but she wasn't about to let her husband forget who was the master in that home whenever she wished.

"You just wait," the father said loudly. "I am going to beat you with a large stick when we're finally alone." He and his wife couldn't stop laughing after that, and the boys and the two sisters laughed with them.

The elder Thorunn was a superb storyteller, and he had a great many tales worth telling. That first day he talked about how he had fought alongside some men loyal to a king named Harald Bluetooth against warlike invaders near the border of Denmark many years ago; there were major battles with shield walls and great slaughter.

However, he said that he had grown tired of all of that, and with some age and maturity he had found a woman and family much more appealing. England seemed an excellent place for trading opportunities, so he brought his family, and he used the Severn River and the salt sea to profit from the desires among the Irish, both locals and Vikings, for fine cloth, silver, and sometimes pottery.

Eadric liked the whole family, even the two girls called Ingrith and Inga, who were about his age, and who seemed to have little to say to him. They were both very pretty, with single blond braids and clear blue eyes, but his mind was on other things, including the stories of adventure from his friend's father. As he walked home he imagined getting ink designs of twisted dragons on his arms like the father, and having heroic experiences to match them.

The next day, the two sons of the tanner, still angry over the incident from two days before, tried to strike back. Eadric and Thorunn were walking down a path between the Dane's home and the river, and talking about the stories told by Thorunn's father. As they were passing between some massive oak trees with trunks looking like the legs of giants, Leofric lunged from a tree on one side and Leofhelm from one on the other, both brandishing thick wooden clubs.

If the two targets of the attack hadn't been alerted by the faint smell of urine coming from the brothers, it would have gone hard for them. Thorunn, the first to recognize the odor, jerked his head to one side to alert Eadric, and then looked around for trouble. He saw one brother swing his heavy stick wildly at him, but he ducked under and ran right at the attacker, knocking him over. Eadric didn't notice the gesture from his friend, so he wasn't quite so lucky. The other brother hit him heavily on the side of the head, hard enough to send him to the ground, and jumped on top of him. Eadric's head was spinning for a while after that.

What neither brother had anticipated was that Thorunn had recently been given a single-bladed seax knife by his father, and he had started to carry it on his belt after the incident in the meadow. He pulled it out immediately and went on the attack. He lunged at Leofric and cut a shallow gash on the boy's forehead. That caused him to bleed like a stuck pig, the red sliding down and almost covering his face, and taking the fight out of him. The Danish boy then pivoted quickly and held the knife to Leofhelm's throat, pressing just hard enough to break the skin.

"Enough," Thorunn panted. "Your brother is going to carry a nice scar from this. Do you want something worse?" Leofhelm started crying, the other brother held his hand to his bloody head, and the fight was quickly over.

Thorunn leaned over to his new friend, whose head was still a bit fuzzy. "Are you still with us, or are you wandering in Asgard with the gods? You look half dead to me."

Eadric shook his head a few times, slowly got to his knees, and stood up with some difficulty. He summoned up the best smile he could under the circumstances, and tried to make light of his situation. "That was ugly! I think I am still alive and breathing, although it looks like there might be two of you in front of me. I feel like a tree fell on me."

The young Dane turned to the brothers, and glared at each one for a moment. "Leave--now. After this, you animals will stay far away from both Eadric and me. Whenever you see either of us, turn away so that we don't have to look at you again. You won't be told a second time. And you really should take some soap to the river and wash yourselves. A dead toad smells better than you two."

The brothers weren't prepared to confront a bigger Dane wielding a seax, and they left with sudden and undignified haste. As Eadric expected, he and his friend had no further trouble with them. In fact, they never saw the tanner's sons in the settlement again. Their family moved out of the area, and another tanner took advantage of the opportunity to bring his work to the settlement.

Eadric really liked Thorunn's toad remark, although he later came up with some other loathsome animals that would have been equally appropriate, and which he shared with the

Dane. In fact, they wound up spending the better part of the next two days coming up with every revolting or outrageous name that they could imagine: different combinations of human and animal body parts, various kinds of decaying or rotting conditions, and physical actions which were humanly impossible. They were inspired, and they alternated between groaning and laughing at the insults that they created. And the two boys became best friends.

Chapter Four
Lessons

Eadric's father, who spent much of his time dealing with King Aethelred's interests--and about which his family knew almost nothing--arrived home one afternoon, laden with small gifts in his saddlebags for all of his children. There was some pretty ribbon for his daughter, and for his sons there was a wooden spinning top, a little musical pipe carved from different lengths of bone, a pair of wooden cubes with dots on the sides that he called dice, and a few nicely carved animals.

Aethelric was a slight man with an almost completely bald head. His family heard him more than once wryly explaining that his efforts in support of the king and country had cost him most of his hair. He prided himself on dressing with some style, his linen tunic displaying borders with multicolored decoration. But he had also made it clear to his children that living with honor--respecting his obligations and his oaths--was his first priority, and it should be theirs as well.

After the evening meal of pork, bread, and greens was finished, and the two kitchen thralls who did much of the work around the main hall were cleaning the wooden bowls and knives, and unobtrusively eating some of the leftover food, Eadric's father invited him to come along as he walked off some of the food he had eaten. Deep in the woods, and out of sight of their home, the father sat Eadric down on a stump and began to talk to him.

"Sit still for a short time if you can. I have things that I want to tell you that might be wasted on my other children. I know that you're a clever boy, and maybe you will have a good future in Mercia. Who knows what is possible but God?"

He paused for a moment, and then he continued, noticably raising his voice as he gave his son a hard look. "However, I do need your undivided attention. That weasel scampering into the bushes over there is enjoyable to watch, but not quite as important as what I am trying to explain. Pay attention while I am talking to you."

Embarrassed by that scolding, Eadric made sure that he didn't stop staring at his father until Aethelric had finished. The boy's father seldom rebuked him about anything, so Eadric understood that his father had something very important to tell him.

"First, I have arranged for you to learn the basics of both Latin and our own English language, so that you can read and write simple things. Many years ago, the great King Alfred required that all who assisted him in the country's business be able to send and receive written messages, and it is no less urgent now that men know how to speak to each other on parchment or vellum when they are far apart."

Eadric thought about voicing his genuine indifference to that lofty goal, but he didn't want to provoke his father again. Why should he care about getting a message to someone who is far away, or receiving a message from a distant place? Direct conversations were all that he cared about. These messages his father mentioned made no sense to him, but he knew better than to question Aethelric when he was this serious. So he responded as he thought his father would like.

"That sounds like it could be good for me. Thank you, father. I will do my best."

Aethelric recognized the lack of sincerity of his son's comments, and decided to ignore them. "I don't know if I will still be alive when you are old enough to make a place for yourself in this world, and I probably could do little to lift you up by myself anyway. I have a certain role to play at the court, and I do see the king from time to time, but I am nothing to the great people there. There are scores, perhaps hundreds of others, just as important as I am. So all I can do for you is try to give you the knowledge and skills which might serve you well."

"I have given a little silver to people at Wenlock Priory, and a learned monk or priest will help to unlock the puzzles of reading and writing for you. You will stay nearby, a few days at a time, with a farmer who owes me many favors. And between times you can come home and be a child again."

Actually, Eadric had stopped paying attention after his father had mentioned his contact with the king. He tried to imagine the excitement of working with a great leader and doing important work, dressed in fine clothes.

He started to stand up, thinking his father was finished, but his father motioned him to sit down again. "Now I have some advice for you, and I want you to remember what I say here. But--and this is very important--you must not repeat what I say here to anybody else. These words could cost a man his head. And not just any head--I am talking about mine."

Now Eadric was really intrigued. "Whatever you say, father. You can count on my silence."

"I saw your eyes--clearly you were very impressed that I see King Aethelred on some occasions, and his several sons, including Edmund. I hear things, and I observe things. I know these people as they really are. And I must tell you that, although the king may look magnificent in his silk and linen and with the crown on his head during special occasions, what I truly see there is a wolf."

"What do you mean? Is he a shape-shifter?"

"No, Eadric, you silly dreamer. Of course he doesn't change his physical form. That only happens in wild stories. Here is what I mean: if you wish to trust him, you must only trust him to act like a beast. When you give him your oath of loyalty, he will accept it, but he is unwilling to protect you as he is honor bound to do unless it furthers his ambition to do so."

He hesitated, his eyes narrowed, and then he started speaking again. "A lord must defend those who serve him. The king will have a commoner or a thegn killed if it is to his advantage, and drink some mead to wash down the deed and do it again. He ignores any responsibility to pay the wergild or death payment for those he has had slain."

Eadric needed to interrupt him again. "Maybe all powerful men are like this?"

"You may be right. I don't know--I haven't seen another king to compare him to. I do know that Aethelred is an animal filled with lust for women. He already has more bastard children than I have fingers on my hand, and I'm sure the other hand will be accounted for before he is done. And his sons, especially Edmund, as they grow, will likely become savage as well. Be careful around them, Eadric: you can only rely on the great ones to be a danger to the rest of us."

The boy thought for a moment. "Father, maybe we are better off by staying away from these people, even though I think we have not been harmed by them yet."

"That's an interesting suggestion, my boy, but they can do favors and lift people up to fame and power. Ambitious men like us take risks when we see large possible rewards." Eadric couldn't help noticing that his father was including him in that category, and it felt like an unspoken compliment. He was both surprised and pleased by the comment.

Aethelric indicated that the discussion was over and started to walk back to the house. When the two of them had returned, the father explained to the rest of the family that Eadric would be learning to read and write, and asked if any of the other children wished to learn as well. None of Eadric's brothers showed any interest, even Brihtric, and his one sister knew better than to ask for herself. She might be able to teach herself to read a little if she wished, but no sane father would spend good silver on formal education for a daughter. Not if he wanted to find a good match for her.

Early the next morning, his father had Eadric ride behind him on his horse, and they arrived at Wenlock Priory after morning prayers. There was a group of limestone buildings with low roofs in a clearing defined by a short stone wall, nestled among the over-arching oak trees that shaded them. At the center of the compound was a small stone church with a whitewashed cross atop the roof.

The boy met Brother Oswith, a short, very thin monk with big ears and a casual manner and, after a brief introduction, his father took his leave, and the teaching began. Every day they met in a room with bare stone walls and some small tables and benches. The cleric always brought out a wax tablet on which he scratched English words with a long pointed metal instrument. He would then slowly pronounce a word and have Eadric repeat the word back to him. This went on for a few hours at a time, with only short breaks for the call of nature and a small midday meal.

In the beginning, the boy simply mimicked what the monk said, but it did not take long for him to recognize the sounds that letters and then words were supposed to make, and he began to learn to read. Words became sentences and sentences became paragraphs.

For the next few months, Eadric spent days at the priory and the farm, and then returned home to go fishing and exploring with Thorunn, and of course fighting the mock battles in the meadow. Everyone was happier that the two sons of the tanner had disappeared, but that experience made the boys more cautious about accepting new fighters into their ranks, so the group stayed small.

As Eadric's father had expected, the boy was a quick study, and had no trouble learning to read and write English. He actually enjoyed the success that he was having. However, Latin was a more difficult challenge, and a priest named Father Morgynnyd, more adept at dealing with that language, was introduced to Eadric as his new tutor. Trying to decipher strange writing on parchment, and then endeavoring to reproduce it on a wax tablet, was the next stage of his education.

Almost immediately, the boy wasn't happy with the change. He had become comfortable with the pleasant instruction of the monk, and immediately felt ill at ease with the priest's strangely friendly behavior. Every day, the cleric asked Eadric about himself and his life at home. He always sat close to the boy, and invariably touched his hand or his elbow or his shoulder.

He would frequently lean closely over Eadric's shoulder, watching him work on his lessons. When the boy moved away from him, the priest found a way to move next to him again. The boy found him repulsive. Father Morgynnyd was a large heavy-set man, whose well-fed appearance belied the adoption of the ascetic life that he had formally accepted as part of his religious vows.

Late one fall afternoon, Eadric was putting away his Latin reading pages in the quiet, almost empty room where his lessons were always conducted, and was preparing to leave for the day. Without warning, the priest came up behind him, bear-hugged him, and whispered in his ear: "You are a pretty boy. Don't struggle--I will make you feel good."

He kissed the boy on the side of his head. Then he began to feel around at the front of the boy's tunic with his hand and found his crotch. Finally he made his way under the boy's tunic, and began rubbing him. Eadric could not believe what was happening. He opened his mouth to scream, and the priest covered his mouth with his free hand.

The priest moaned, and whispered in the boy's ear. "Let me take you to my private cell. If you will share my bed with me, I promise you both pleasure and a certain place in Heaven. Surely you know that the Lord and the Church have given me special powers. I will pray to Him for your salvation, God will hear me, and I can assure you that when your days have ended, you will enter into His presence and be with Him forever."

Eadric, who was having a difficult time breathing, was both furious and panicked. There was nothing exciting about any of this. In fact, he thought he might faint. The priest was hurting him, and the discomfort seemed to be lasting an eternity. He was able to keep Eadric's mouth covered, and bent him over a table, exposing his bare bottom. The boy felt something press against him, and then suddenly he thought he was going to be split open by something inside him. The pain was terrible. It felt as if the priest was trying to kill him.

After what was probably only a few moments, but seemed much longer, the loud creak of a door opening interrupted what the priest was doing to Eadric, and someone nearby loudly cleared his throat. The priest moved away from him and the pain suddenly diminished. The boy looked around, and noticed a strange silence in the room. He saw an unfamiliar young priest standing there, looking at the two of them.

He smiled, and spoke. "Father Morgynnyd, surely your

student needs to leave now in order to be home by dark. And it is almost time for vespers."

Eadric barely heard the big priest whispering softly in his ear. "If you tell anyone what happened here, I will know about it, and I will see to it that your family suffers."

The young priest turned his head away, and waited for the boy to straighten his tunic and walk out the door with him. Eadric was visibly upset, but the priest who had ended his torment said nothing to him. He was still in considerable pain, and felt like he might be bleeding, so he had difficulty keeping up with the long strides of the cleric.

When the boy had reached the short wall marking the border of the priory's property, he looked around. He found that the young priest had already left him, and was making his way to the grey stone church for late afternoon prayers. Eadric angrily guessed that he had already dismissed what he had seen. It took a long time before the boy stopped shaking, and he vowed never to return to the priory. He washed himself as best he could in a stream that he always passed on the way to his lessons.

Eadric said not a word to the farmer or his wife during the evening meal, and afterwards, he told his host that he would not be taking any more lessons at the priory, and he would not be coming back to the farm. He had trouble falling asleep that night, and when he did, he dreamed about a terrible animal that had trapped him in a corner. Eadric left early the next morning, and did not look back. However, he never forgot Father Morgynnyd. And he never forgot the silent priest, who had stopped the assault, but had never offered a word of comfort or sympathy to him.

When he got home, still disturbed and confused by what had happened, he thought about what the priest had whispered to him about keeping silent, and the threat to his family. However, he didn't believe that his family would have anything to fear, and decided that he needed to tell his friend about the assault.

He was still sore, so he took his time walking to Thorunn's home. They met at the front door, and Eadric asked his friend to accompany him. They went some distance away, deep into the trees. After some silence, he tried to explain to his friend what had happened. Thorunn listened intently as Eadric began to describe his experience, and his eyes widened when his friend told him in detail what he thought the priest had done to him.

After Eadric was finished, Thorunn covered his face with his hands and was silent. Then he made a strange noise, sounding almost like a growl. He angrily pulled out his blade, slammed it into a tree standing next to him, and gritted his teeth. "When we are older, we will kill that priest after we cut off his balls."

Chapter Five
Sailing and Oaths

Eadric never told anyone else except his friend about what happened at the priory, and just told his father, the next time the busy thegn came home for a visit, that the priests had taught him as much as he wanted to learn. He was able to read and write, and to understand some Latin. That was all that his father needed to hear, and the subject was dropped. However, Eadric's disgust with the Church grew very deep roots.

Finally at home again for good, he found himself spending a great deal of time with Thorunn and his family. The two boys continued to have their mock battles with other area boys, but as both began to look and think more like young men, exploring became more interesting to them.

Thorunn's father invited Eadric to accompany his son and him on a sailing trip. "It's about time that you and my son start to see more of the world. I have a small longship called a karve that I use from time to time, sharing ownership with four other Danish families. We take goods to sell down the Severn and then across the salt sea to a settlement in Ireland called Waterford. Come with Thorunn and be surprised by a different place. See the world, young man. It's exciting." Eadric didn't hesitate for a moment before agreeing, and two days later he found himself on a lap-straked boat floating on the river.

The boy had never been on a vessel of any kind before, so the first time the big square sail caught the wind and began to drive the vessel downriver, Eadric laughed with delight. He had never experienced a feeling of speed like this, of being rushed through a place in a blur. He remembered his father once taking him for a gallop on a horse, but it was nothing compared to this. The six other men on the ship had obviously done this many times before, but even they looked to be enjoying themselves, and caught up in the moment.

Later, the wind got stronger and the vessel's motions became more erratic in the choppy water. He tried not to be amused when he observed young Thorunn looking like he might share his previous meal with the fishes. Seeing what was happening to his son, the father brought him to the stern and held his shoulders as the boy purged himself. Didn't all Vikings have a natural comfort on a sailing ship? Wasn't that something they were born with? When the unhappy boy looked over at him, Eadric quickly put a look of serious sympathy on his face. Surely, a friend should not laugh at a friend's distress.

Once out on the open sea, all of the men kept watching for storm clouds, but the clear skies promised fair weather, and the white tips of the waves glistened like silver in the sunlight. They were also alert for the possibility of running into a Viking vessel filled with raiders, but there were no large sails anywhere to be seen. Thorunn the elder took turns at the tiller with another Dane who called himself Anlaf. He was another storyteller who lived nearby and, during the voyage to the Irish coast, he admitted to Eadric that he had been involved in raiding coastal areas some distance north of Shrewsbury perhaps twenty years earlier.

"Yes, boy, I went a-viking as a young man, and I had no problem at that time with anything I did. The settlements we attacked had people who spoke different, looked different, even smelled different, and most believed in a different god than those that we knew. They were not our family, they were not our friends, they were not our blood. And they had silver and slaves that we wanted. The churches near the sea were like piles of treasure waiting to be taken. I was young. What has changed for me? I know people here now. My family and I are a part of this place. That makes a big difference."

He said that he had been so taken by the beauty of the area that he stayed, found a wife, and became a trading partner with other nearby Danes. However, he still kept a Thor's hammer pendant hanging from his neck, hung a lethal-looking axe on his belt, and talked about getting enough wealth to return to Denmark a powerful man.

When the vessel arrived at the port called Waterford, just a short distance upriver from the salt sea, everyone on board helped to unload the bolts of fine linen and wool cloth, as well as some interesting green pottery that they had picked up in the settlement of Bristol.

While Thorunn's father negotiated with two Irish traders who were eager to buy everything that the ship had carried, the two boys wandered around the settlement. It was even bigger than Shrewsbury, and had started to expand beyond the fortifications that had protected the western part of the town. Even some of the area marshes were being slowly filled in to allow more expansion.

Outside of an alehouse, two dark-haired girls, at least a couple of years older than the two boys, gave the boys a friendly greeting. The shorter one spoke first: "Why don't we take you behind the building, so we can show you what a true Irish welcome can be."

Both of them had pleasant faces, with bright eyes and pug noses, but covered with freckles, and they could probably have been a little cleaner than they appeared to be. Perhaps the Irish had not learned from their Viking intruders about the virtues of a weekly bout with soap and water.

The taller of the two was particularly enthusiastic about her hospitality, in exchange for a piece of a silver coin. "If you haven't had a local girl, you haven't really lived, now have you?" She was an artful talker, and made a good case for herself and her body. However, the boys, who had never had any sort of girl at all, looked at each other, and broke into embarrassed laughter.

They were quick to politely thank the girls and almost ran down the wooden walkway towards their vessel at the edge of the settlement. During the handful of similar trips to Waterford over the next year, they received similar invitations from the two girls. At some point, the boys stopped laughing and actually thought about accepting their tempting offer, but the time never seemed right.

Eadric's father broached the subject of honor to the boy during one of his unexpected visits home. They were relaxing in front of the open stone hearth in the middle of the great hall. The low flames were the only light to be seen in the entire home, except for the occasional firefly trying to find its way outside. Everyone else was asleep except for them, so the two started talking.

"My son, tell me what it means to give an oath." His father spoke slowly so that Eadric would have time to think about an answer to such an unexpected question.

Eadric paused. "It means to say something that you take seriously."

"All right," his father continued. "And why is it important? Why does it matter? Think for a moment."

The boy wasn't sure. "Because it is important for you to be true to your word?"

"Eadric, oaths are an essential part of our world. The Church helps to keep order, and to encourage men to act as they should. However, oaths create a web of obligations that helps to keep our society whole." He paused for a reaction from Eadric.

"I don't understand the meaning of this web that you mentioned. Is it like a trap, like a spider web is made to trap bugs?"

"It's interesting that you'd say that. Indeed, sometimes people who swear oaths do feel trapped. Honoring a vow can be very difficult at times." His father continued. "Thralls, or slaves, which is what they are, do not make vows. They are possessions, and we can do almost anything we want except kill them—and then we would need to pay a wergild in silver to the owner. The free born men who work on my estates take an oath to be true to me, and I try to protect them."

"Thegns like us—you will become one when you reach the beginning of your twelfth year—will swear an oath to a representative of the king. If there were an ealdorman standing between you and the king, you would swear fealty to him as well. However, there is no ealdorman in Mercia, and hasn't been for some years now."

"You'll swear to support your lord, with your life, if necessary. When you marry, you will swear to support and defend your wife. Every oath is a commitment, perhaps to the death. Your word is everything. Am I making sense?"

Eadric was starting to feel drowsy in front of the warm fire, but he heard and understood what his father told him. He needed to honor his oaths. What he did not ask about was the possibility of one oath being more important than another. Or, could changing circumstances or somebody else's actions kill the strength of an oath? He wished much later that he had explored some of those complications.

After that discussion, it was inevitable that Eadric, who shared with Thorunn what his father had told him, suggested that the two share an oath of friendship with one another. The young Dane was delighted, and in turn suggested that they seal the oaths with blood. After all, Thorunn had a sharp knife, and he thought they should involve it somehow in their solemn ceremony.

He smiled at Eadric. "What is the point of having a seax if you don't use it sometimes? Let's get ourselves bloody!" They both started laughing.

So, behind Thorunn's longhouse, as far away from the family's cess pit as possible, the two boys swore an oath to each other: to support and defend each other, until death, and to make an enemy of one the enemy of both.

Thorunn touched his friend's shoulder. "Do we both mean this? We need to mean it if we say it. An empty oath is worse than no pledge at all."

Eadric blinked. "Of course, you ugly Dane. We must say what we mean, and mean in our hearts what we say." He was certain. Thorunn indicated that he was as well. Each made a small cut on the palm of his hand, making sure not to cry out, and then let it bleed a little. They clasped hands, said in one voice the words they had chosen, "Brothers forever!" and it was done.

Told of this ceremony, Thorunn's father was pleased with both boys, and happy that they each had such a good friend. He made it clear that a Dane took oaths as seriously as any English man. "I served a jarl named Eardwulf when I fought at the Danish border, and I swore allegiance to him until we had defeated the outsiders and pushed them out of our lands. I fought in three shield walls because of that oath, when each time I wanted to be away from there, especially the first time. Only after we had won did he release me from my oath to him, and I was free to go."

"Your oath to each other binds you together forever. If, Eadric, you can someday believe in the stories of Asgard and the realm of Odin, I hope that you both die honorable deaths with weapons in your hands, and can fight together in Valhalla until the end of the world."

Eadric wasn't any more comfortable with the Norse beliefs than he was with the stories of the Christ, but he was happy to believe that both Danes and Christians shared a respect for their word. And that he had a friend for life.

Chapter Six
The End Of The World

There were rumors everywhere that the world was coming to an end. It was November, and the year 999 was almost finished. When Eadric and Thorunn walked to the Shrewsbury settlement early in the morning on a market day, they could hear small groups of people speaking quietly of the possibility that January might never come. That, after a thousand years, the Christ would come again and there would be nothing left of this life. They talked of priests proclaiming this in their churches.

Interestingly, there seemed to be no shortage of people looking to buy food for the approaching winter months. Flour for brown bread was a popular purchase. Farmers were putting away seed for the spring planting. And the boys never saw any public signs of panic. If people were convinced that the world was coming to an end, they had a strange way of showing it.

Thorunn didn't understand any terrible apocalypse that didn't include the battle called Ragnarok, so he didn't take the Christian prophecies seriously. Eadric also thought the whole idea was silly, and he suggested to his friend that they ignore the worrying talk and instead do some exploring on foot along the bank of the Severn River. There was a well-worn path to follow. They had passed some interesting settlements on their sailing trips to Waterford, and Eadric brought a silver coin in case they found something worth buying.

It was a strange weather morning. There was a light misty rain coming straight down, but the sun was shining brightly, making the branches and the few leaves left on the trees and bushes glisten. The two boys thought they could see a rainbow to the west over the river, and they decided to rest for a moment. A kingfisher was gliding overhead and then lower, just above the water, looking for a late breakfast.

Then they saw it, almost beneath their feet, and both of them at virtually the same moment. Something gray and metallic was shining in the mud, something in that glaring sunlight that looked like tarnished silver. Eadric whooped first, and then Thorunn yelled, and they both dropped to their knees and began digging into the wet dirt with their hands.

First, there were dark gray and then bright silver coins, a lot of them, some displaying faces of kings that they did not recognize. Several had a strange three limbed cross on them. There were a number of small silver bars with tiny markings on them. There were twisted silver rings, and then two gold rings. There were silver armrings with a myriad of punch marks covering them. There was a similar gold armring. There were more silver coins. And then another gold armring. A flat gold ring with punch marks everywhere and a knot on the back. And even more silver coins, plus many pieces of what looked like silver jewelry which had been cut into small chunks.

They used sticks to dig around what they had already found, making sure that they had uncovered everything of any value. After washing the mud off of everything they had piled up, the two boys sat there on the wet ground, stunned. What lay in front of them was a great fortune.

Thorunn spoke first. "This is Viking treasure. I know this from the markings on the bracelets and the twisted rings. Someone gathered his wealth and hid it here, someone of importance. Or this may have been the holdings of an entire war band. How one man could have owned all of this by himself is difficult to imagine!"

"I wonder how long it has been here," Eadric said. "It looks like it has been sitting in the earth forever."

There was a mass of tiny triangular punches with dots inside covering most of the surfaces of the jewelry, and the markings on the gold glittered in the sunlight. Thorunn was sure that all of the silver would do the same after it was cleaned with sand and burnished bright. He said that his father had owned a fine silver armring similar to the larger ones in the pile that he had been given after the battles in Denmark had ended. In fact, he had seen it once before it was used to invest in the boat they had sailed in.

There had been traces of rotting cloth around the mass of silver and gold, so someone had buried a large sack many years before, intending to return for it. Whoever it was had surely died, as nobody in his right mind would neglect to retrieve such a treasure unless death took him first.

The boys were excited beyond words. Grinning, Eadric reached down, grabbed a handful of mud, and threw it at Thorunn, hitting him in the chest. The Dane quickly retaliated with two handfuls, and their battle continued until both of them were covered with muck and had run out of breath from laughing.

Eadric and Thorunn resolved that they would rebury the hoard near one of their homes, and wait for the day when they could use it to change their lives for the better. Neither family was in need. Eadric's father owned more than one large estate, and Thorunn's father had a profitable trading business. So the boys knew that this discovery had been meant for them. When they were a little older, when they had reached manhood, they would surely know what to do with it. Everything would be clear to them then.

The two boys had not gotten very far down the river before their exploring was abruptly interrupted, having uncovered that large pile of treasure, so a few days later they returned to where they had been diverted from their adventure, and continued to walk along the Severn at a leisurely pace. They were certainly in no hurry to get anywhere that afternoon, although they hoped to find some food at a settlement along the way.

Both Anlaf and Thorunn's father had warned the boys that Bristol was a major port for sending slaves from Wales and the north across to Ireland, and then to unknown parts of the world. So, of course, that river would be a convenient pathway for Vikings and others searching for captives to sell. However, they had forgotten all of that, and like many young people, they could not imagine anyone deliberately harming them.

Some light rain did not discourage them from continuing their journey on the path next to the river, and the drizzle lasted only a short while. They were approaching the settlement of Wribbenhall when Thorunn noticed in the distance a long slim vessel that he knew to be a drakkar, or Viking longship, tied up at a piling on the riverbank. There appeared to be two armed men on board having a conversation, but the boys were too far away to determine anything else.

Only a few painted shields were displayed on the ship's gunwale, so it was obvious that there were other Vikings nearby. They saw an unusual amount of smoke rising above the trees surrounding the settlement, but from a distance, they observed no unusual activity. Everything seemed normal--until they started hearing loud screams. First it was the high-pitched shriek of a woman. Then it sounded like two young children, and then a shout from somebody, which ended abruptly. They knew that they were hearing terror and pain.

The boys quickly darted away from the riverbank and ran into the trees and the thick understory growth that surrounded the settlement away from the water. Thorunn led the way, slowly weaving through the brush towards what were now many different sounds: men's loud voices in a language that neither boy understood, women and children crying, the thud of wood and plaster being hit by something hard, and everything punctuated occasionally by cries of agony.

They hunched down close to the ground as they got closer to the chaos in the settlement. They wanted to see exactly what was happening, although they already suspected the truth from the many stories about raiders they had heard. They were afraid, but they were also curious, and their curiosity won. Getting to the edge of the brush where the settlement began, they saw a terrible scene.

There were Vikings everywhere, perhaps twenty or thirty of them. Scattered between the buildings were the bodies of several men and women, mostly old, although a few looked like younger men who had apparently fought back, and died for it. Two buildings were on fire. Several women and children were being separately dragged toward the longship, where a few forlorn people were huddled together with their hands tied. A few older boys and young men were being guarded by a single raider. He stood over them with his unsheathed sword shining in the afternoon sun.

"I'm sure these are Norwegian Vikings, and probably from Ireland," Thorunn whispered. "I do not understand a lot of what they are saying to each other, but the meaning of this is clear. The captives will be taken across the Irish salt sea, and then sold and taken to a foreign place far beyond anywhere that we know."

Eadric looked at him with wide eyes and quietly hissed. "Horrible--this is horrible. I can't believe that this is happening right in front of us. Is there nothing we can do?"

His friend grunted. "Are you serious? If we were fully grown warriors, armed with long sharp swords, we could charge these raiders and perhaps kill a few before we would be cut down in our tracks. But we are years away from being able to save even a single person. I think we need to pull back deeper into the brush and go back where we came from, avoiding the river until we are safely away from this trouble. Let's go, Eadric. We are worthless here."

Eadric nodded. He thought about the possibility of returning home and getting a group of men together to try and rescue the captives, but he knew that attempt would not work. In the first place, the odds of quickly finding fifty or sixty men willing to travel down the river and attack a score or more of Vikings were slim. It would take that many men to have a chance against this band, and some would surely die.

More importantly, by the time a group of fighters could get to Wribbenhall, the Vikings and their captives would be long gone. That was the magic of the longships. They could slip into a vulnerable place, pillage and kill to their hearts' content, and be gone like a ghost in the night.

Suddenly they both heard a shout. A large bearded man with a vicious-looking broad axe in one hand was standing in the middle of the clearing, and pointing at the boys with his other hand. Obviously, they had not been as invisible as they had believed, crouching in the brush. Another Viking nearby with a sword in his hand grunted a brief reply and nodded, and they started walking towards the boys.

"Quick! Run!" Thorunn hissed, and his friend needed no further encouragement as a blinding fear washed over them. They both crashed wildly through the bushes, their faces, arms and legs lashed by the tips of branches as they ran. Moving their legs as fast they could, they could hear behind them the sounds of two larger bodies moving heavily through the underbrush. They knew better than to slow down to look behind them at their pursuers, and saw ahead of them a large clearing in the forest, where they could run even faster.

Suddenly, just ahead of them, they saw a young woman, eyes wide with terror, cowering in silence under the low cover of a cedar tree. They knew instantly that there was no time to do anything for her. If they stopped, they would all be taken, so they did not even hesitate. They raced right by her and kept running.

The boys were breathing so hard and making so much noise themselves in the woods that they could not hear the pursuing men behind them. However, after they had run as fast as they could, and as long as they could without a rest, they stopped, and turned to look back at where they had fled. Far behind them, they saw the two Vikings, having found a much easier catch, making free with their hands all over the struggling young woman, and dragging her back to the settlement.

Turning away from that appalling scene, they tried to make no sound as they walked as quickly as they could, hoping that there would be no other raiders nearby. They tried to put as much distance as they could between themselves and the settlement. Watching for danger behind every tree, afraid they would spy a Viking where they hadn't just looked, they were almost home before they both felt safe. Eadric had nightmares for three nights after their return about being trapped in a dark cave with a creature that he could not see.

Neither boy wanted to think about the young woman they had seen, and who had unwittingly saved them both from the terrible life of a thrall, a slave to whoever would have bought them. Surely she was repeatedly raped by the Vikings, and then, if she survived, taken to Ireland. She would have her hair cut short, like all thralls, and then she would disappear as someone's possession.

The two boys never talked about that woman, but Eadric discovered after that experience that he found it impossible to treat the thralls in his family's home as simply useful animals. He knew that he had been within a hair's breadth of becoming a slave himself. Eadric had never imagined the lot of a thrall before, but now he could do it quite easily.

He asked the slaves already in the family home what they called themselves, and started addressing them by those names. The same was true for every thrall bought after that. Probably without realizing it, other family members began to use their names as well, and began to treat them better. Another blanket, somewhat better food--the thralls noticed the change, although they never knew why things had improved for them.

To almost nobody's surprise, the world didn't end, and the priests and others who had made that prediction tried to forget that they had done so. Of course, everyone else was expected to forget as well, or at least say nothing more about it.

The next year and more went by slowly for Eadric. He and Thorunn continued to grow towards physical manhood, and the practice shield walls became more aggressive and bruising for everyone involved. The two boys checked on their hoard, hidden near Eadric's stead in a hollow under a flat rock, on a few occasions at dusk. Eadric began to look with increased interest at Thorunn's two sisters, now grown pretty and more willing to talk with him than before.

They were named Ingrith and Inga, and Eadric didn't know which of the two he liked better. They were a Dane's dream of beauty: blond hair braided in the back, large crystal blue eyes, and there was no mistaking either the shapely form or the physical strength of each of them. Of course, Thorunn threatened to geld Eadric if the English youth ever went near either one of them, but neither boy took the threat seriously. Surely bedding a friend's sister was not a terrible thing, if they were very good friends.

Chapter Seven
St. Brice's Day: 1002 A.D.

Thorunn reached the age of manhood on his twelfth birthday before his friend did, but nobody in authority came to ask for his oath of loyalty to the king. His family didn't think anything of it, but Eadric's father, on one of his rare visits with his family, seemed concerned about the apparent oversight.

"I don't understand why a king's reeve would not have been dispatched to administer the frankpledge a month ago in October. Thorunn and his family live in this land, they're clearly intending to stay, and a vow of fealty to Aethelred is expected of every young man. I am certain when Eadric reaches the age of manhood, it will be required of him. This is a mystery, and I do not like mysteries."

Both boys shrugged their shoulders. The omission seemed trivial, and any issue relating to a king in a distant land, about whom they knew very little, was of no concern to them. Eadric asked when the evening meal would be ready, and through the front entrance watched one crazy squirrel chase another around the oak trees near the house.

Thorunn and his father were going to be traveling south to Oxenford the next day, and would be gone for a few days while looking there for goods to sell in Waterford. Naturally, Eadric wanted to give him a final jab before they departed.

He winked at his friend. "By the time you get home again, your two sisters will have become women with my help, so enjoy your journey. I certainly will!"

Thorunn pretended that he was furious after looking at the smile on Eadric's face, pulled his seax blade, and chased him around the house, just like the insane squirrels running after each other. The thralls served the family a hearty meal of lamb, bread, and some fine eels, and Thorunn left to prepare for tomorrow's journey.

The next morning, Aethelric woke up his sons and daughter so they could get up and attend church with him. It was an obscure saint's festival day, someone named Saint Brice, and the father was feeling guilty that he hadn't been to the local church for quite some time. However, none of his children were eager to bestir themselves for a long ride, and then a service inside of a cold church, plus he had a small headache from drinking some ale late in the evening. So he had to settle for saying a long prayer before the morning meal.

Thorunn and his son rode into the prosperous town of Oxenford early in the morning. The father had visited there a number of times, and each time he had been able to purchase well-made products to sell in Waterford: silver jewelry, fine bone combs, good linen cloth. He expected the wide streets to already be busy with traders and sellers, but the town was very quiet. The two Danes rode past a Christian church that seemed to be holding a service, although they could hear no music. It was full, with people standing at the door. One bearded man turned and stared at them.

They went looking for the weaver with whom the father had done business in the past, but the man was not at his stall. Another man who had sold him some rings fashioned in a Viking style was not at home. They were able to buy four eggs from a passing farmer, who seemed uninterested in selling to them until the father showed him a piece of silver worth twice what the eggs typically cost. So they sat and ate by the side of the town's main road, waiting for the expected sellers to appear for the day.

English men and women in small groups walked past them on the other side of the road, presumably coming from the crowded church. Most looked past them or down at the ground, but a few glared at them and seemed to be muttering something. They looked angry, and the father and son didn't know what to think.

The street seemed to empty very quickly, and stayed that way for some time. If nothing changed, and the place did not return to normal, Thorunn and his son would have to consider this a wasted trip and return home. They both wondered if there was some spreading sickness in the town, with half of the people coughing in their beds. What other explanation could there be for the absence of so many?

The two Danes started hearing the sounds of people in motion: feet hitting the ground, the quiet whispers of heavy breathing. They looked down the street and saw numbers of fellow Danes, men, women, and older children approaching them, perhaps two score in all, and they were walking rapidly, all in the same direction. However, their movements looked strangely erratic; they were obviously frightened, even the men. The panicky behavior, the fear in the air reminded the father of something he had seen many times: animals being driven to slaughter.

And then the father saw much farther down the road an almost silent mass of people walking behind the hastening Danes, and clearly following them. There had to have been hundreds of them. He could already see that most of the men were carrying tools that could be used as weapons: meat cleavers, farm sickles, axes, and even a spear or two. A few looked like the very same English who he had seen walking away from their church.

The father recognized one of the Danes at the front of the first group, a trader named Einar. Perhaps he knew what was happening. He yelled, "What in the name of Odin is going on? Have the English gone berserk?"

Einar shook his head. "We have no idea what this is about, but we already fear for our families and our own lives. Nobody has said anything, but they are obviously following us, and their actions seem threatening. The trader next to me suggested that we go to the Christian church nearby and ask for sanctuary, a safe place that the English will respect. I believe that's their tradition. Then maybe cooler heads will prevail, and we can return to work."

Thorunn and his son quickly looked at each other and nodded their agreement with that idea. They joined the group hurrying toward the large building with the cross at the top. When they arrived, the door was open, but there was nobody inside to offer them safety, so they entered and filled the open area of the church. Everyone watched through the doorway as the English crowd slowly arrived and began to surround the church. Men holding weapons were the closest to the building, but there were women behind them.

The father closed the door, and turned to the other Danes. "Let's not give them a reason to attack us. I suspect somebody will soon knock on the door to treat with us."

Everyone inside the church was silent and motionless, and they listened. Nobody outside seemed to be saying anything, as though they were waiting for something or someone. A few minutes passed, and then a number of people heard the crackling sound of a fire.

A tiny finger of smoke appeared under the edge of the door, and then another one appeared at the base of a wall. A tiny flame emerged from another wall near the front of the church where a table sat, and a large metal cross with the figure of a man on it. Clearly, the fires were no accident, and everyone inside seemed stunned--even paralyzed--by this turn of events. Little yellow flickers of light became larger flames; then the smoke started to billow around them.

Somewhere at the back of the crowded building a woman cried out. "Help us, for pity's sake." But nobody answered.

Next to Thorunn and his son, a mother was holding her young daughter in her arms, and the child was sobbing against her mother's breast. Nearby an old man with a wiry gray beard was blinking as he looked around, and watched the scene as though it was something from a bad dream. A few families were there: parents and children.

As a youth, the father had heard frightening tales of hall burnings, when Viking enemies torched a meeting hall to trap people inside, but those had always seemed like whispers from a Denmark of long ago. Surely hall burnings were just a distant memory, along with dragons. This was Oxenford, here was a church, a place of worship, and nobody was at war in this place. He brought his son to him, and placed his forehead against that of his son.

He looked into the boy's frightened eyes. "I am proud of you. You have become a man, and you deserve better than this." He smiled grimly, and whispered: "We are not going to stay here to die in the fire. Draw your seax, I will break a spindle from this railing to arm myself, and we will battle anyone who goes against us out there. I will see you after."

He turned to the others and shouted, loud enough to be heard inside the church and in the crowd outside. "They want to kill us like cowards, without seeing our faces, without a fight. Let's not make this easy for them. If we are to die, let us go to meet our forefathers as Vikings, with our heads held high."

The father and son were among the first to fling open the door of the church and begin running from the fire, and into the armed and angry mob that had retreated some distance from the rising flames.

Thorunn and his father did not return when they were expected a few days later. Eadric visited their home, and, although the mother had not heard anything, she was not concerned. She was confident that her husband and son were good people, and kept out of trouble unless they couldn't avoid it. The two sisters flirted with Eadric, and he stayed for the evening meal. He kept on looking at the doorway, expecting the two Danes to come walking in, joking about the ugly English women that they saw in Oxenford.

Two days after that, as Eadric was thinking about visiting their home again, he saw from his front door a lone rider coming towards their house. He quickly recognized that it was Anlaf, the Viking who often sailed with Thorunn and his father to Waterford. He was surprised to see a sword hanging from the horse's saddle as he went out to greet him.

"Hello, Anlaf. You are welcome here. How can we help you? Is there a problem?" The Dane had never visited the family estate before, and his sword suggested trouble.

Gazing off into the distance, Anlaf spoke haltingly, sharing the rumors that he had heard: that an English mob in Oxenford had murdered a large number of Danes at a church two days ago, and vague stories of other massacres of Danes in other towns. He was gripping tightly the hilt of his sword as he spoke, his white knuckles revealing his anger. He looked for a moment at the boy's shocked face. Then he leaned over and rested his hand on top of Eadric's head for a few moments. Slowly turning his horse, he left the boy alone with his tears.

Eadric had almost stopped listening after Anlaf had confirmed that his best friend and his father were still missing. Truth be told, he didn't care about other towns. His oath-brother may have been brutally killed, and there was nothing else worth thinking about. He went inside the house and shared what he had been told to his father. After listening quietly for some moments, Aethelric had his horse saddled, and he rode into Shrewsbury to find out what he could.

He returned less than three hours later, and Eadric saw immediately that his father was deeply troubled. The news was not good. "I am having difficulty believing what I was just told. Although I learned nothing definite about Thorunn and his father, it is possible that they were among the many victims of a decree from the king. A leading man in Shrewsbury received a message which seemed to be from Aethelred's own hand, and may have been sent everywhere in the land. English people were instructed by the king, who said he feared for his life and the survival of the kingdom, to kill all of the Danes in England."

He looked directly into Eadric's watery eyes. " It is impossible to know exactly what happened, and in what places, but I fear for any Danes living outside of the Danelaw, where they are too many to be in any danger. The fact that your friends haven't been seen for days suggests that they did not survive. And I really fear that, in the future, the consequences of these events will harm this kingdom in terrible ways."

Thorunn and his father never did return, and so Eadric mourned. For weeks, he was impossible to talk to or be around. When he was by himself he cried, and muttered terrible curses directed at everyone living in Oxenford. He lost his appetite, he had no interest in the old battle game, and he simply refused to laugh or even smile for a very long time. His world had suddenly changed, and had grown much darker.

His father, who was reluctant to return to London because of possible retaliation from the Danes in Mercia, used his considerable influence to learn some facts about what had happened at Oxenford, and elsewhere. He was able to confirm what Anlaf had heard. A church had been burned down with Danes inside, and those who fled from the fire, men, women, and children, had all been cut down. There were attacks in many other towns, and among the dead were Gunhilde, the sister of Sweyn Forkbeard, the king of Denmark, and her husband and young son. These deaths and the other murders were certain to be a huge provocation to the Vikings.

When Eadric could finally bear to do so, he walked with a heavy heart to visit the grieving widow and her two daughters. Ingrith and Inga were very sad, and neither was willing to talk about their loss, but the widow Ilsith was angry.

"What a stupid, stupid waste. They were good men, both of them. Now we are left on our own, women unprotected in a dangerous world. And this was no way for them to die. My husband didn't carry a weapon of any kind, to avoid creating fear among the English, and they took advantage of that. My son at least carried a small seax with him, and I'd like to think that he died fighting, but whether either of them have a chance at Valhalla we will never know on this earth. Curse the filthy English! They are sorry animals!"

As soon as the words left her mouth, she regretted them. "I apologize for the insults. We cannot believe that this happened, but we know that you and your family could not be a part of this hatred. Please forgive me for what I said."

The boy walked over and put his arm on her shoulder. "I am furious too, and my anger is not going to fade like a morning mist. How will you live without your husband's trading?"

"Don't be concerned--that is the least of our worries. Our friend Anlaf has already made it clear that the other Danes who shared the boat with our family will continue to give us the same portion of their profits that my husband had earned. Danes take care of Danes: we will not starve."

However, Eadric intended to talk with his father, when he next visited, about providing their family with any supplies that they might need. As far as he was concerned, Ilsith and her daughters would now be under the protection of Aethelric, the king's thegn, and himself. Of course, he thought about the treasure that he and Thorunn had found.

The gold and silver that we found was ours, his and mine. I always thought that we would use it together, so we never talked about whether we each owned half, or if a survivor should get the whole thing. Death was the farthest thing from our minds. If half of the hoard belonged to Thorunn, should that part be given to his family?

I care about Ingrith and Inga and their mother. I'm not going to allow anybody to starve for the sake of my own desires. That's why I'm relieved that the Danes will take care of the family and continue to share their profits, and I'm certain that my father will watch over them.

For the time being, I can keep the entire treasure for myself. I can keep what I have, and think about both my future and my desire to avenge the killing of my friend. But--what if things change? What if the family really needs some of that silver?

I am going to do nothing for now. If hunger threatens Thorunn's family, I will need to think again about what to do.

A week later, Eadric asked his father to ride with him to Oxenford. He wanted to see where Thorunn and his father had died, and he wanted to look at the people who had done it. The thegn tried to talk his son out of this, but the boy insisted. They left at dawn and arrived late, staying at the estate of a friend of Aethelric, who was welcoming and a generous host, but he steadfastly refused to talk about what had happened.

The next morning, they went into the center of town, and watched and listened as people went about their business. Conversations were strangely brief, and people seemed aloof and quiet. It was rare for anyone to look at the faces of other people. There were a number of empty stalls for traders that showed signs of having recently been used for buying and selling. Of course, for Eadric and his father, the absences were easily explained.

They found without any difficulty the burnt-out ruin of the large St. Frideswide's church, which had been a familiar site in that community for many years, and which now seemed like a black mark on the town. There were a few half-burnt timbers standing, but what remained there now was blackened rubble. Nothing resembled what it had once been. They knew that was where many Danes had been killed.

Eadric whispered to his father. "What did they do with the pile of bodies? Where were they buried? Where is the guilt for what has happened? Who will be punished for these murders? No justice, not even the paying of wergild?"

His father had no good answers for him. There was no sign, no acknowledgement, no gesture of regret, nothing to show where people had been inhuman to other people. The citizens of Oxenford had moved on. It was as though nothing had happened in that place. It was a learning experience for young Eadric, who had believed that the past stayed in the memories and thoughts of everyone else just as it did with him. He guessed that forgetting was an appealing refuge when the only other choice was shame.

Although the boy was still mourning for his friend, he had watched how other people could have strong feelings after losing someone they cared about, but that sense of loss seemed to disappear over time, and the person who died was forgotten. Eadric was determined to prevent that from happening.

I remember that we joked some months ago about how we were always together. We were sitting next to each other on the river bank, dangling our feet in the cool water, and I commented that we had been at each other's side almost every day since that incident with the sons of the tanner. It was early afternoon, and we could clearly see our reflections in front of us in the river. Thorunn remarked that he and I were like a boy and his shadow, and we each jokingly claimed to be the real boy and the other person the shadow.

If I am able, I will remember my friend years from now as I do at this moment, and remember what happened to him at the church in Oxenford. Whenever I see my shadow in the sunlight, I will be reminded that I must keep those memories alive, and I will keep my friend alive so I can do something about his murder. I know he would have done the same for me if I had been wronged, let alone foully murdered. This is a test of my strength.

Chapter Eight
Love and Power

The idea of revenge, a seed that had been planted at the news of Thorunn's death, began to grow more substantial as Eadric approached his twelfth birthday. He told himself that he was certain about who was responsible. Although every English man or woman in that mob had a hand in killing his friend, it all led back to the king, to Aethelred: the wolf that his father had warned him about.

There was nothing he could do now. He was young, and he did not know a lot about the world and how it worked. However, every day he remembered the wonderful hoard that he had found with his murdered friend. He suspected it would become useful when he entered the adult society, and hopefully provide him with the means to avenge Thorunn's death.

Eadric quietly began to favor some Danish ways over English ones. He remembered some of the words that the widow had cried out: "Curse the filthy English." Perhaps she unknowingly meant that in a direct way. He knew that the English and the Danes had very different views of cleaning their bodies. Based on his experiences with his family members, as well as other English that he knew, bathing was something to be avoided more than three or four times a year.

Danes, and other Vikings he had encountered, believed in some sort of bathing at least once every weekend: a bucket, a stream, perhaps a lake or a river. Soap was a popular resource, and most Danes used a comb to look their best. Eadric decided that they had the better argument, having heard on a few occasions how women seemed more interested in spending time with a clean, well-groomed Dane, than a typical English man, so he began to wash himself with regularity.

He had also begun to wear his hair longer, and bound in the back, like most male Danes tended to do. One day he was leaving the settlement at Shrewsbury, and passed by two boys with short-cropped hair. Thralls always wore short hair, and Eadric wondered whether they were simply free born workers or if they were slaves, and their owner had left them without supervision.

As he walked by, one of them looked at him and muttered "Viking shit" and both boys made rasping metal noises with the metal shears for cutting sheep wool that they held in their hands. There was no trouble, but Eadric was reminded once again of the hostility between some English and the Danes who were their neighbors.

That winter, he found himself visiting the widow and her daughters almost as much as he had done when he and Thorunn had been friends. What had begun as a concern for the women's welfare became a matter of youthful physical attraction. The girls had both become *wynlic*: beautiful. Truth be told, he spent most of the time with Ingrith, the older of the two sisters. Although he liked Inga very much, he knew that dealing with two energetic Danish girls at the same time was more than he could possibly handle, so he selected the elder girl for his attentions, and tried to ignore Inga's obvious jealousy towards her sister.

Ingrith taught him how to play a Danish board game called hnefatafl, which he mastered very quickly, and beat her the second time that they played. In fact, he won every time after that. He seemed to instinctively have the ability to plan attacks and defenses. However, he had no interest in humbling her, and told her that he enjoyed every minute of their battles together.

Although Ingrith was an obvious beauty, she frequently surprised him with her toughness and her strength. One afternoon, they were sitting together on a bench inside, and she grabbed his hand. "Let's go find food for the evening meal."

He shook his head. "What do you mean? Are we going to

kill a chicken by wringing its neck?"

She made a sweet smile. "That's too easy. Come with me and I'll show you what I mean." She picked up something that looked like leather thongs and a pouch of some kind, and gently pulled him out the door. They walked into the woods for some minutes, and then she stooped down and picked up a stone.

"Watch this," she said, and put the stone into the pouch. Whirling the pouch around her head with the thongs, she release one, and Eadric watched as the stone flew through the air and hit something with a thud. The couple ran over to the spot, and there was a dead rabbit still twitching among the leaves.

"Did you just do that?" Eadric asked. He was amazed.

"Of course. Let us find one or two more animals for our meal."

"What is that weapon you used?" Eadric whispered. "I have never seen anything like that."

"Some people call it a sling. It has been used by many people for a long long time."

Ingrith was so good with the sling that she was able to bag another rabbit, a squirrel, and a quail. And when she brought the kill home, she was able to skin every one except the quail, and she plucked and burned the feathers off of that. Finally, she helped her mother to make a tasty stew, which the family enjoyed with some hard wheat bread. Eadric had never paid much attention to what the kitchen thralls did at his home, so this was all new to him, and he was impressed by Ingrith's skills and knowledge.

After the meal, the two young people walked down to the river. Each had an arm around the other's waist, and as they strolled along, Eadric felt the girl's strength. She was delightful to look at as a female, but she was almost his equal in strength, and he liked that about her. When they stopped at the riverbank, he gave her a little kiss on the mouth, and she gave him a bigger kiss back. He felt her firm breasts press against him, and he wondered what she would look like without her clothes.

After a few weeks, he got up the courage when they were alone to slip his hands under her shift and slide them up and down her body. She seemed to enjoy that, especially when he found his way between her legs. She initially let him do as he wished, but when she shivered a little, she stopped his one hand with hers.

"I think we should take our time with this," she whispered. "My body is telling me one thing and my mind is saying something else. I have seen my parents in bed together--keeping things private in a small house is not easy--so I know the pleasure that a couple can have when they lie together. But we do not need to hurry. We have plenty of time. Also, there is the possibility of babies to consider, and I'm not ready yet for the great joy and also the great burden of being a parent."

Eadric assured her that he only wanted what she was willing to share with him. He had never seen a man and a woman together, his mother having died a long time ago, and his father having no woman in his bed since her death--at least while he was at home. He wondered if Aethelric might have bedded either of the female thralls at some time, but Eadric had never seen any signs of intimacy at all.

He noticeably blushed as he blurted out a confession. "I don't know anything."

She looked at him closely. "What do you mean? That's a big statement to make."

"I know nothing about a man and woman together. Nobody in my family talks about it, and my mother died long ago, so I haven't seen a couple's passion with my own two eyes. However, I'm not stupid, Ingrith--I know that people think about it."

She smiled and put her arm on his shoulder. "Nothing to worry about. I think it's like riding a horse. Once you've learned how, you never forget."

Eadric ruefully shook his head. "That's probably a good comparison, but I haven't learned how to ride a horse yet either.

She started laughing. "Ok, I give up--you're worthless." She pulled him to her and hugged him, which made him laugh as well. They provoked each other's laughter until they had to stop and catch their breath.

He pulled away from her. "Seriously, I hope that you will be patient with me. I want to make you feel pleasure, but I may need your help at the beginning."

Ingrith giggled. "People have been figuring out how our bodies work together for a long time, and they seem to have found some success, so it does not seem like unusual cleverness is required. Look around. There is no shortage of babies. We will learn what we need to know together."

As they returned to her home that day, they both felt warm and slightly dizzy inside. This was very new to both of them, and their dreams that night, both of their dreams, were full of mysterious discoveries and passions.

A special celebration marked Eadric's twelfth birthday on Aethelric's estate. His brothers and sister had always understood that he was the favorite, but there were never any open complaints. His father gave him some breeches to go under his tunic; it was time for the sake of decency that he begin wearing them. He also put on his son's shoulders a handsome woolen cloak, which a thegn would be expected to wear for public occasions. Finally, he promised Eadric that when he had grown a little taller and broader, he would receive a good sword, and lessons about how to use it effectively.

After Eadric received some other gifts from his brothers and sister, Ingrith smiled and whispered, "I have a very special gift for you as well. Please come for an evening meal at our home when it is convenient for you." Eadric's mind raced, and all he could think to do was smile and thank her. He committed himself to visit her the very next day, but some other things intervened.

His father took him aside after the birthday meal of venison and some ale. "The king has ordered a meeting of the witan, a gathering of rich and powerful men, where the business of the kingdom will be approved of and witnessed. You and Brihtric and I will ride to Worcestre early tomorrow morning, and you will attend. Get some rest."

It took the three of them the entire day to get to the property where the meeting would be held. Having little experience around horses, Eadric was given the slowest mount his father could provide, so the thirty miles were covered at a comically slow pace. His brother had great difficulty refraining from laughing at his struggles with a horse that was surely close to death. They were guests that evening at the estate of another thegn, and the next morning they joined a meeting in the main hall, which clearly included some very wealthy lords, and important men of the Church.

Eadric and his brother were introduced to Archbishop Aelfric, a well-fed cleric who wore beautiful embroidered vestments, and the finest linen that the boy had ever seen. He looked at Eadric and spoke very slowly. "My son, we are here to do the Lord's business. The Church seeks to strengthen itself to better represent Jesus in a world full of sin. Be ever mindful of that truth."

He walked slowly away, with his linen gown making a whispering sound as he walked, and the strong smell of incense trailing after him.

Finally, from a distance, he was able to see King Aethelred, surrounded by a few advisors. Here was the man who was apparently responsible for the death of his friend. Eadric became preoccupied with watching the king's movements carefully. He was a monarch, and therefore in reality he held great power, but from a distance, he looked like a man with no confidence in himself. When he spoke, it looked like he was asking for approval, rather than demanding agreement. He appeared nervous, like he was expecting to be startled at any moment. He did not look steadily at a person, but his eyes darted around.

Eadric paid little attention to the proceedings, understanding almost nothing of the discussion. There were a number of Latin expressions used, but his basic background in that language was of no help to him. In fact, he fell asleep briefly, and his brother needed to nudge him to stop him from snoring and thus calling undue attention to himself. Finally, the exchange of comments ended, and then they were all required to place their signatures on a document placed before them. Aethelric informed his sons that it was called a charter, which involved the transfer of land.

As the three began their return home, Aethelric rode next to Eadric, and asked him his impressions of the proceeding. His son was quick to respond. "I was surprised by the obvious wealth of the men attending the witan. I also thought the king and the archbishop had impressive appearances, although the cleric seemed to enjoy hearing himself speak. The brief legal signing seemed like a necessary formality, and it made me feel important to be a part of it. Were these men chosen by the people to represent them?"

His father chuckled. "Let me begin to introduce you to the real world of power. Sometimes things are not as they appear to be. Recently, this archbishop married King Aethelred to his new bride Emma, from Normandie, so the king owed him a favor. In order for the Church to expand its land holdings to the south of us, a shire court presided over by a cleric found a woman guilty of adultery, and thus her lands were forfeited to the king. And the king is now granting her lands to the Church."

"What is unfortunate is that this woman, who is elderly, could not defend herself, and her husband is gravely ill. She probably was guilty of nothing more than owning lands in her own name. Finally, the grant specified a vague sum of money to be paid to the king, so his personal coffers were enriched from this transfer by charter." He paused for a moment. "And no, those men represent nobody but themselves. They support their own interests."

For a few moments, Eadric was dumbfounded. "Unbelievable. Could we have done nothing to help that old woman? Where is the fairness in that situation?"

"My son, she was already found guilty by a Church-controlled court. You cannot challenge the Church, at least directly. The king supported this charter, and you cannot challenge the king directly. This is how arrangements work in the kingdom. Gold and political power always tip the scales. Always."

During the long ride home, Eadric kept thinking about three things. First, he was uncomfortable with the role of his father and brother and himself in the witnessing of that unjust charter, although he realized that their signatures had not really been necessary. Many others had signed as well. Second, he thought about the treasure that he and Thorunn had found, and which in time was going to be his to use. He had silver, and gold, and a lot of both--and he hoped to tip the scales in his favor some day.

Third, he had a birthday gift to collect from Ingrith. That was probably the dominant thing on his mind. Just thinking about her and the dreams that he'd had about her aroused him. He hoped that his father would not notice. Eadric was a young man, and females had finally become an especially fascinating subject for him.

Chapter Nine
Sex and Mortality

The next afternoon, the young thegn walked to the stead of Thorunn's widow Ilsith, and her two daughters, his mind in a whirl thinking about what the evening might bring: his desire for the girl waiting for him, and his small fear of the unknown. The mother met him at the front entrance.

"Welcome, young man. You are looking well. Inga, please tell your sister that Eadric has come to see her." The younger sister looked a little amused by her mother's unusual formality, but also a little sour as she went inside. Her jealousy was obvious.

"Please thank your father for us. You might not know that he has had a free man from another of the family estates to check on us, to make sure that we're safe and that we have everything that we need. We're grateful for his concern, and it reflects well on both him and you."

Eadric had not known about this, but the boy was grateful for his father's willingness to protect these women.

After some minutes, Ingrith, dressed in a green shift and a white linen overdrape, met him near the front door and hugged him. She smelled of soap and some flower water, and she was more beautiful than he had ever seen her. Eadric was so excited that his head ached a little.

They ate a modest evening meal. Afterwards, the widow took him aside, and put her hand on his shoulder. " You are welcome to stay here tonight if you wish. If Ingrith chooses to share her bed with you, that is between you and her. And when there is a child, I trust that you will defend and support it as your own. Our men are gone, and you are our best hope for an honorable alliance." And then she added, "That small area on the one end of the house was a place for my husband and me. You may stay there tonight."

He knew that Inga was not happy with him, cleaning up after the meal with unusual care and attention, but Ingrith giggled a little, and asked him to walk in the woods with her until it was dark. After they returned, Eadric bumped into a stool with a loud crack; finding their way with only a single candle for light wasn't easy. And a female voice from the far end of the house was heard: "Just like a man." Inga made sure that she was not being forgotten.

As soon as Eadric heard that, he realized that whatever he did with Ingrith, her mother and sister were going to be able to hear the sounds of their passion. There was no help for it. Although he was on the other side of the house from the two women, there were no walls between them, no barriers of any kind, and the house itself was a small one.

In his family's large home, he could not remember having heard the sounds of a man and a woman sharing pleasure, because his mother had died long ago, and no woman had replaced her in his father's bed. However, as big as that house was, he still got awakened by family members snoring, farting, or coughing like they were close to death. In this small place, noises would be shared with everyone. He was not happy about that, but not enough to consider foregoing a night with Ingrith.

While they got comfortable together on the straw-filled mattress, Eadric realized that he had no idea what to do. He did know that he and Ingrith had to remove their clothes, so he began with that, removing his leggings and tunic. Her shift was easily slipped over her head. He could not see her breasts or anything else, but his hands slid over them, over everything, and she giggled again. Then the giggles turned to heavy breathing.

He could tell that she was as excited as he was, and when she guided him into her, they both groaned quietly. His pleasure ended quickly, and she seemed to experience some very sharp pain at the start of their merging, but they were determined to try again. Later that night, they were far more successful. And when he left the next morning, he had a broad smile all of the long walk home.

The young man suddenly discovered that there was more intense pleasure to be had than could be found in eating, playing games, or even meeting interesting people. And he found himself paying more attention to bathing and combing his hair, because other girls he encountered in Shrewsbury seemed to be taking more notice of him. He was finally taller than all of them, and he enjoyed watching them walk differently, moving their hips in an interesting way, when they saw him looking at them.

The next few years were a time of learning for Eadric. True to his word, his father bought him a sword and scabbard. Convinced that Viking swords were of better quality than English ones, he paid handsomely for one with the classic three-lobed pommel that an old Dane, who had no sons to pass it on to, sold to him. The father provided lessons for Eadric with an experienced warrior, who tried to teach him how to fight with that sword, but the young man improved much more by learning Viking battle tricks from Anlaf, the old friend and former partner of Thorunn the elder.

The Dane showed him how important a sturdy shield could be, both for defense and to use as a blunt weapon. He demonstrated that watching where an opponent stepped, putting his weight on that foot, could show a place to attack. Anlaf talked about where on his body an adversary could be distracted, where he could be disabled, and where he could be killed. Finally, he emphasized that a serious blow is best struck when the attacker follows through, that the sword destination should be past the point of impact.

He also talked about battle panic and the killing fever. "The easiest thing to do in a battle is to let fear overcome your efforts and make you an easy victim for a fighter with a cooler head. Fear can make you alert, or it can paralyze you. Paralyzed soldiers die. But you can also go to the other side, and become so caught up in the joy of killing that you forget where you are, what your surroundings may be, and an attacker right behind you can kill you without you knowing he was even there. A good warrior balances his fear and his blood passion."

Although Eadric understood that practicing, even with a good teacher, was not the same as actual fighting, he learned something important about himself. Without anyone telling him, he realized that he would never be a battle champion: one who could cross swords with another great warrior and defeat him. His arm was reasonably quick and his reflexes good, but he knew his limitations: his strength and his agility were only average for a man of his size. He would have to use his wits and guile more than just his sword arm to make his way if he found himself in a fight.

He also became much more comfortable with women. Although he continued to share a bed with Ingrith at least once a week, he began to appreciate that different women had different things to offer, and the virtue of variety was soon obvious to him. As it happened, Ingrith's own sister taught him that lesson. Early one morning, when her older sister was out getting some water at the nearest stream, and Eadric was lying half asleep, he felt Inga slide into the bed next to him. She looked at him with a crooked smile, put her finger to her lips, and embraced him, shift hiked up around her waist. He discovered very quickly that she was a naturally creative lover, and she was a welcome partner when she found the occasional opportunity to share a bed with him.

There were also a few squandered opportunities to be with other women as well. A pretty girl with dark brown hair named Wenda, who lived on the family estate, saw Eadric walking nearby while she was picking mushrooms, and she contrived to lean over and have her loose-fitting garment open to partly reveal her breasts. His eyes widened, pretending to be shocked, and he grinned as he signaled with his outstretched hands that he was flattered, but not able to join her at that time.

Another woman traveling through the settlement made it clear to Eadric with few words that she found him appealing. However, nothing came of that quiet offer.

As attractive as these openings were, Eadric realized that between Ingrith's passion and the occasional surprise from her sister, he had no need of other intimate companionship. In fact, trying to put anything more on his plate might endanger either his health or his personal safety. Danish women were not strangers to jealousy.

In truth, his greatest learning came from having more and more personal contact with those who wielded power in the kingdom. Eadric and other members of the family were called to attend a number of witans. They were witnesses to numerous charters being ratified, some of them clearly involving transfers advantageous to King Aethelred, and others dealing with land forfeitures which would mean lucrative rents and power going to the Church.

Although he never spoke to the king, he was introduced to many lords, among them Aelfham, the ealdorman of Southern Northumbria, whom he liked immediately. He was an exuberant Dane who loved his mead and his food. His two sons, who accompanied him, loved jokes and pranks. And at home in York there was a reputedly pretty daughter called Aelfgifu.

His father brought him to London, a city so large that Eadric couldn't imagine seeing the other end of it. All manner of people, both English and Danes, flooded the open areas with their noises and voices. There seemed to be hundreds of stalls and sellers with small tables offering materials and products of all sorts: completed articles of clothing in various colors, pieces of jewelry in silver and what looked like gold, although the latter were probably a base metal covered with a thin gold coating.

There were sellers who specialized in knives of various sizes, and men who were able to sharpen the knives or anything else with a turning stone wheel. He saw two or three artists who were willing to draw a person's face or a building or an animal on parchment with what looked like a burnt end of a stick. Anything that he could imagine was for sale. And food! There were delicious smells of cooking meats and spices, of unknown delicacies. However, there was also the stench of sewage along the edges of the wide streets.

Aethelric had warned his son about the whores standing next to some ale houses and alleyways, but Eadric just grinned. His father didn't know that he had already seen professional women like them in Waterford, and he found it strange that men would want to pay to bed a woman when there were enough both pretty and interested ones to go around. At least that was his experience. However, he also did not like the idea of money being involved in the passion between a man and a woman.

Late in the day, Eadric and his father were startled to hear loud yelling, and the sounds of iron striking iron. Insults in English were accompanied by shouts that Eadric could identify as Danish, although the exact meanings weren't clear. People moved to one side of the crowded road or the other, and the two Mercians could then see what was happening.

Four men with long hair tied behind, two of them with elaborate ink markings on their arms, were fighting with long seax blades or axes against five or six men who were similarly armed but looked English. It didn't last long. The Danes were probably more skilled with their weapons, but they were outnumbered, so the result was inevitable. Two of the Danes lay still on the road with terrible wounds on their bodies and blood all around them, the other two fled, and the English men hooted in triumph and then separately disappeared into the crowd.

Eadric was appalled. "Why did they fight like that? And why didn't anybody try to stop the fight?"

His father shook his head and sighed. "Was it a conflict over a pitcher of ale, or perhaps somebody's woman? Maybe it followed an insult about somebody's religion? Who knows? But there's some real hatred between English and Danes in this country, and I fear that there are terrible times ahead before things get better."

He covered his face with his hands for a moment. "I'd guess that if the Danes had outnumbered the English, armed men would have stopped the fight very quickly."

Eadric was relieved that they left the city immediately and began the long ride back to their home in Mercia. His first visit to the great city of London was more disturbing that he had expected, and he couldn't imagine a reason that would justify his going there again.

In the spring of 1005, his father Aethelric sickened and died very suddenly. He had been involved with some sort of legal negotiation for the king in Winchestre, which involved the land holdings of a ward of the king. Without warning he became sick with a fever, and his life ended. As often happened, nobody knew how he became ill, what the malady might have been, or if any available medical procedure might have been able to save his life. There was no time or opportunity for either bloodletting or cautery with a hot iron. He was dead within twenty-four hours of the first signs of distress.

His body was quickly returned to his estate, and within a day he was buried in a nearby Christian graveyard. Many local men and women attended his hasty funeral, and his children heard for the first time stories about Aethelric's generosity to his neighbors. Providing farmers with seed in the spring when there was a shortage, forgiving debts when crops were poor, helping a widow after her husband died, legal advice to someone who needed it. He had given numberless gifts to those in need. All of his children were sad, and many tears were shed, but such sudden and unexplained deaths were commonplace, and at times like these, life seemed unbearably short.

After everyone else had left, Eadric still stood by the grave, his hands folded, and waited for the right moment for speaking. Eadric briefly found himself feeling angry because his father had left while his family still needed him. He had always taken care of things that needed to be done, things that Eadric knew were important, but too complicated at the time for him to understand. Who could his family count on now?

Although Aethelric spent a great deal of time away from home, the man had been a rock, and the rock was suddenly gone. However, he knew, thinking about it calmly, that blaming him for dying was folly, and gratitude was Eadric's strongest feeling. He knew that his father had always supported him when he needed support, and gave him freedom when he needed choices to help him grow. That was what a good parent was supposed to do.

His tears expressed themselves in small words. "Goodbye. I hope I can make you proud." Then he returned to his family. As the future unfolded, he knew that he would have to play a more important role in the lives of his family and the functioning of the family estates.

Chapter Ten
Royal Invitations

Just as he had found himself years before leading when the boys were playing at combat, Eadric became a leader of his family and its interests. Now a mature man of sixteen years, he became involved with some family land holdings that he had only recently learned about. He met with estate managers to ensure that the rents would be paid by the laborers working on the properties. He also encouraged people on the estates to be armed and vigilant, to protect themselves from raiders from Wales. And he began to consider how to increase his family's standing in the kingdom.

Although Eadric had by no means forgotten the murder of his friend, he understood that a relationship with King Aethelred was the easiest road to power, and he discovered that getting access to the king and his close advisors was most easily accomplished with the giving of gifts.

When he addressed Oswith, one of the king's men, before a session of the witan in Gloucestre, the thegn had almost nothing to say to him. That surprised Eadric a little, as people typically seemed to enjoy talking with him. However, when he was at a subsequent witan and he discreetly gave him a gift of a twisted gold ring from the hoard that he and Thorunn had found, Oswith's attitude changed dramatically. In fact, he was happy to introduce Eadric to the king, walking the young man across the hall to meet him.

"Lord king, this is the young son of Aethelric of Mercia, whom we all mourn. He was a thegn who performed important service to you and the kingdom."

The king nodded to him, and Eadric bowed, and gave him his best smile. The monarch, a thin-faced man with a small beard, was elaborately dressed, wearing a dark blue linen tunic and a white cloak with gold embroidery along the edges, but Eadric was not impressed.

Having attended a number of witans, he had seen a quietly nervous monarch who was determined to present himself as self-assured and in control, but wasn't entirely successful. Eadric wondered how someone like this could have ordered the massacre of the Danes three years before. Would he have made that decision by himself? Eadric was not at all sure about that.

The king looked him up and down, stared into his eyes, and smiled. He seemed to take a liking to Eadric immediately. "Although I didn't know him very well, your father was a thoughtful advisor and a loyal thegn. I wish there were more like him, and I hope you will follow in his footsteps." He paused and began again. "I invite you to visit me in London, and I will show you the same hospitality that I would have shown that good man if I'd had the chance."

Eadric knew better than to ignore that casual invitation, and quickly agreed to journey to one of Aethelred's residences within the week. He knew that getting closer to the king might both open opportunities for him and his family to improve their connections with the royal court, and also possibly begin to provide him with more information about the St Brice's Day massacre. He knew that he needed to remain patient about this, but the loss of his friend still haunted him.

Six days later, he arrived at the large stone building at the edge of the city, which served as one of Aethelred's primary estates, and a thrall took charge of his horse. He identified himself to the two helmeted and well-armed guards outside, and was allowed to enter. Inside the main hall, the high walls were covered with cloth hangings showing Bible scenes, and strong oak beams supported the ceiling. There was a long board for eating, many stools, and two chairs with carved backs. However, other than the greater size, the hall didn't look that different from that in his own home.

He was immediately confronted by a big, plainly dressed

man, perhaps ten years his senior, with a thick beard, wide eyes, and short brown hair. The man strode over to him, stood up straight, and frowned. "Who are you? I was not told to expect a visitor. I am Prince Edmund, and I'm destined some day, God willing, to become the king of England. I expect people like you to bow when you meet me."

Startled, Eadric quickly tried to do what the man had demanded, and began to introduce himself, but the prince clearly had already lost any interest in him, and had walked away. Although he was sorely tempted to respond to the insult, he remembered that he was a guest in that house, so he swallowed his pride and said nothing.

He saw the king talking to two other men, one of whom he recognized from the witans, and there was an attractive woman with long brown hair who kept trying to interrupt King Aethelred. She was obviously frustrated because she was speaking very loudly, but appeared to have trouble making her meaning clear to the king.

After a few moments of discussion, Aethelred saw him, smiled, and waved him over. "Eadric, I'm delighted that you could come and visit us. I hope that your long ride was uneventful. Let me introduce you to my beloved wife Emma, who came from Normandie. You will quickly see that she has her small challenges with our language."

Eadric bowed. "Your royal highness."

She looked at him and smiled. She was beautiful, and she had the eyes of a cat. "Je suis content, um, happiness--to meet vous. Vous etes un bel--mans--men." She stopped, looked around, and shook her head to indicate that she had finished.

The king summoned four of his sons and his daughter Eadgyth, a slim young woman with thick dark brown hair and large brown eyes, and introduced them to Eadric. With the formalities out of the way, they all sat down together at the board. His son Edmund must have chosen to eat elsewhere, since he did not join them.

Eadric was intimidated at first. He was surrounded by English royalty, all dressed in linen tunics or gowns, and decorated with the finest gold thread and colorful embroidery he had ever seen. And, since the only person he had met previously was the king, and Aethelred was not the easiest person to talk to, he decided it would be wise to watch and listen before opening his mouth.

He noticed very quickly that eating was more elaborate in the king's hall. Servants had provided sharp knives for each person to use to cut and eat a few varieties of meat set on the table, and nicely carved wooden spoons for the thick stew that was served as well.

In addition, a clean cloth was placed next to each person's dish, which Eadric assumed was used for wiping your face or hands. At home, soup and stews were eaten by lifting the bowl to your mouth, and each person was responsible for having a knife, or did without. Eating with your hands was expected, and certainly considered civilized, and wiping cloths were unknown.

Watching his hosts begin to eat, he observed that they tended to put smaller portions of food in their mouths at one time, and he started to cut a piece of chicken he'd been given.

"Aren't you hungry, Eadric, or does the look of the food not please you?" Edgar, the eldest son and heir, looked concerned. He was a tall man with brown hair and a serious manner.

"Not at all, lord prince. I am a little tired from my journey, but everything looks delicious."

"Please, in our home we cannot stand formality, so just use our names here, except for our father the king. Save the titles for public gatherings."

Eadric grinned broadly. "You make me feel like I belong here. All of you are welcome to be my guests in Mercia. I can promise some good hunting."

Another brother, Eadred, who always seemed to have a amused expression on his face, spoke up. "Take that invitation back! This family eats like locusts--everything in our path disappears in our bellies. Spare yourself the famine at home that our presence has forced on the entire city of London."

With that, the rest of the family started laughing, and pretended to attack the food on the board as though they were starving.

The sister Eadgyth, who sat next to Eadric but had said

nothing until that moment, smiled. "Tell us about your family. I know that your father died recently, and you have some brothers. Are they all as friendly as you seem to be?"

He talked about each member of his family briefly, mentioning their best features, and he noticed that the king was watching him--listening to his comments and observing how well he seemed to get along with Aethelred's royal children. Eadric was at his best in a social setting, and he appeared to be impressing a man who was not easily impressed.

After the meal was over, the king and queen asked the children to be good hosts to their visitor. Aethelred said that they were tired, bid Eadric good night, and left the hall together. Eadred winked at the others and smirked at the earliness of the hour. Night was almost upon them, and many candles were lit to keep the darkness at bay. A large fire had been built in the hearth, which was central to the main hall, and the royal sons and daughter and Eadric sat around and enjoyed the warmth. As the smoke rose and found the hole in the roof, Eadric was feeling very cozy, surrounded by these amiable people.

He couldn't help thinking back to his father's warning about members of the royal family, how they were all inclined to become beasts as they acquired power. Although the immediate circumstances were unlikely to provoke their worst actions, these did not seem to be evil men--or woman. Edmund was perhaps a different case altogether.

Edgar was curious about the affable visitor. "Tell us about yourself, Eadric. I understand that you are from the distant forests of Mercia. This must seem like a different world to you."

Eadric smiled. "I think you might be surprised at how similar things are here and there. Your hall is bigger, and our estate is farther away from its neighbors, but our needs are the same: food, shelter, safety, and good company. I like London, but it is beautiful and quiet where I live."

The daughter, who had been quieter than her brothers during the meal, smiled and asked to be excused, and left the rest of the conversation to the young men in the family.

Aethelstan, another son, spoke up after she was out of

earshot. "Despite her departure, I think she likes you. She probably talked more with you than with any other visitor that we've had. That's one for you. However, it would seem that you have already met with Edmund's disapproval. Truth be told, our father is the only family member that he is civil to, and that is solely because he is the king."

There was a chuckle from Eadred, whose sense of humor had brightened the evening meal. "Edmund is the family troll, and he is convinced that he will be king some day. Quietly spoken, we are happy that three of us still stand between him and the crown. Although one son has already died, what are the chances that the fifth in line would emerge as the next monarch? In this case, England would be the sorrier for it."

The youngest son, Eadwig, who was about the same age as Eadric, seemed willing to agree with whatever his brothers said, but otherwise added little to the evening conversations. He watched and listened with interest, and Eadric wondered if he had a similar perspective about his surly brother as did the others.

After returning to his home in Mercia, he had many roles to maintain. He continued to help his brothers to oversee the family estates. He spent occasional evenings with Ingrith and her family, and found her passion in bed undiminished, her younger sister apparently having given up her hopes of supplanting Ingrith in Eadric's heart. However, Inga did not hide her disappointment well.

He even found the time to develop a friendship with Aelfham, the Ealdorman of York, whom he had met and talked to at a number of witans. He got to know his children, travelling to that city on two occasions. The lord's two sons were funny and clever, and his daughter Aelgifu had become a beautiful and clever young woman. She loved making fun of Eadric's consistently well-combed hair, suggesting that he had as fine a mane as she did.

Eadric invited the ealdorman to visit his family home before the spring was over, and told him that the hunting, for deer and even an occasional boar, was excellent in the area. After consulting with his children, the ealdorman arranged the trip. Aelfham and his two sons would come, and perhaps the daughter would accompany them. She was hesitant, saying that she wasn't sure if she would enjoy watching animals being killed.

Visiting the king and his family again in London a few weeks later, Eadric started to suspect that Aethelred was already seeing him as a potential suitor for his daughter, as the young man and woman were given considerable time to become better acquainted with each other, and they were again placed next to one another at the evening meal. Eadgyth was friendly, but he saw nothing to suggest that she had any romantic feelings toward him.

Queen Emma smiled constantly, but it was clear that most of the mealtime conversations were beyond her understanding. Prince Edmund was no more welcoming than he had been when Eadric first met him, but the young thegn understood that some people simply don't like each other, and he and Edmund were never going to get along.

As the meal was ending, Eadric mentioned that Aelfham was going to come to Mercia soon to go hunting with him and his brothers. There was a strange silence for a moment, and then he noticed that the king and Edmund looked directly at each other. While the rest of the family resumed their conversations, the two excused themselves, leaving the board for a few moments to have a quiet conversation away from everyone else.

Something had just happened. Their discussion seemed very animated from his vantage point, but he didn't think there was anything to be gained by wondering about it. Everyone in the family except Edmund appeared to enjoy his company.

Later that evening, while Eadric slept in one of the several small rooms off of the central hall, he dreamed that he and his friend Thorunn were walking along the river, saw the glow of tarnished silver, started digging, and found in the mud a treasure far greater than the one they had found in real life. There seemed to be no bottom to the silver and gold hoard: masses of coins and jewelry and silver dishes and gold inlaid knives and even a small gold crown. Then Eadgyth walked up wearing a glittery golden dress, put her arm around Eadric and told him that there was more treasure to come. Thorunn said something quietly that sounded like a protest, he tried to step in front of her, and then the dream ended as Eadric woke up.

When he arrived home again, he informed his sour old aunt that they would be having a distinguished family visiting in a few weeks, and she needed to organize the house so that they would feel welcome. She had grown comfortable having little responsibility except for watching the thralls prepare meals, and making sure that the wooden floor was swept periodically, so her laments over these new duties were energetic. The family had purchased two more thralls to reflect Eadric's new status as a favorite of the king, so the aunt's everyday duties were diminished, but that did not lessen her dissatisfaction.

Chapter Eleven
A Firestorm and An Opportunity

There was a large, undisturbed forest near Wroxestre not far away from the family estate, where the red deer were abundant, and the tender new leaves on the low vegetation brought on by the warm Spring weather had begun to fatten the deer into quarry worth hunting again. Eadric made certain that a number of good yew bows would be provided for his guests, and shortly before the visit, fish were caught from the river and placed in water-filled troughs to keep them alive and fresh until needed for a meal.

The ealdorman and his two sons, Wulfheah and Ufegeat, arrived without ceremony. Aelfham was a rarity: a powerful man who seldom took himself very seriously. He had spent a lifetime enjoying himself, when he was not fulfilling his responsibilities, and his large belly was a source of amusement for both his sons and himself.

Aelfham's first words inside the great hall were comically dramatic. "Ah, young Eadric! Just in time! I am really starving after our long ride--could I be close to death's door? Sadly, I was much fatter before we left York. Perhaps my sons are famished as well. Lead on to the board! We have mountains of food to consume!" His greeting had his host and the rest of the family doubled over with laughter.

After a good meal and a long night's rest, the guests and Eadric and three of his brothers happily set off to have some good sport finding and taking down some deer. Wulfheah, the older of the two sons, told a ribald story about an old miller and his unfaithful young wife, and Ufegeat sang a few songs about true love. Both of them and their father were enjoyable company, and Eadric hoped that they could return for another visit before too much time had passed.

The day was overcast and there was a mist in some lower areas of the forest. Within a short time, they sighted a group of deer, perhaps five or six, and they all dismounted, getting their bows in hand for the kill. As the younger of the two sons, Ufegeat held the horses. They made sure that they were downwind from their quarry.

Suddenly, from behind a massive oak tree, a man with a wild beard in rough brown clothing rushed at them, running straight at the ealdorman, and hacked at him with a large carving knife. Blood flew everywhere, and the man immediately fled towards an overgrown area of the forest. He never got there. Three arrows, one from the bow of Eadric, struck him down, and he died without uttering a word.

It was obvious before they were able to get to Ealdorman Aelfham that he was dead as well, his open but unseeing eyes and the pools of blood next to his body making that clear. His two sons were horrified by the murder, and Eadric was shocked. None of them recognized the dead killer, and the only thing of note that they discovered was that he had twenty silver coins in a purse tied at his waist. That was a huge amount of money for someone who looked to be nothing more than a free born laborer, and it suggested a disturbing mystery.

Aelfham's distraught sons took him back to Eadric's estate. The other man's body was flung over the back of one of the horses and brought into Shrewsbury, in hopes that someone could identify him. It didn't take long. An old weaver recognized him as a butcher named Godwin, called Porthund, the "town dog" for his crude habits and slovenly appearance. However, no one Eadric talked to could explain why such a man would attack an important figure as he did. Godwin was not known for any erratic behavior; it didn't make sense. Also, nobody in the settlement mentioned anything about the butcher having a lot of silver to spend.

Although Eadric had been caught up in the suddenness of the attack and the aftermath, when he finally had time to react, he was sick to his stomach, and blamed himself for Aelfham's death.

The man had been his guest, and the extremity of his failure as a host was beyond measure.

The ealdorman's sons departed for York that day with their father's body and buried him, thankful that their sister had not accompanied them on their trip, and thus was spared witnessing the killing. However, as disturbed as Eadric was by the terrible murder he'd witnessed, he was in no way prepared for the next horror. He was told by people that he trusted that, soon after the funeral, a number of armed men came to the ealdorman's estate, bound the two brothers, and took them to Cookham, near London. There the men blinded them, cutting open their eyes with knives and leaving them there.

A rumor was voiced, and by more than one of Eadric's sources, that the men that committed this deed were sent by someone at the court of the king himself. In fact, the king was staying nearby when it happened. Eadric recalled the strange moment during his visit to the king's estate when the royal father and son had a quiet exchange after he had mentioned the ealdorman's upcoming visit to Mercia.

After the killing near his home, and especially after the following atrocities, Eadric decided that he should stay close to Shrewsbury for a while. He was informed that the slain ealdorman's daughter was blaming him for her father's murder, claiming that he had planned the attack, and she shared this with anyone who would listen. Certainly the blinding of her brothers rendered her unable to think clearly about who really might be responsible.

Eadric was no fool. He reluctantly believed that the royal family was behind the recent events. Removing a Dane as ealdorman and replacing him with an English man perhaps more likely to be trusted could explain the murder. And permanently disabling his sons would eliminate the possibility of their taking revenge with their own hands. Obviously, the unexplained silver on the body of the killer suggested a powerful sponsor. After a short interval, an English thegn named Uhtred was named the new ealdorman for York.

Thinking about the recent events for some days, Eadric concluded that exploring any suspicions was pointless. Kings are not subject to interrogations from those who serve them, and the young thegn remembered very clearly what his father had told him about the dangers of living with royalty. He would bide his time, and learn about how the world worked, and still remember his oath to his dead friend.

For several months, Eadric attended to local concerns and interests. The family estates were prospering, the Welsh were staying within their own borders, and, to no one's surprise, Ingrith announced that she was pregnant. Her mother sacrificed a goat to the Viking gods, asking that the baby be born whole and healthy, and soon enough, her request would be granted.

Shortly before that happy day, though, the king's messenger arrived, informing Eadric and his brothers that a witan would require their attendance in Gloucestre, although he made a special point of telling Eadric that his presence was especially needed. He, Brihtric, and two other brothers made the long ride south the next day, and he was personally invited to attend the king as soon as they arrived at the host thegn's estate.

Entering the main hall, he saw the king surrounded by other members of the witan, and he approached. Bowing, he waited for his presence to be acknowledged, and Aethelred motioned him and his eldest son Edgar, the atheling, over to a far corner.

Eadric smiled, and began. "Lord king, you wanted to see me? How can I serve?"

The king's son grabbed Eadric's hand and shook it. He liked the young Mercian, and had shared more than one cup of ale with him. "My father has some interesting proposals for you. Maybe we should find you a stool so you can be sitting when he tells you what he has in mind for you."

Based on the prince's tone of voice and the grin on his face, it didn't sound like what was on the king's mind was likely to be troubling, so Eadric continued to smile and nodded. He thought nothing could shock him after recent events. He was wrong.

"Young man," the king began, " I and the rest of my family have spent time with you, and believe you to be a good man and true to me and to this nation of England. I relied upon your father for many years, and I think I can rely on you to represent the crown and our interests in Mercia. As you may know, there hasn't been an ealdorman there for over twenty-five years, since the last one was exiled for treachery. I think perhaps it is time for Mercia to have a leader again. Almost every member of my family believes that you would be a good choice, and we need to know your views about this."

The Mercian's eyes widened. "A thousand pardons, lord king, but are you serious about this?"

The king looked at him solemnly. "Young man, I do not joke about power. I never joke about power. I am offering you a chance to make a real name for yourself. What do you have to say?"

Eadric had to resist the temptation to laugh out loud. This was a huge opportunity. He knew exactly what he needed to say at that important moment, what the king would expect him to say, and he said it: "I am humbled by this offer, that you would even consider me for this high position. I am still very young, still learning about the ways of the world, and have no experience governing. However, I and my family would be honored for me to accept this position."

The king nodded and smiled, clearly pleased by Eadric's response. However, he was not finished. "In addition, we are suggesting that you consider the advantages of marrying my daughter Eadgyth, who already has told me that she would not be opposed to this union."

Here he moved closer to Eadric so that no one else could hear him. "I am duty-bound to explain something to you about her. My daughter has never expressed a great interest in marrying. Frankly, she is not the most passionate of women, but your formal connection to the royal family should force anyone who might consider challenging you to reconsider. If you discreetly choose to find other women for your pleasure, I will not be displeased." It looked like the king winked at him.

Although he was taken aback by the king's comments about his daughter, he was stunned by the unexpected offer of the powerful position, and even more shocked by the suddenness of the king's proposal of his daughter in marriage. However, he was delighted by both offers, and he understood what needed to be said.

"How could any young man object to a marriage with your beautiful daughter? She is a wonderful woman, and I would be honored with this match."

Although Eadric had not had an occasion to explore any physical intimacies with Eadgyth, he had no reason to doubt what the king said to him in confidence. He was not concerned. His relationship with Ingrith, as well as the interest that other young women living in the area of Shrewsbury had shown towards him, left him indifferent about the state of his betrothed's passion or lack of it. She was what he clearly understood to be a "power bride." The status that she brought to him would be much more important politically than any physical pleasure she might bring to the marriage.

Aethelred was not finished. "There is something that you will need to understand. My father King Edgar--God rest his soul --supported the Church in its desire to gather power, and he supported a number of charters that gave it increased authority over both lands and fighting men. This was especially true in the area of Worcestre. The bishop there has many annexed properties and fighting men who owe him fealty, men who used to look to the ealdorman of Mercia for orders and direction. The fyrd in those areas obeys the bishop."

"Therefore, it is likely that you will need to reassert the government's authority, and that will be at the expense of the Church. I will support new charters, which will slowly reduce the bishop's power. However, the bishop will not be happy, and the other ecclesiastical authorities will not be happy either."

"They will use every ounce of their power to prevent these changes, accusing you of stealing Church lands and their dominance. Who knows what they might do to punish either of us? Do what you need to do, and we will let history be the judge of our efforts. I need a strong leader in Mercia. Am I being clear?"

Eadric nodded. "Lord king, I understand the issues with Church dominance in Mercia as you've explained them. A bishop should lead his flock, but he should not rule the land. That power should belong to the king and his deputies."

He paused for a moment. "However, I have an important

favor to ask of you, which I hope you will not deny."

Aethelred's eyes narrowed. "You want something more? Is it a matter of silver, of payment? Aren't you happy with what I have offered you?"

The young man was quick to reply. "Lord king, not at all. I am simply concerned about proceeding with a wedding without the consent of the intended bride. Surely a woman desires at least the appearance of a choice in her mate. I would like to get your daughter's approval of this match in person before the wedding takes place. Would you oppose my doing that?"

The king smiled. "Perhaps you understand women better than I do, Eadric. They remain a disturbing mystery to me. I know that my daughter will obey me, but that may not be enough. You will have an opportunity to ask her for her agreement face to face when you are installed as ealdorman, and then we can finalize the wedding plans. We will proceed step by step."

The king's son Edgar shared with Eadric that his strong-willed wife had taught him much about getting along with women, and agreed with Eadric's idea. The three discussed a possible date for the wedding, shared a cup of ale to toast the agreement, and the witan proceeded without anyone else knowing of the changes that would be coming. Afterwards, Eadric gave the news to his brothers, who were as stunned by the turn of events as he had been. They shared another cup of ale to celebrate, and returned home to tell the rest of the family about their suddenly improving fortunes.

Brihtric suggested that the existing hall in their home should be expanded to provide the proper place for an ealdorman to have meetings and feasts, and workers were found to begin the work. However, Eadric had another improvement to their home in mind. Having seen windows with small glass pieces assembled with lead strips into large panes at the king's hall, Eadric had learned from the king where on the continent the glass had been obtained, and arranged for a number to be installed on their house as well.

He had to wait several months for the glass to arrive, and some days for the experienced workers to make the proper openings in the walls. However, after the windows were installed, every visitor remarked on the sunny brightness of the great hall, and the astonishing luxury that they represented. Local people had never seen such a thing. Eadric was a rising star in the kingdom, and it was obvious to all.

Chapter Twelve
Courting And The Shire Court

His beautiful Ingrith, who had given birth to a healthy son while he was gone, was predictably much less delighted by Eadric's political and marital plans than his own family had been. He had dreaded telling her, with good reason, and he avoided looking directly at her face as they sat around the board in her family's hall. Nothing had changed there since his very first visit, including the stark simplicity of the furniture and a complete lack of decoration on the whitewashed walls. Perhaps he should make some improvements in the home where his woman lived.

Her first response to Eadric's affectionate greeting was silence. She refused to talk to him. He asked her how the end of her pregnancy had gone, and she said nothing. This lasted long enough to make him uncomfortable, and then she spoke.

"I have been going through the agonies of childbirth, and you greet me with the news that you're getting married to another woman in a Christian church? Is that my reward? I am going to begin crying because of your grand generosity. You are too good to me!"

He looked at her. She actually had the whisper of a smile on her face, but her blue eyes were flashing, and Eadric knew that he needed to explain the practical realities of the situation so she would soften her heart. Danish women were dangerous when they were angry, although he was fairly confident that his life was not in any imminent danger.

"My sweet love, I understand your anger. You are only paying attention to the news that I am to be married to the daughter of the king, and are worried that that will turn me away from you and our new child. Nothing could be further from the truth. This will be a ceremony that will make me and my family more powerful, and that will benefit you and our son as well. I just turned seventeen, and we have so much to look forward to together. In fact, as soon as the workers have finished the great hall on our family home, I will tell them to begin working on a fine extra room on your family home as well." Her eyes widened when she heard that, and he began again.

"As for the passion in bed, I suspect that there will be little of that after the first night. Even the king her father admitted that she is not a woman with a great fire inside, and she will probably be content with pretty dresses and a prominent place at formal occasions."

She glared at him, and appeared skeptical. "Really? Is that the truth? Are you being honest about this? The bride-to-be is a lady without passion?"

He put his arm around her neck and pulled her to him. "I would not deceive you, and I have no reason to doubt her father's words. Why would he lie about something like that? As far as I know, he is not aware that you or our son exist."

Ingrith pushes him away with her head so that she could look in his eyes. "About that new room," she said, "Can it have walls high enough so that I cannot reach the beams with my hand?" She smiled, and he was finally able to relax. Clearly, he was in no physical danger from her.

As soon as he saw the baby, it touched his heart powerfully and never left. They named the baby Thorunn, to remember the father and son that they loved. And Eadric told himself once again that he would never forget St. Brice's Day.

Soon after, there was a small ceremony at the king's estate outside of London. Eadric was formally declared to be the primary judicial authority in Mercia, and the commander of the fyrd. He was given a silver chain and medallion to wear at witans and hearings and other occasions. The king was there, as well as a couple of his sons, and of course, Eadgyth, his intended bride, dressed in light blue linen. A local priest gave a blessing, Aethelred formally declared that Eadric was now the ealdorman of Mercia, and everyone present shared a meal together. As expected,

Edmund was absent.

After the ceremony, Eadric went to Eadgyth and asked to speak to her privately. She walked with him to a pleasant garden nearby filled with colorful flowers, and sat down on a small stone bench.

He began cautiously. "I am thinking that the king your father has told you about a discussion we had recently concerning you."

She had obviously been expecting this. "My lord, this talk is not necessary. My father has made clear to me for many years what he expects of me, and he didn't need to order me to accept the marriage proposal. I know my place, and I know my duty. Fortunately, your looks are pleasing, and your manner courteous, so I am not offended at all by the match. I thank you for consulting me, and I agree to marry you. However, I intend to stay here in London. I'm sure that will be convenient for you as well."

A much less intelligent man than Eadric would have realized that she was far from delighted with the prospect of being married. He did not know if marriage itself was the issue, or if she had a problem with him personally. However, he hoped that he would not be a source of unhappiness in her life. And he had a sense that she was an important piece in the puzzle of his career, wherever it would take him.

As he was leaving her, he saw his long shadow in the bright afternoon sunshine, and he thought of his friend.

There was much to do when the new ealdorman returned home. Although Eadric had been generally aware that Viking raids in England had been going on for many years, his new responsibilities forced him to learn more about what was happening in the rest of the country. There had been no attacks in Mercia for longer than he was alive, but that could always change. One of the first things that his soon-to-be father-in-law required of him was that he begin to organize the building of ships, which ultimately might be used to fight the raiders. Other ealdormen had already been given that order. Three of his brothers became involved in the project, and Brihtric led the way.

As King Aethelred had warned him, the Church had

become the dominant political presence in the general Worcestre region, having taken advantage of the previous king's generosity and the absence of an ealdorman for many years. Bishop Wulfstan, both the Bishop of Worcester and the Archbishop of York, was in control of many estates which had traditionally been controlled by the ealdorman. And he required fealty of many thegns and free born men who had previously been oath-sworn to the secular authority.

The new ealdorman began to petition the witan to approve charters which started to return power to his office: small estates and minor properties. However, the private responses by the bishop and his representatives were immediate and shrill. They were outraged that the king and the witan would consider the removal of even one foot of ground from the absolute control of the Church, let alone tracts of land.

Although the bishop did not speak about the changes in open witan, clerics quietly talked about property being stolen from them, and quietly they called Eadric "the ealdorman thief." Because the charters were each modest in their scope, the king and the witan approved them, although Aethelred continued to assure the bishop that he remained a loyal and devout advocate and man of faith. It would not do for the Church to see him as a threat to their supremacy. He had no problem with the blame falling on the broad shoulders of Eadric.

The new ealdorman learned to his dismay that the king had failed to tell him about another problem. Although he was responsible for strengthening the military readiness and defense of Mercia, he was also required to fulfill a more judicial duty. He was expected to preside jointly with the local bishop, or the bishop's representative, over the shire court of Mercia, and to attend those assemblies twice a year. He was to provide justice to the poor and unfortunate, and to deal with criminal behavior.

The problem resulted from the fact that there had been no ealdorman in Mercia for over two decades, and so the Church exercised sole authority during that time to judge all issues throughout the realm. Bishop Wulfstan was the preeminent churchman in England, and busied himself with composing religious sermons and political and legal writings. As a consequence, he handed over his duties as a magistrate to an assistant named Leofsige, whose primary mission seemed to be to favor the Church and all of its worldly interests in his judgments whenever possible.

Eadric still vividly remembered his discussion with his father after attending his first witan. An older woman had been implausibly found guilty of adultery by a court presided over solely by a churchman, and some of her lands had been transferred to the Church. Such abuses needed to be stopped.

His first shire court assembly was a memorable one. It took place in the home of an English thegn named Aeldwulf, located in the north of Mercia near the large town at Chestre. The large manor had been fortified, as it was near the seacoast, and the area had suffered a number of Viking raids in the past, so entry to the great hall was through the narrow opening of a high earthen palisade.

Having just arrived, Eadric was met by his friendly host, an impressive-looking man--tall with graying brown hair and beard. He was surprised by the thegn's first words. "My lord, you are a welcome sight. I am a good Christian, but this priest has been unchallenged in court for too long. Every opportunity to fill the coffers of the Church is used, and everyone except a cleric is at risk of losing silver or land. It is good to have an ealdorman in Mercia again." He was direct and honest, and the ealdorman liked him.

Eadric bowed. "I thank you for the greeting. I am a young man, with much to learn. This is my first assembly, but I intend to deal with people in this court fairly. Grant me the favor of your counsel, please. If I say something that might create a serious legal problem, kindly shake your head with as much energy as you can muster. I will then require that the proceeding be stopped so I might answer nature's call, and you can explain to me privately where I have gone wrong."

His host made a slight bow. "I will give you a clear sign, if it's necessary, even if people think that I have the palsy."

He met the bishop's representative Leofsige a few minutes later. A very thin man with closely cropped hair, the priest was dressed in a long black gown. His face had a solemn expression on it during the whole assembly, indicating to all that he was aware that he carried the huge burden of the Church's will on his shoulders.

"Lord ealdorman, Bishop Wulfstan sends his greetings. As is his custom, he allows me to preside at these court proceedings. Since there is much to be done, let us forgo the small talk and pleasantries, and begin hearing the cases before us. I have been told that you are inexperienced in these matters, and I will give you what guidance that I can."

"I agree, father. There is much for us to address this day, so let us get started without delay. And I look forward to hearing your thoughts as these trials are presented."

There were three cases to be dealt with, and about a dozen people having an interest in those cases waiting to get a hearing. These were typically cases about which a lower court had been unable to reach a judgment. The shire reeve, a tough-looking large man responsible for dealing with situations until the court convened, kept seven people off to one side of the hall, and waited for the priest and Eadric, sitting together at one end of the hall, to begin.

The shire reeve called forward a man with his hands bound, accused of killing a free born man, a carpenter, when he was drunk. The reeve pointed out that the accused had killed another man under similar circumstances two years before, and the lower court had permitted him to pay the family of that first victim 200 shillings as compensation, called *wergild*. However, given a second offense, the case was sent to the shire court for a resolution.

The accused, a slave trader with a large business, freely admitted that he was responsible for the man's death, explained that he had not realized what he was doing at the time, and had volunteered to pay another 200 shillings to the new victim's family. However, the victim's brother complained that the family, a widow with six children, would have difficulty feeding themselves for very long with that award, especially given the tithe to the church and a small portion of the money kept by the shire. Also the brother pleaded that the accused had little respect for human life, and deserved to die.

After hearing from the admitted killer and the brother, the priest and Eadric withdrew to discuss the matter. Leofsige immediately declared that that there was no choice: the accused had to be put to death. And although the ealdorman agreed that the man deserved to die for his crimes, formally condemning him was a difficult step.

Eadric hesitated before replying to the priest. He had never deliberately killed a man before, but it could be argued that putting one of the arrows into the body of Aelfham's killer was almost the same thing. And that act somehow made Eadric's decision easier.

"Although we need to be very careful about handing out death sentences as though they are loaves of week old bread, the man has done violence to another man, and then repeated the offense. Paying the wergild didn't discourage the offender, so we seem to have no other choice. I agree--he must die."

That was a promising beginning. However, Leofsige proposed that the family should receive 200 shillings, minus the two fees, and that the trader's remaining assets should be completely forfeit to the Church. After listening carefully to the cleric, Eadric calmly but emphatically disagreed with that disposition of the case. He instead recommended that the Church's only payment would be its portion of the 200 shillings, and that the victim's family should receive the killer's remaining possessions and silver.

The priest was outraged. "My lord, that man committed a mortal sin with that killing--and for the second time within recent memory. The Church should be given the resources to make its defense of morality stronger, and more able to help the flock to resist the challenges of the Devil. Surely you agree."

The ealdorman was quiet for a time, and the priest wondered if he had fallen asleep. However, Eadric was thinking about the Church in the real world, the question of morality, and the memory of his terrible experience at Wenlock Priory. He was certain that more money to the Church would not make priests less sinful, and he knew exactly how to negotiate a financial compromise that Leofsige would not refuse.

"Father, the Church has its own moral challenges.

However, that is a subject for another day. The killer has no wife or close relatives himself, so his wealth can be seized by the shire. I am more concerned about the family that lost a husband and a father than I am about the coffers of the Church. Therefore, I propose a middle way: that the Church should receive a tithe for the entirety of the killer's assets, which will be a considerable sum, and the remainder will go to the victim's family. I would strongly suggest that you agree to this disposition of the case--I speak for the king on these matters."

The priest initially protested, but that arrangement would mean more money for the Church than Eadric's original suggestion, so he reluctantly found it acceptable. In addition, he was simply not used to dealing with disagreement from another authority in the court, so he gave in without an extended argument. The assembly reconvened, and the priest announced the judgment of the court. The killer bowed his head and was led away without protest, and the brother hugged the widow--who then applauded the court before leaving the hall.

The second case involved a boundary disagreement between two farmers, each insisting that the other was stealing land belonging to him. Eadric suspected that the younger farmer was lying about the boundary, but the other man could not prove it. After a very brief consultation, he and the priest stipulated that each farmer would get an identical part of the disputed land. Neither farmer was happy with the decision, which Eadric suspected was a good sign that their verdict was a fair one.

The final case concerned a young woman who had been accused of casting dark spells on people, and who must therefore be in league with Satan. She was called a wicce, a maker of magic and potions, by the wife of a man she was supposed to have cured. Clearly, these were serious charges.

Leofsige took Eadric aside and quietly explained to him a particular problem with the case according to his perspective. "One early Christian position was that women like this should simply be put to death. Another was that she should do penance for a full year, living only on bread and water. Do you have a position about these two choices?"

Eadric covered his face with his hands, and shook his head.

He tried not to think about the terrible judgements that Leofsige had rendered when there was no one with the power to disagree with him. He certainly had a problem with the priest's immediate offering of those alternative penalties. Eadric put his hands down and looked over at the priest.

"Father, you have given two options for punishment, but we have not established whether the woman is guilty yet. Perhaps we should consider that question first?"

"Of course she is guilty. Look at her."

Eadric looked. She was an unusually pretty young woman with dark brown curly hair and dark brown eyes. From what he could tell, given her almost shapeless clothing, she had a body guaranteed to arouse a man's desire. She saw Eadric glancing at her, and she looked steadily back at him with confidence--she was a woman certain of herself.

The priest saw her glance. "You see, this is a woman full of the devil's pride. Does she dance in the moonlight with the horned one? She should be chastened and brought down low, so that she is forced to show a good woman's humility. Just like her, Eve forced Adam from the garden of Eden."

Eadric was having difficulty listening to the pious speech that the priest was making, and was beginning to lose his patience. He took a deep breath, and stopped clenching his teeth before he spoke. "The accused has rights. Any guilt needs to be established before punishment can be considered." With that, he loudly announced the resumption of the public hearing.

The ealdorman asked the woman who had made the accusation to come forward. She was an older woman, probably in her thirties, who had seen her youth disappear long ago, and who seemed eager to testify. She said that her husband, who was not in attendance at the assembly, had become very sick with a fever, stopped eating, and she was convinced that he would die before the week was over.

According to her, the accused, named Hilde, came to their home, apparently gave the man a healing potion, and he survived. However, the wife noticed that after her husband's condition had improved, he became enamored with Hilde, wanting to send her gifts, and looking at her with longing when she walked by him in the settlement. The wife was convinced that the wicce had given him a love potion as well, and she wanted the young woman punished. Neither judge asked the woman any questions.

The accused was called forward, and Leofsige was direct: "Young woman, are you a follower of Satan, and a maker of spells and unnatural cures and potions?"

She was just as direct. "Reverend father, I am none of those things, but a good daughter of the Church. My parish priest is here, and he can testify that I attend mass every week."

Leofsige went on. "Why is her husband not here today? Did you threaten him with a terrible spell if he was willing to speak against you?"

Hilde smiled. "That woman's husband is surely ashamed of himself for allowing his wife to bring these charges. Or perhaps his wife did not want him to contradict her. I have enough to respond to without being blamed for the absence of another."

With a sigh, Eadric realized that he needed to enter the discussion. "Perhaps you could explain what you know about the illness of this woman's husband, and his behavior since."

She shifted her gaze from the priest to him. "Lord Eadric, I will tell you what I can. When I was a little girl, I was taught about which herbs and flowers had the power to improve or even cure health problems. My mother, who lost her husband and my father to a farming accident involving a horse, was able to feed herself and me by providing remedies to people who needed them. There are many neighbors who owe her their lives."

"I heard that this woman's mate had a high fever, so I went to her and offered my help. I made a thick broth made from yarrow leaves and flowers, black elderberries, and a tiny bit of catnip. Within one day, his fever went down quickly, which I observed when I visited again to see if the broth had done its work. At that time, she welcomed me to her home, and was grateful for my curing her husband."

"However, she changed her view of me after her man was feeling well again, and began to look at me with carnal desire. I did not encourage him in any way by word or action, I refused his offers of gifts, and I used no magic or spells or any other black arts. So his lust should be his wife's concern, not mine. He is certainly much too old for me, and he is not even very clean. Why would I want this man?"

Leofsige was not finished. "Can you prove that you are innocent of these charges? The testimony of the wife is troubling, and there is still the smell of brimstone about your story."

"Holy father, how can I prove that I did not do something with magic? I know about herbs and roots that can help the body to cure itself. Find me someone suffering from a high fever, and I will show you that this remedy does work. Otherwise, I am at your mercy."

The priest and Eadric withdrew to discuss the case. As soon as they were alone, the priest ignored his earlier judgements, and started talking about a fine to be assessed against the healer because she offered medicine without authority--and because it was a woman who did it.

The ealdorman resisted the urge to start laughing, but he had heard enough: he was adamant about dismissing the charges. No real evidence had been provided, and thus no guilt had been proven, at least to his satisfaction. Leofsige was unhappy about that, but Eadric made it clear that, in his view, these had been weak accusations, and quite unworthy of their review.

When the finding was announced, the wife bit her lip and frowned, but she knew better than to protest. Eadric nodded to Hilde, who thanked the court and smiled as she walked out of the hall. Watching her leave, he knew that he could have desired her without the benefit of any sort of magic potion. She was very attractive, and he appreciated strong women. However, his marriage was almost upon him, so he needed to let that thought go.

Other shire courts brought different challenges, and Leofsige approached each one like a stubborn child might: expecting to get his way no matter how many times before he had been refused. The priest anticipated at every session that he would be allowed to rule on cases solely according to his view of things, even though Eadric was never willing to accept that, and the priest always seemed surprised that the ealdorman could not be bullied.

Eadric had no trouble admitting to himself that he enjoyed

not only thwarting the priest's attempt to dominate him, but also getting his way with almost every verdict and financial disposition that the shire court was called upon to decide. The old man was predictable in his refusal to accept either evidence or secular logic in his judicial dealings. However, as much as Eadric liked to see fairness prevail, he also delighted in winning for its own sake, especially when the Church was the loser.

Chapter Thirteen
Marriage and a Brother

The wedding of Eadric and Eadgyth took place at the small king's chapel on his estate near London. Guests crowded into every inch of the stark gray stone interior, except for an area directly in front of the altar. Everyone in the kingdom with political sense wanted to attend, and it was so crowded that two of Eadric's brothers were forced to stand outside of the chapel door to listen to the ceremony.

The bride wore a long sleeved gown of pure white linen with a bright blue sash at her waist, and the groom wore a new tunic made for the occasion, edged with elaborate embroidered designs in the same bright blue. His blue breeches were much more colorful than what Eadric was comfortable wearing, but the bride had insisted, it being her favorite color. However, during the long ceremony itself, Eadgyth looked extremely nervous, and seemed almost disbelieving that this was happening to her.

The reception was held in the king's great hall, and the only unexpected element was that Edmund attended it, as he had attended the wedding. The expression on his face made it clear that the king had ordered him to be present for both events, and he was obviously angry that his presence had been required.

He had seen Eadric as someone grossly inferior in status at their first encounter, had not changed his opinion since, and was mortified that a sister of his would lower herself to marry a country thegn like this. He was supremely indifferent to the reality that his father and brothers liked Eadric, and had happily welcomed him into the family. Even Emma, the king's wife from Normandie, occasionally made an effort to converse with him, despite her limited knowledge of English. She was as friendly to him as she was to anybody, saving only the king himself.

The wedding night went about as badly as the young ealdorman had expected. After he gave his bride time to don a shift and become relaxed in their bed, he entered to find her softly weeping. He asked what was troubling her.

She hesitated. "I know what this evening should be, and I am willing to submit to you as your wife, but I am not—comfortable—with this side of things. I have always been very particular about my grooming and being clean, as I know you are, but my delicacy in these matters is quite extreme." Her pretty hazel eyes looked very sad. "Please do what you are expected to do tonight, and we will talk further about this soon."

She was an attractive woman with a slim body, and Eadric longed to enjoy her, but he was determined to be patient, using his hands gently under her shift to try to arouse her interest. She lay there as if she were asleep, allowing him to touch her however he wished. Unfortunately, as softly and considerately as he caressed her, she remained completely unresponsive. Finally, he entered her, causing some slight discomfort, and the event concluded quietly. Neither said anything afterwards, and they went to sleep.

When Eadric next came to visit his wife and the royal family, a few weeks later, the sun was already down. He was met in the doorway by a pretty free born girl with blond hair like Ingrith's, and startling green eyes.

"My lord, you must be Eadric. My name is Brita, and I have been brought to this royal house by your wife, my mistress. I am to attend to your needs when you come to our great city. Think of me as your hostess. The princess is a very sensitive woman, whose desire for privacy and peace in her daily life needs to be respected."

Eadric looked at her carefully. He was on uncertain ground now. "Perhaps you could be more specific. I am very tired after a long ride, and my mind is a little slow at the moment."

She smiled. "When there's something that you need, I will provide it, as much as I am able. Can I begin by offering you something to drink? I am sure you would like something to refresh you after such a long ride."

She brought him a cup of ale, which he downed in a few gulps. He was still somewhat uncertain about this situation, but that uncertainty was short-lived. After the two exchanged words for a moment or two, she took his hand, and walked with him to the same room where his bride and he had stayed recently, and closed the door.

She was clearly a woman whose experience with men was at least the equal of Eadric's experience with women, and he was delighted with that. Standing up on her toes, she kissed him, and they wrapped their arms around each other. They were moving together almost before they realized it. They made the battle last as long as they could, and then surrendered to it.

When they emerged fully clothed from the room into the great hall, he saw his wife across the room speaking to a servant. She turned and smiled at him, and the family shared a pleasant meal together. Brita became a familiar face in the king's home, and there were no further discussions between Eadric and his wife about the marriage bed.

When he returned home after the very public marriage, he found Ingrith and their son sitting in front of the open hearth, her arm around him, telling him a story. They hadn't noticed him come in, so he stood in the evening shadows and listened to her weave a fanciful tale about a hero and some nasty trolls, and he was interested to hear her talk about the hero's love for his mother and his father.

Eadric wasn't sure that he deserved to be thought of so warmly given the recent events in London, but he decided that he wanted to make an effort. He would try to resist any further intimacy with Brita, and give Ingrith the loyalty that he knew she deserved. He stepped out of the shadows, startling both of them for a moment, and then almost smothered them with a loving hug. They felt so warm after the cold days riding from London.

Ingrith pulled away a little and looked at him. "Are you back?" It was a leading question.

"I am back. It is good to be home."

The two of them sang a gentle song to Thorunn about

seeing shapes of things among the stars, and the boy fell asleep with a contented smile on his face. After a naked battle in their sleeping area, the two of them slept very soundly as well.

With the cooperation of King Aethelred, and the reluctant consent of the witan, Eadric continued to increase his control of land in Mercia previously taken from secular owners by the Church, and added many men who now swore their fealty to him. Every important cleric in the land was angry about these changes, but Eadric understood. People do not miss what they have never had, but once they have something, they do not ever want to give it up.

His older brother Brihtric was pleased for Eadric and his new political status, and for the sudden prominence of the family. However, he was constantly aware that it was his younger brother who had surpassed him, and he was hoping for an opportunity to become important in his own right. He broached the subject after an evening meal, when they were sitting alone at the board, except for Leina, the thrall who was cleaning around them.

"I thought the meat was over-cooked and very tough to chew. What did you think?"

Eadric smiled. "I think I have to agree with you. Even the bread was hard to get down. However, I don't think that's why you waited for everyone else to finish and leave before you started this conversation with me. Talk to me. Is there something on your mind?"

Brihtric groaned. "Either we have been together too long, or you are becoming too clever for me." He put his head down and rested it on his hands for a moment. "I am taller than you, but I am feeling small standing near you. You have become an important man in the country, you are married to a noble woman, and I'm nothing but an overseer of our estates."

"My brother, you're not giving yourself enough credit. You have taken on many of the family responsibilities while I am dealing with issues relating to the whole of Mercia. I could not do what I am doing without you. Understand that."

Brihtric expected him to say that, and he was not going to be placated so easily. "I want to do something more. I want to make a name for myself, and not stay completely in your shadow. Help me find a good opportunity, and I will be very grateful to you."

Eadric promised that he would be alert for any opportunity, made several inquiries, and three weeks later, he spoke again with his brother. "The king has considered what you asked of me, and has said that he is willing to appoint you as commander of the northern fleet of our navy. Your leadership in building some of the ships is to be rewarded. You will need to plan with Wulnoth, a thegn who heads the southern fleet, to ensure that the shores of England are properly protected. Is that a big enough job to you?"

Needless to say, Brihtric was overwhelmed and happy. In his eyes, the opportunity seemed perfect. He traveled to Sussex to meet Wulnoth and was gone for about a week. When he returned, he asked his brother to sit down with him, that he would have much to tell him.

He looked unhappy and troubled, and more than a little angry. "I will be blunt with you, Eadric. I believe that this Wulnoth is more interested in filling his own purse than in defending our shores. Further, I suspect that he is in contact with Viking leaders, and for a price may be willing to hand over his ships and betray his king and country in favor of raiders. A messenger arrived while I was there, and Wulnoth met with him privately. Frankly, the man looked like a Viking warrior or jarl from across the sea."

"If you are confident about what you are saying, you should take your accusations to the king. Are you?" His brother nodded. "Then I will endorse your visit, and Aethelred will give you a fair hearing."

Brihtric was able to speak to the king within a week, which was most unusual. That Aethelred made time for him was a loud statement about his affection and respect for his younger brother. Not only did the king listen, but a trial was immediately held, and an absent Wulnoth was found guilty of treason and exiled. Completely ignoring the judgment of the court, but confirming the correctness of its verdict, the thegn took twenty-nine of the ships from the country's fleet and began raiding the southern coast, including his home area of Sussex.

Seeing an opportunity for personal glory, Brihtric got the king's approval to take a mighty fleet of eighty ships from the English fleet and set sail, pursuing the raider in the south near Southampton. Confident that his forces were far superior to the ships he was pursuing, Brihtric began to imagine the great honors that his victory at sea would bring him. The king would recognize him, other thegns would respect him, and pretty women would suddenly find him attractive. He would be an important man like his brother.

Unfortunately, the forces of nature did not cooperate. A massive storm developed over open water, and before any of the ships had time to prepare for the onslaught, the unearthly winds and waves brought terrible destruction to the fleet. Open sails capsized many ships or, in some cases, drove them into other nearby ships, and one hull stove in another. Dozens of ships were sunk, and for some sailors desperate to save their own lives, there was no alternative but to beach their vessels.

When Wulnoth, whose ships somehow avoided the worst of the storm and survived it, found the shore littered with abandoned ships, he burned many of them, and fled. As a result of this two-fold calamity, the English fleet was devastated, and greatly reduced in size. These losses made the coast much more vulnerable than before to new attacks from abroad, which everyone knew were coming.

A week after the storm, Eadric had still heard nothing from his brother. After more than two weeks, he correctly concluded that Brihtric had been lost at sea, along with a large number of his ships and men. As was the case with so many on board those ships, his brother's body was never found and identified, and the funeral at the estate involved an empty grave.

Knowing that it would have meant a great deal to Brihtric, Eadric paid a poet to write a song about his brother's bravery, and his battle against the winds and the water. It began thus:

Angered by open treason,   brave Brihtric called to arms
the best of England's fleet   to heed the direst need
of king and country and face   the harshest battle
against the deadly seas and foes   unwilling to fight.

Full eighty ships laden with men   in war-gear well equipped
Went forth angry and resolute   to search and find
The traitor and those who sail   for gold and not for country.

Eadric paid a monk to make copies of the verses, and had them shown to attendees at the next witan. Unfortunately, the writing was uninspired, and the narrative was far from a moving story. The purchased eloquence stirred nobody's imagination, the verses were ignored, and the brother was quickly forgotten by everyone but his own family. There were many other families who had lost sons, especially along the seacoasts, and they had their own losses to remember.

After the naval losses and the family tragedy, Eadric became much less willing to provide opportunities for public advancement to family members. He already understood that a public life exposed a man to much greater dangers than a private one. Hereafter, he hoped that he would be the only member of his family vulnerable to the winds of power and politics.

Chapter Fourteen
Visiting The West

The death of Brihtric was a real blow to Eadric. They always had the closest relationship of all of the brothers, and the two always played together as children. When his older brother had been eager to do something significant with his life, just as Eadric was doing, the ealdorman had used a little of his Viking treasure to make a couple of the king's advisors more receptive to giving Brihtric a position of responsibility within the English navy. So some of the responsibility for his brother's death fell to him.

Brihtric's death also served to remind Eadric of his own mortality. Although he was not sure that a priest or monk could despise him enough to be a threat to his life, he knew that the Church hostility was real and substantial, and he didn't want to take any chances. Anywhere close to the home estate near Shrewsbury, he was comfortable riding alone. However, when traveling any significant distance, he started to ride with a small number of armed companions, typically anywhere from two to five men.

His dead brother had been overseeing the family estates until the brief naval commitment began, so Eadric decided that he should visit a few of the holdings himself. One of them was near Westburh, a minor fortified settlement perhaps eight miles from home--but also no more than a couple of miles from the manmade boundary with Wales that many called Offa's Dyke. The border had been quiet for some years, perhaps because of the common practice of removing an ear of any Welshman found east of the border.

It was late spring, and the wild flowers were on colorful

display everywhere. The day promised to be sunny and cool as the mounted party started out from Eadric's home early in the morning. Traveling on a well-worn path towards their destination, the six men were unconcerned about losing their way. In fact, two of the men had relatives living near the settlement.

The ealdorman started talking casually with Weolfran, a free man who worked the land on the home estate, as they rode next to each other. The young man thus far had met with little success in finding a woman interested in marrying him, and his willingness to find humor in the situation did not mean that he was happy about it.

Eadric tried to begin gently. "Who do you have your eye on now?"

Weolfren groaned. "Lord, I have made little gifts for Uma, the daughter of a neighbor of the estate, and she has returned each of them. She must have her pretty eye on somebody else, and I think that I will have to keep looking for a mate."

Eadric knew who Uma was, and he thought that she looked like someone who must have had a curse of ugliness placed on her, but he kept that to himself. "Have you started to wash yourself in the river with soap as I suggested to you some weeks ago?"

Weolfren was momentarily silent. "No, lord."

"Are you afraid of the river?"

Weolfren smirked. "No, lord."

"Are you afraid of the soap?" Eadric began to laugh.

"Perhaps, lord." He waited until Eadric stopped laughing. "I have heard from more than one person that washing yourself too often makes it more likely that you will get sick. And sick people die."

Eadric smiled. "I have heard that story from other people as well. Do I look sick?"

"No, lord, but you are a powerful man."

"Do the Danes, who all wash themselves like I do, look sick?"

"No lord, but they are Danes, and they all seem strong and healthy."

"Smack yourself on your forehead--but not so hard that you rattle your brain." Without even thinking about it, Weolfren followed precisely the order of his ealdorman. "Danes seem to do very well with the women, is that not so?"

"Lord, you can talk about women like this because you have landed a real beauty. But there are not many unmarried women within a reasonable distance, and my family would murder me if I tried to marry a Dane."

"I can do nothing about your family's hostility towards the Danes. But I can continue to encourage you to begin to wash yourself clean more frequently, and perhaps the lovely Uma may change her mind."

Weolfren looked at Eadric and wondered if the thegn was being sarcastic, and then he shrugged his shoulders and stared down the path as he rode. Alas, Eadric did not see much hope for the banns being posted as a prelude to marriage any time soon for the young man and Uma.

As they approached the settlement, the front rider saw through a stockade entrance two men running in different directions, and alerted the others. Something looked amiss. Eadric pulled out his sword and spoke quietly to the others. "Stay alert. If there is trouble, we want to surprise whoever is in the town and doesn't belong there."

His sword was the only one among the group, but each of them had a weapon an enemy would have to take seriously. Three of the men carried battle axes, another had an unusually long seax knife, almost a short sword, and the last held a short wooden haft with a sharpened spearhead on the end. None of them were helpless lambs.

Leading the way, Eadric saw four sad-looking horses hobbled and standing wearily together as he approached the opening of the palisade, and he heard a loud voice saying something urgent, but he couldn't understand the words. He did recognize the language: Welsh. Clearly, there were bandits from across the border in the settlement, and probably five or six, looking for food, silver, and better horses. If nobody hindered them, they would probably also take young children and women back with them to keep or sell as slaves.

He dismounted, left his horse with Weolfren, and quietly crept up to the entrance into the settlement. There appeared to be a small number of men looking around, and two of them were thus far trying and failing to break into buildings. The locals were nowhere to be seen, and had probably hidden themselves behind doors that they had barricaded. Unfortunately, that escape would likely prove temporary if the raiders were determined.

He retrieved his horse, mounted, and had the other men get as close to him as they could before he started giving quietly whispered instructions.

"There are probably a few more thieves inside than our number, but they are on foot right now, and probably less well armed, so we can afford to be confident of success. When we get inside, spread out, find one or two of the brigands, and run them down with your horse. If you need your weapon, use it well, and any deaths that may result will be well deserved. Capture them if you can. I hope that at least one raider will survive and be returned to Wales with a story about a border settlement being defended with serious force."

Without a moment's hesitation, the six men rode quickly through the entrance and fanned out. Eadric spotted a man in a tattered brown tunic holding a knife and leading a woman towards the open center of the settlement where the raiders' nags were standing unsteadily. The Welshman heard the horses, saw Eadric coming after him, and forgot the woman, running like the devil was after him. He didn't get far, as Eadric's horse knocked him off his feet. The ealdorman's sword stayed out of its scabbard until it became clear that the man was hurt, and beyond resisting.

The other Mercians had different degrees of trouble with the Welsh thieves they went after. One of Eadric's men named Durstan found himself dealing with a gray-bearded raider with a knife, who was obviously willing to use it. Avoiding a battering from the horse by staying close to a building and then keeping a tree between himself and his attacker, the man then charged with his knife raised over his head. Durstan brought his axe down and hacked at the man, slicing into his neck and sending blood everywhere.

Another of the Mercians chased a raider between two buildings and could only get him to stop running by striking him on the top of his head with the butt end of his axehead. That dropped the intruder in his tracks, although he only looked to be dazed by the blow.

The rest of the Welshmen were taken down without further injury or loss of life. In fact, the Mercian with the sharpened spearhead only needed to brandish his weapon, and two thieves surrendered in an instant. All of the surviving Welshmen were herded over to where Eadric was standing over his sitting prisoner, and their hands were bound. There were seven of them, and none of them said a word in any language.

Looking them over, Grimwald, the man with the spearhead, had one comment: "I have seen harder men drinking in an alehouse." He shook his head.

As soon as the settlement had been retaken, local people began to emerge from their hiding places: some from the surrounding forest, others from inside buildings. One woman had hidden herself in a pile of wet hay, and looked a little like a porcupine before she brushed herself off.

There was obvious relief that the raid was over, but also anger. One older man was already shaking his fist at the captured thieves, and the woman who had been grabbed by one of them started speaking loudly about hanging them. A small boy tried to kick one of the thieves as he walked past. Over a score of people quickly gathered, and Eadric knew that he needed to speak.

"People of Westburh, I am Eadric, the ealdorman of Mercia, and I have been given authority by King Aethelred to judge and set punishment for any who break the king's peace in this domain. We need to learn the truth about what happened, and then to respond if necessary with an appropriate punishment."

As he was talking, the group of residents got very quiet, a few people bowed, and most looked at each in astonishment. Some didn't even know that they had an ealdorman in Mercia again, and they certainly had never laid eyes on someone of his rank and power. Typically, disputes or personal offenses in this area were dealt with privately, and personally.

Eadric began again. "The timing of our arrival was fortunate, as I believe that the damage could have been much worse, but we need to deal fairly with these men. They are clearly Welsh, so they have already violated our border. However, let us gather what information we can."

"Durstan, you have relatives in this area. Do you know any Welsh? We need to question these men."

"I do, lord. I am not happy speaking the language of this filth, but I have dealt with some of them before this."

"Then I suggest that you ask the man with the dirty green tunic what they were doing here. He probably leads them, if anybody does."

Durstan walked over and spoke quietly to the man Eadric had singled out. The man said nothing, and just glared at his interrogator. Durstan turned back to Eadric. "Now what, lord?"

"Tell him that we believe that they came to murder everyone in the settlement, and we plan on hanging all of them shortly."

That message was conveyed to the Welshman, who immediately went into a long rant that only Durstan could understand, and even he probably missed some of the details. However, this was better than the previous silence.

Durstan pursed his lips. "He says that they came to take horses, and maybe a few chickens. He also says that the man taking the woman was hoping that, if he brought her back with him, she might be willing to marry him." He sighed. "As it happens, the woman is already married to my cousin, and happily so. Needless to say, I do not believe that there is much truth to his story."

"Fair enough. He admits that they came to steal, and probably to do more than he is saying. Livestock, silver if they could find any, and probably some young people to take as slaves."

Some loud murmuring from the locals began after those comments. A man in the rear of the group spoke clearly: "They should hang--all of them."

Eadric abruptly raised both of his arms, and everyone stopped talking. "Let us continue with the inquiry. Was anybody injured by these outsiders?"

Nobody said anything.

"I understand your silence. It is clear than no one was injured. Were any of your animals killed or harmed by these men?"

After several quiet moments, a man in the front looked around, heard nothing from the group, and replied. "No, lord."

Eadric went on. "So there are no injured parties. The only harm was to the king's peace, which is no small thing. Grimwald, what did this trouble cost the raiders?"

"One dead and one injured, my lord. The man you took down has a broken arm, and perhaps some damage to his shoulder. Seven thieves remain alive."

The ealdorman looked at the assembled residents. "Who among you still believe that these men should hang? Any of you?" People looked at each other, and said nothing.

"Then here is my judgment. Attacks on peaceful English settlements like this one need to be discouraged. And a second offense is intolerable. I order that each of these Welshmen should have one ear cut off, so that if any of them return to this side of the border again, their repeated guilt will be obvious, and they will be executed. Durstan, explain the punishment to the prisoners, and what it will mean if they return." Durstan did so.

"Grimwald, does your spearhead remain sharp?"

"As sharp as a razor, my lord."

"Then I charge you to take these men behind that blacksmith's forge, and remove one ear from each. They can select which ear to lose. I trust that, afterward, they will still be able to hear the jeers of their family and friends. The rest of my men should accompany you, and assist you in carrying out this punishment."

He turned back to the residents. "Do any of you wish to keep the unfortunate horses that these men brought with them?" There was no answer. "I thought not. Grimwald, let these Welshmen return to their sorry lives with the sorry horses that they rode getting here."

After the sentence was carried out, and the cries and groans of the offenders diminished, they were escorted to the border by Eadric's men and their bonds cut. While this was being done, Eadric received for his efforts the praise and gratitude of the people who called the settlement home. A small pig was killed and roasted to provide a proper reward for Eadric and his heroes upon their return. After that feast, they visited the ealdorman's nearby estate, the real reason for their visit, and then turned eastward towards home. And the settlement of Westburh returned to normal.

Chapter Fifteen
Enter Thorkell the Tall

Viking raiders had a genius for looking for and recognizing weaknesses in potential targets, and the loss of so many ships when the great storm devastated the English fleet in the spring made the coastline much more open to attack. To no one's surprise, in early August 1009, a large Viking fleet led by Thorkell the Tall, a Dane oath-sworn to King Sweyn Forkbeard but acting on his own, began attacking coastal towns.

The shires of Kent, East Anglia, and much of southern Wessex witnessed burning, killing, and plundering. Mercia remained mercifully spared from these attacks, but Eadric realized that the situation might change in the future, so he directed some warriors loyal to him to visit farms and estates to ensure that if the fyrd needed to be called, men would be armed and trained.

During those attacks in the south, a formal edict written by Bishop Wulfstan was issued by King Aethelred to the entire nation, which called for a three day period of penance, asserting the conviction that the Viking raids were the result of the sins of the English people. The royal announcement stipulated that, during that period, all men, women, and children could consume only bread and water. No exceptions were made for the sick or elderly. Further, people were ordered to walk to church barefoot, a small offering must be made to the Church by all landowners, and everyone must attend mass on every one of the three days. Anyone not fully participating in these was to be fined or whipped.

Priests throughout the country noticed a slight increase in

church attendance during the period of atonement, but their disappointment with the general lack of observance was keen. Needless to say, very few people living in the Danelaw observed those requirements, and the Danes living near Eadric's home ignored them.

Eadric himself was informed of the edict, but he did nothing to enforce the penalties. In fact, he invited Ingrith's mother, sister and Inga's Danish lover to the estate for a midday feast, and they ate perhaps a bit more venison and chicken than they should have. In addition, a considerable quantity of ale was consumed. He was sure that a report of his leniency and disobedience reached the ears of the bishop, but nobody said anything to his face.

In 1011, the raiders of Thorkell captured both the city of Canterbury and the archbishop himself, a man named Aelfheah. Eadric knew the cleric fairly well, having dealt with his priests at the witans when Bishop Wulfstan and his clerics did their best to resist and prevent the transfer of some property to Eadric. There was no meanness or evil in the archbishop, but Eadric could see that the man was convinced that his vision of things and his goals for the Church were miraculously an exact match for the vision and goals of God. And that meant that he was incapable of making compromises with anybody.

Shortly after learning about the seizure of the archbishop, King Aethelred asked Eadric to begin negotiating with Thorkell for the possible ransoming and release of Aelfheah. There were two likely reasons for the king's selection of the ealdorman for the task. First, Eadric knew the archbishop, although the cleric had opposed his efforts to strengthen the secular authority in Mercia. Second, the king had learned that his son-in-law had a Danish woman and son living near Shrewsbury, and he might have a better chance of succeeding given his personal experience with Danes.

The possibility of the English paying money like this was no shock to Eadric. He had learned that over a hundred years before, King Alfred had paid money to Vikings to get them to withdraw, and he was informed that Aethelred had made similar payments in 991, 994, 1002, and 1006. Some called it danegeld, but it was actually heregild or "army money," used to pay off raiding armies to stop attacking. Eadric didn't think much of the practice, but the tactic had become a comfortable one for King Aethelred.

He first met Thorkell the Tall at an alehouse in Canterbury, where the Dane had demanded the meeting. What surprised Eadric was that Thorkell wasn't especially tall at all. In fact, he was probably only slightly taller than most Danes that the ealdorman had met, so he assumed there was perhaps some small humor involved in the nickname. Or perhaps it was a comment about Thorkell's importance as a Viking leader, since one of the nicknames for Odin, the Viking god, was "the Tall."

A broad-chested man with long pale hair tied back behind his head, he had smiling blue eyes and a laugh to match. He shook hands with Eadric, brought him a cup of ale, and quickly informed the ealdorman that he preferred to be called Jarl Thorkell, and just Thorkell to his friends.

"So you have come to talk about buying back that stiff-necked Christian high priest, yes? You know, you could pass for a Dane if your beard was a little longer. What do you know about that?"

Eadric grinned and shrugged. "The truth lies buried with my mother." The possibility of being part Dane amused him. "However, we have some business to discuss."

Thorkell shook his head. "I don't think this thing is going to happen quickly. Let us drink a little more, and then I will show you the priest to prove that he is in good health."

Eadric was curious. "Why do you expect our dealings to take a while? I don't have the authority to hand you whatever outrageous payment you might demand, but I directly represent the king and the interests of England."

"Bargaining, my English Dane. We need to bargain. What is the fun of selling the priest like a cow with a fixed price? After a little more ale, you can go back to Aethelred and ask for a price that is acceptable to him to free the old man. He will probably offer little, and I will have to turn it down, and we will have to start again. And of course we will have a chance to get to know each other."

He took Eadric to a house that one of his crews had taken, and they had some fish, a chicken, and something that Eadric had never tasted before: roasted horsemeat. The Mercian liked the chicken much more than the horsemeat, which he found tough to chew, and less tasty than the other offerings, but he made sure that he appeared to be enjoying it.

Thorkell informed him that horsemeat was a very familiar food for Danes and other Vikings, and Eadric realized that he had never heard that in his dealings with Thorunn and his family. Perhaps Viking warriors had their own ways. He did know that there were actually laws forbidding the eating of horsemeat in some parts of England.

After they had finished their meal, they played a few games of hnefatafl, the same board game that Ingartha had taught him. Although Eadric had learned the game quickly and had beaten his woman many times, he was no match for Thorkell. He had some understanding of the basic tactics of the game, playing on offense and on defense, but he found that he simply didn't have the sense of timing that his Danish adversary had.

Thorkell has perfect instincts: when he should attack and go after the king piece, and on defense when to plan an escape for that king piece. He sensed when to make trouble, and when to avoid it. Eadric had always believed that his sense of timing was unusually good. He would have to consider revising his views about that.

Chapter Sixteen
A Danish Interlude

After more than four years as the ealdorman for Mercia, Eadric had become an important man in the kingdom. He had strengthened his political authority by retaking by charter some properties which the Bishop of Worcestre had become comfortable owning. However, to hear the complaints of his priests, the "ealdorman thief" must have stripped the Church of all of its earthy possessions, which was very far from the truth. He presided at the shire court whenever it assembled. And he got along well with his father-in-law the king and Aethelred's other advisors, except of course for the clerics.

Two of the king's sons had died, meaning that Edmund was closer to being the atheling, heir to the throne, but he was no more willing to be civil to Eadric than he had been when the Mercian was a country thegn and a stranger. His wife remained content to sleep by herself in her bed, and Brita, her substitute, proved to be an interesting occasional bed partner, although his loyalty to his Danish woman encouraged him to sleep alone more often than not when he was away from her. Ingrith was a big part of his life, and he seldom had any desire for another woman.

He was almost certain that Thorkell had prolonged the negotiations for the ransom of the archbishop because he enjoyed Eadric's company. However, he had also become involved in negotiating the amount of the heregild that Thorkell and his raiders would accept to stop attacking towns in the south of England, so that complicated the dealings as well. The two talked about the wealth of England, and the Dane indicated that he might, if the payment was rich enough, consider becoming an ally of

Aethelred and supplying over forty of his ships and their crews to now defend the English kingdom against other Viking raiders. Eadric was told, in fact emphatically ordered by the king, to attempt to make that deal as well.

During one of Eadric's several visits to Canterbury, he was feasting with several of Thorkell's warriors inside a large church, and the Dane abruptly stood and raised his cup to propose a toast. "Here's to one of the finest Danes alive, Cnut Sweynson. I have taught him everything he knows, and I think, like his father, the king of Denmark, he will become a great man."

Eadric had no idea why Thorkell was saying what he was saying. The two had just been making comparisons about English women compared to Danish women, and they agreed that the Danes were more beautiful. Suddenly a tall man wearing a plain brown cloak stood up, shrugged it off, and Eadric was facing a handsome figure wearing a dramatic scarlet tunic with dragons embroidered with gold thread on the borders.

Immediately certain that this was Cnut, the son of the Danish king, Eadric had not realized that he had been eating and drinking with Viking royalty. Thorkell gestured Cnut to join them, and he introduced them. They were certainly within a few years of being the same age, although Cnut was the taller of the two: unusually tall in fact. Other than having a very thin nose, the prince had the perfect appearance of a Viking warrior. He seemed pleased to finally meet the English ealdorman.

"Lord Eadric, I've heard much about you from my warrior-tutor Thorkell. He tells me that you are an honorable man, you have a Dane woman and son, and that you seem to have some grievances against the King Aethelred, despite having married into his family. You may know that my father's sister and her husband and her son were murdered on the same day that so many other fine Danish folk were murdered. We share a grievance. I would suggest that you might consider serving my father and me when the time comes. We are stronger than this king, and whenever we choose, we will lead England as we now lead Denmark."

Eadric paused for a moment, and then spoke. "What Thorkell has told you is correct, up to a point. I will consider what you have said, and who can say for sure what the future holds? We do not know what Fate has determined for us."

Cnut leaned forward, his blue eyes glittering, and waited for him to continue.

"However, I have swore to serve this king, and could only abandon that vow under the most extreme circumstances. Further, I am still not satisfied that Aethelred was the one to decide that Danes should die on that day. It seems out of character for him. He is a fear-ridden person. Look at how he continues to pay Viking raiders to cease their attacks and leave, knowing full well that the peace is only temporary. I am not sure that he was to blame, and I still hope to learn the truth."

Cnut sat back and smiled. " I think you will know when the time is right to join us. And I hope, as you do, that we learn the identity of the mad dog that was behind the order to massacre innocent Danes."

Eadric had been curious about something for a long time, and this seemed to be a good opportunity to ask a question. "Thorkell, I need to satisfy myself about a mystery. About three years ago, my brother accused a thegn named Wulnoth of plotting against England, and the man afterwards raided the coast. His actions resulted in the destruction of much of our fleet, and the death of my brother. Did you have any conversations or business with that man?"

Thorkell hesitated before answering. "Wulnoth is long gone, so he cannot be hurt by the truth. Of course, yes, he was in contact with me about joining my fleet, and we were close to agreeing on it. Although I could have used his support, the destruction of much of your navy was much more helpful than Wulnoth could ever have been. I am very sorry your brother was lost."

The three men raised their cups to Brihtric, and enjoyed more excellent mead together. After more discussion about the merits of English versus Danish women, they parted in a friendly fashion.

On the long ride back to Mercia, Eadric reflected upon the encounter with Cnut. He suspected that the entire meeting was carefully planned by either Thorkell or Cnut, and perhaps both of them. Thorkell had made certain that Eadric had eaten well, and had already drunk a few large cups of ale before he even knew that Cnut was there. When the prince revealed himself, his appearance was dramatic and impressive, and that was probably deliberate.

Thorkell had obviously provided Cnut with every detail about the death of his friend during the St. Brice's Day massacre in Oxenford, as well as information about Ingrith and their son. Then Cnut used that information to try to convince him to defect to the Danish side, and was quite persuasive. Clearly, Cnut was a man to be reckoned with, and Eadric needed to keep his wits about him when dealing with the prince. He knew from playing the board game with Thorkell that the man was excellent at tactics and planning. Already he suspected that Cnut might be even better.

Finally, after several months, and a number of negotiations involving Eadric, Thorkell and some of his crews agreed to stop raiding and to actually join the English cause for 48,000 pounds. After the money had been paid, Eadric assumed that his work was done. He was wrong.

Some of the leaders in Thorkell's army were not completely satisfied with the deal. Because Archbishop Aelfheah had been so difficult to deal with, insulting their Norse gods and continually demanding that every Viking that he met must convert to Christianity, they demanded an additional 3,000 pounds for his release. He had been an irritating captive, and Thorkell's men did not forget that.

Once more Eadric returned to Canterbury to treat with Thorkell. When he arrived, the Viking could not be found. He finally appeared after a long wait, looking extremely unhappy. "My lord Eadric, things have changed since you were summoned. Sadly, the priest is dead."

The young Mercian was stunned. "What? Did he try to escape? Did he insult the Danish gods again? Did he offend some warrior personally? Please tell me that there was a good reason for his death."

Thorkell thought for a moment about the best words to use

before replying to his friend. "The stubborn old man refused to be ransomed. He said that he was unwilling to add to the financial burdens of his people by permitting more heregild to be paid for his freedom. Either the payment already having changed hands would be enough, or he would place his life in the hands of his Christian God."

Eadric waited. "And then?

"And then some of my men, who learned of his stubbornness, became angry, got quite drunk, and began throwing large cow bones from their feast at him. He was knocked down, he was very badly injured by a cow skull, and one man mercifully finished him off with an ax butt to the head. I only learned about his death after it was too late to do anything. Can I assume that the 3000 pound ransom we were talking about will not be paid for his body?"

Shocked by this sudden turn of events, Eadric couldn't believe his ears. He hoped Thorkell didn't intend that last inquiry to be a serious question. Surely nothing would be paid for the cleric's corpse. It was several moments until the Dane smiled broadly and shrugged his shoulders--his sense of humor had failed him this time. The ealdorman was relieved, having wondered briefly if he had been wrong about the Dane. He didn't like dealing with stupid people, and he had always thought that Thorkell was a clever man.

As good as his word, Thorkell immediately began defending the English coast against other Vikings with his forty ships and hundreds of warriors, and peace was quickly restored to the kingdom. After reporting to the king in London, Eadric returned to his home near Shrewsbury, and started to believe that he could finally enjoy the fruits of his labors as ealdorman, and live in peace with Ingrith and their son. He wanted nothing more than that. Not power, not fame, not even more women. Of course, the Fates laugh whenever men with power anticipate a life without challenges in their future.

Chapter Seventeen
The Church Revisited

A witan was held at Amesbury in mid-1012, and Eadric was startled to see a familiar face, one which could have been long-forgotten, but wasn't. From across the hall, he was not sure that he knew the man, but on closer inspection, he was certain of his identity. He was the young priest who, some years ago, had interrupted his assault by the other priest, the molester of children who had been asked to tutor him in Latin. During a pause in the proceedings, he walked over, greeted the cleric, and gently pulled on his sleeve to get him away from the others.

"What is your name, reverend father?"

"I am called Father Winoth, and I serve in the north. How may I help you?"

"You probably do not remember me, but I was a student at Wenlock Priory some years ago, and I had a tutor then who I wanted to thank for helping me with my education. His name was Father Morgynnyd. Could you tell me where I could find him?"

The priest looked puzzled for a moment, and then suddenly recognized the boy who had grown into a man. A moment after that he recalled what he had witnessed so long ago. He quickly glanced around, looking for a way to leave the hall, but he realized that an easy escape was not available to him.

He returned his attention to Eadric and answered quickly. "He has gone far away. He is no longer at the priory."

Eadric was not going to be satisfied with that, and he hoped to make that clear to the priest. He held the cleric's ample sleeve a little more tightly. "And where has he gone? I need to see him."

"I do not know where he went. He was assigned to another

diocese." He stopped speaking for a moment, and seemed to be weighing his words. "I cannot tell you anything more. Remembering what happened so long ago, and seeing the look on your face, I know that you want to kill him, and I cannot help you."

Eadric pulled the priest closer to him. "Listen carefully to me, reverend father. If I did want to murder that priest, I would get you to tell me where he could be found, and I would cut his throat. However, I swear that I will not kill Father Morgynnyd. I am willing to give you my solemn oath on that. He will leave my presence alive. And you do not want to make an enemy of me. You must certainly know who I am now."

The priest was silent for a time, and then spoke slowly and deliberately. "He is no longer a humble priest like me. He is now Bishop Morgynnyd, and he is the head of St. David's monastery on the Welsh coast. He has been there for a dozen years, and is a beloved leader of the Church."

"So you never reported what I know that you saw that day to anyone, and he has prospered in the Church since then? You don't see a problem with that?"

The priest looked and sounded confused. "I think that you are not a true believer--you do not understand the religion of Christianity. Why would I tell anyone? His sins are between him and God. I'm sure he confessed and asked for forgiveness long ago, and he has done his penance. That book is closed."

Eadric shook his head. "Not for me, father. I have another small chapter to write." He released the priest, who immediately walked to the other side of the hall. As difficult as it was for him to remain at the witan until it ended, that time gave him a chance to contemplate what he needed--and wanted--to do with the information he had coerced from the priest.

He returned home immediately after the witan had concluded. He did not know if the priest he had just met would try to warn the bishop about an unwelcome visitor, so he needed to do whatever he intended to do without delay. He assembled a dozen men on horseback that he knew were skilled with weapons, just in case they encountered any armed Welsh men on their journey. Then he led them south and west towards the wide salt sea separating Wales from Ireland. Two of his warriors had been to the monastery in recent times, so he relied on them to get the group close enough so they could happen on the place without too much trouble.

It was on a tip of land jutting out into the sea, perfect for Viking raids, so finding St David's would not be difficult. Exactly what Eadric was going to do when they arrived was something he would need to make a final decision about before then. Thorkell had recently given him a very special sword, one of the finest anywhere, which had the name ULFBERHT inlaid on the blade, and Eadric wasn't certain if he would be using it when they arrived at the monastery. He had imagined meeting that priest once again, but he had never pictured what he would do when they met.

They stopped for the evening at a prosperous-looking farm stead. Appearing outside of their front door, the humbly-dressed owner and his wife acted like Eadric and his men were intending to kill him, rape her, and steal everything in the stead, and seemed almost too afraid to speak.

Eadric wanted to make clear that he did not want to cause any trouble. "Could you provide a meal and lodging for me and my men? We have traveled a good distance."

The man's response was not very hospitable. "We have little to eat ourselves, and our two small children would certainly starve if we give you what you want. Please spare our family, and try another farm closer to your destination. God go with you!"

However, after Eadric showed them two silver coins, they instantly smiled, warmly invited the men inside, and provided a good meal of a hearty stew and good rye bread. As he learned during the evening, these people lived comfortably, they really had no children at all, and based on the large look of them, hunger seemed a very distant problem. Glancing inside the family's larder after the meal, Eadric estimated that the couple could have fed a hundred men without straining their resources. He and his men all found a comfortable spot to sleep near the hearth, and left early the next morning.

Arriving at the monastery at about midday, Eadric inquired of a passing monk where they might find the bishop, as they had some business with him. Eyeing the armed men who had accompanied the ealdorman, the cleric said that the great man had been called away from his church for a few days. Realizing why the monk had answered as he did, Eadric shook his head at his own stupidity. He ordered his men to withdraw to a copse of trees some distance away, and asked another monk the same question.

"I believe that he is preparing for a mass, so you can surely find him near the altar in the church." With that, the monk continued on his way. Eadric motioned to his men to follow his lead, and he quietly entered the large stone building.

After his eyes got used to the dim light, he recognized his old assailant, despite the elaborate bishop's vestments and a strange pointed hat on his head. The cleric was placing a chalice on the altar in front of him, and he appeared to be running his hand through the hair of a young acolyte who was standing beside him.

"Bishop," Eadric said loudly, "We have come to have counsel with you. We are troubled, and perhaps you can be of some help to us."

The priest jerked his head up, removed his hand from the boy's head, and looked sternly at Eadric and his men, who walked slowly towards him. "This is the house of God, and the weapons of war are not welcome here. Please remove them, or remove yourselves."

They kept walking towards him, and the priest looked closely at Eadric. "My lord, whoever you are, this is most unseemly. Your weapons are an offense to the Lord." He started shaking his finger at them, and only stopped when Eadric was a short distance away.

"Don't you recognize me, bishop? I was a little boy named Eadric, who came to you to be taught, and now I am Ealdorman Eadric. That last time we saw each other, you had one hand covering my mouth and your cock somewhere that it didn't belong."

The bishop's face went deathly pale. "Eadri--Lord Eadric, I did not look to see you again—"

"Of course you didn't. But the Lord has put you in my path once again, and I intend to make good use of his guidance."

The ealdorman knew that he needed to act quickly. He spoke quietly, but with some urgency. "Wenric, take one of his arms. Aethelstan, hold the other one." Without a moment's hesitation, they quickly did as he had ordered. The priest was now unable to move from the spot where he had been standing, and was completely at his mercy. He remembered the acolyte, told him to leave the church, and the boy ran down the aisle and out the door.

"Bishop Morgynnyd, I have thought a great deal about you since we last saw each other. I believe that I owe you something, and I would like to pay that debt." With that, he pulled a small thin knife from its sheath on his belt.

The priest shivered and wailed. "Surely you will not kill me, my lord. I always confess and atone for my sins after I commit them, so they are my sins no longer. I am like a newborn lamb, as white as snow."

Eadric looked at him with disbelief. He had not been a proper Christian for a long time, but he knew that penance and atonement were not tricks to be used to conveniently dismiss the evil that one might do again and again. "Bishop, I don't believe it works like that. Perhaps you do not understand your religion as well as you think you do." He looked at the men at his arms. "Hold him fast."

What he had decided to do didn't take very long. He got close to the Bishop's face, put the tip of the dagger against the man's forehead, and slowly made some shallow cuts in the skin. After a few moments, and some loud yelling from the cleric, five small letters now remained there. A considerable amount of blood had been let, but he knew that he had done no great physical harm. The cleric would simply have a permanent scar on his face, one spelling out the old English word meaning "monster": E-G-E-S-A.

Eadric had a grim smile on his face. "Release him." The bishop collapsed to the floor weeping, his hat flying under a nearby bench. "Perhaps you can get used to wearing your bishop's head covering a little lower on your head."

He looked around. All around the front of the church were glittering gold and silver ecclesiastical objects: candle holders, tiny plates and goblets, and other things that symbolized the wealth and power of the church. He had been inside of other churches, and he had never seen such a show in any of them. Clearly, Bishop Morggynnyd enjoyed displaying those beautiful things. They obviously meant a great deal to him, and he would miss them if they were gone.

Eadric smiled. "My friends, take whatever you like. The bishop wants you to have some of these beautiful things for yourselves. Isn't that right, Bishop?" There was only silence.

"And Bishop, I would suggest that you keep your hands off of young boys from now on. Someone is likely to be watching you. I now know where you are, and if I need to return, you will not find me as merciful the next time."

His men took what they could easily carry away and load on to their horses, and they rode east at a leisurely pace in the direction of Mercia.

As he rode towards home, Eadric thought about the way that some Christians seemed to play a game with their religion. A man--even a priest--could do terrible things to other people over and over, and each time go to confession, say some prayers, and believe he was forgiven. Then he could continue to repeat his evil, seemingly without any risk to the soul that he was certain he possessed.

One of his thegns named Wenric, who had become a friend, rode up next to him. "I didn't like how that priest was touching that boy near the altar. I hope whatever offense you punished him for, he stays away from children after our visit."

Eadric gave him a serious look. "He probably deserved worse than a few scratches on his forehead, but I suspect that he'll keep his short staff under his tunic for a while." He made a mental note to have a man visit the church from time to time. However, whatever the priest did in the future, the ealdorman knew that he could finally turn the page on that chapter of his life. At twenty-two years of age, he was free of it.

Chapter Eighteen
Peace

For almost a year, Eadric was able to spend much of his time at the family stead in Mercia, and his disciplined approach to his duties as the ealdorman freed up time for more pleasurable things. Ingrith's sister had finally married her Danish lover, and they lived with their still youthful-looking mother in her enlarged longhouse. However, Ingrith and their son Thorunn spent most of their time with Eadric and his family. Their home now included an even larger hall, suitable for entertaining the now frequent guests, and there were several woven hangings from across the sea adorning the walls.

Eadric sometimes made time to take his son fishing at the Severn River, although the boy, like most children of his age, lacked the patience to sit for long in one place. On occasion, he tried to show the boy how to use a sword and shield using pointed sticks and woven baskets. And he ordered Owen, one of his recently purchased thralls, who seemed to have some experience with weapons, to play at combat daily with the boy. Thorunn wanted to let his hair grow like a Dane--and like his father--instead of keeping it short, and Eadric saw no reason to discourage that.

In fact, he acknowledged to himself that he was becoming more comfortable with Danes than with his own English people. Obviously, Ingrith and her family had put a Danish imprint on his private life. Thorkell had become a trusted friend, and Cnut already seemed like he could be a stronger and more decisive leader than his father-in-law the king could ever be. On the other hand, the mutual dislike between Eadric and Aethelred's son

Edmund, who was now the second in line for the throne, had grown into something bordering on hatred. Many of the English clerics with whom he had contact addressed him with politeness and deference, but were clearly hostile because of his modest property annexations within Mercia. Some of them might even have blamed him for the death of the Archbishop at the hands of Thorkell's men. He had no friends in the Church.

As complicated as Eadric's life had become since being named ealdorman of Mercia, this was a golden period in his young life. Because Thorkell's ships patrolled the English coast, small companies of raiders were discouraged from attacking the countryside. More significantly for Eadric, Welsh bandits had stopped venturing into areas in western Mercia. That was probably because some of them had been made to understand that there was once again a leader there who could summon warriors to defend local families, or violently punish those who attempted to pillage and burn. There was peace in the land. The Bishop of Worcester and his clerics sulked in their modestly reduced domain, but publicly said nothing.

In the middle of the summer in 1012, Eadric decided to provide a harvest festival on his estate for his tenants and neighbors. It had been an extremely good year thus far for the growing of crops, and no wolves had come to take any of the estate's lambs, so the larders were going to be full that winter. He knew that the early English people had celebrated a pagan harvest-time celebration called Lughnasa, and the Christian Church had created a version of it called Lammastime, and had a church service involving "first fruits". Therefore, neither Christians nor pagan Danes would be likely to object to the festival.

He asked Ingrith and her mother to organize the food, most of which would be cooked on a large open hearth in a clearing near the family home. A weir made of wooden strips woven together was constructed in a nearby stream to hold fish that were caught until the feast arrived. A cow that had just gone dry was fattened up. Early wheat and rye were cut and the grain milled so two different breads could be baked.

The kitchen thralls were busied making butter and cheese, and then placing it in a small stone cellar, which kept food cool. Three barrels of ale were set aside, and some mead was purchased from a Dane living near Shrewsbury. Finally, some apples and a few bowls of tiny wild strawberries and blackberries were picked for a sweet end to the feast.

The day before, Eadric sent three men out to hunt whatever large game they could find, and they returned with a couple of plump deer. They were all disappointed that a wild boar hadn't been found. In truth, it was a clever animal as well as a dangerous one, and was not easily cornered and downed. However, having already imagined a delicious pig roasting on a spit, they had to make do with slaughtering a tame one. Ingrith helped the thralls to clean and cook some onions, cabbage, and some nice white carrots, but she knew that meat and bread and ale were going to be the primary attractions.

People started arriving at midday, and Eadric was startled to see how many would be his guests, but some had walked considerable distances to share in the feast and the company of other festive visitors, so he ordered that several chickens should be killed and prepared in case more food was needed. Nobody would be sent away, or leave hungry or thirsty. Perhaps a quarter of them were Danes, so the host asked a few of the free men who worked on his estate to be alert for any trouble, but the plentiful food distracted anyone who might otherwise have caused a problem. The only issue was a shortage of the mead, which guests trying it for the first time found very appealing.

Many of the people ate beef for the first time--and probably the last time. It was a rare treat: few people could provide the feed necessary to raise a cow until it was big enough to slaughter. Cow's milk was equally dear, but Eadric made sure that the few small children in attendance were given a nice cup of it instead of appropriately diluted brown ale.

Trying to be a thoughtful host, Eadric had come up with a series of diversions, hoping to involve as many of his guests as possible. He had planned contests of strength, games involving pitching iron horseshoes near a target, and short races for the children. However, he quickly discovered that everyone was so absorbed in eating and drinking with abandon that they had eyes only for their food and beverages. And after they'd had their fill, many of them were in no condition to move about safely, let alone with any agility.

As darkness approached, three bonfires were lit. A tall man with intense-looking eyes and wearing a multicolored tunic appeared as if by magic, and began to strum on a small harp. Most of the guests, incapable of consuming anything more for a while, drifted over and sat down to listen. Aethelwine had been able to find and hire a traveling story-teller to bring some entertainment to the festival, and the host was as eager to see what was in store as anybody else. The man had a good reputation.

Waiting until all of the talking had ceased, the scop began to speak in a deep, distinctive voice. "My name is Crispin. I am a teller of tales, and I can be bought for just a few scraps of silver." There was widespread laughter. "I thank ealdorman Eadric and his family for inviting me here, and I hope I can earn their--he paused and noisily shook some coins in his purse--satisfaction." There was even bigger laughter. Then he dramatically cleared his throat.

"About twenty years ago, there was a battle on the shore of the eastern sea between some English men and some Vikings. No matter the end, a long poem was written soon afterwards about that fight. Called The Battle of Maldon, it is a story about bravery and loyalty, and how men choose to deal with difficulty--some well, and some poorly. I hope that you will find the telling interesting."

It was not a long story. Eadric had listened to much more elaborate tales. However, he was captivated by the speaker's manner, and the power of the words, and the absolute silence of everyone else during his presentation indicated that they too were entranced. There were fireflies floating all around, which decorated the night sky and mingled with the stars. After the teller had finished, he received loud applause and shouts of praise from his audience, and afterward Eadric paid him something extra for his efforts. Although the story was told through the eyes of the English men and their cause, the Vikings won an overwhelming victory, so both sides in the audience had something to cheer about, and went away happy.

Everyone who lived close and was sober enough to make it home safely later in the evening did so, after thanking their generous host and his family. Certainly, that was the majority of the guests. Those who remained found a comfortable place on the ground to sleep, and the warm night air made their slumber an easy thing. The last guest departed before noon the next day.

Things could not have been better. His Danish woman was happy raising their son Thorunn in a much larger and grander home than she had ever known, and Eadric had time to spend with both of them. His relations with the king and his absentee wife Eadgyth were cordial. When he visited them, she was friendly and talked to him about his other family. Her marital bed replacement Brita was proud of his well-earned importance, and understood his new loyalty to Ingrith.

Significantly, Aethelred was pleased that Eadric had consolidated some of the power in Mercia in his hands, and believed he would be a worthy ally if the need arose. Eadric thought that his world was exactly as he wished it could be, and imagined that it could be so for a long time. He would be profoundly disappointed.

Chapter Nineteen
Royal Exile

In July 1013, everything suddenly and drastically changed. The Danish king Sweyn Forkbeard and his son Cnut brought a large fleet carrying a Viking army to England. Within a few short weeks after landing, the king had absolute control of the eastern areas of the country, primarily filled with residents having Danish origins. In fact, without leaving his new headquarters at Gainsborough in Lincolnshire, he received the fealty and offers of support of every thegn and leader in the Daneland. Hostages were provided to ensure their loyalty, and the Vikings turned their attention to the rest of England.

The citizen fyrd of Mercia was perhaps two weeks away from fighting readiness when Sweyn went west and crossed the Daneland into a few border districts of English Mercia itself. Although the Viking army ravaged a few border settlements, it did not pursue its opportunities to the west, so most of Eadric's realm was left undamaged, and the army quickly went south into central Wessex. Oxenford and Winchestre surrendered without a fight. Perhaps Wessex was seen as a bigger priority than Mercia. Whatever the reason, Eadric continued to raise the fyrd, and sent out daily scouts to watch for the Viking king's next move.

Trying to finish his conquest with one blow, Sweyn took his army east to London and attacked, but was repelled by soldiers loyal to Aethelred and warriors allied with Thorkell, and many of the Vikings were drowned in the Thames after trying to ford the river when the water was too deep. Failing there, Sweyn took his army west, forced the rest of Wessex to submit to his authority, and again collected hostages. He then returned to

Gainsborough where his fleet awaited him. London was the final holdout. A total assault on that city using the ships was expected before long.

Eadric received an urgent message from London asking him to bring to the king as many warriors as he could assemble in two days or less, and it indicated that the safety of the entire royal family depended on him. Gathering roughly fifty men, he was able to avoid an unwelcome confrontation with any of the Viking forces, taking a direct route from Mercia to the capital. After three days of hard riding, the armed party arrived without incident at the king's London home.

Inside the hall, Thorkell was waiting for him, as usual with a cup of ale in his hand. "We have got a serious problem, my lord Eadric. Well, perhaps not a serious problem, but a changing situation. I assume you've heard about King Sweyn?"

Eadric shrugged his shoulders. "I know that all of the Danelaw accepted him as king right away, and he has taken control of the west. Do you know why I was called here? It's always a pleasure to see my wife and my father-in-law, but I had little time to respond to the summons. What can I expect to hear?"

"I think you should let the king tell you himself, as this is state business, but I am confident that you can expect to take a short sea voyage on one of my ships very soon."

Eadric was intrigued. "Then I expect I will be hearing an interesting story shortly. Is there any more of that ale to be shared with a tired friend?"

As it happened, Thorkell had brought the ale for him, and decided to share a bawdy riddle with him, hoping to lighten Eadric's mood. It had recently been told to him:

I am a strange creature,   *for I satisfy women...*
I grow very tall,   *erect in a bed,*
I'm hairy underneath.   *From time to time*
A beautiful girl,   *the brave daughter*
Of some stout fellow   *dares to hold me*
Grips my reddish skin,   *robs me of my head*
And puts me in the pantry.   *At once that girl*
With plaited hair   *who has confined me*
Remembers our meeting.   *Her eye moistens.*

Thorkell smiled. "A priest shared this with me. Can you guess what it is? Can you? Of course, it's an onion."

Eadric chuckled. "Of course." They both rolled their eyes.

After a few minutes, King Aethelred swept into the hall with his white cloak trailing behind him, and looking more anxious than Eadric had ever seen him. His eyes were blinking quickly, and the lips of his small mouth were pursed tightly together, perhaps to prevent his teeth from chattering.

"My loyal son, I am so happy to see you, and whatever men you could bring with you on such short notice. As I'm sure you know, the kingdom is crumbling down around our heads. Many thegns have become disloyal traitors, and I will remember everyone who betrayed me when I return in triumph. The damned Vikings already have every outlaw with Danish blood siding with Sweyn, and the western lords have just bent the knee to him. For now, we have to withdraw."

Eadric gently interrupted him. "Lord king, where can we go? We can probably return to Mercia, where I can gather some more warriors to defend you, but the Viking army will simply turn north and pursue us like hounds after a fox. Surely, that isn't a good option."

The king shook his head emphatically. "That's not it at all. Normandie, across from the narrow English Sea, will take us in. Perhaps I should more accurately say that it will take you, your men, and the rest of my family right away. My wife Emma remains a beloved sister of the current duke Richard, and he will shelter you until I can reassert our authority against these barbarians."

He stopped to catch his breath. "I plan to stay here as long as I can, if necessary go to the Isle of Wight after that, and then join you in Normandie. Thorkell will take you as soon as my family members are all prepared to leave. I hope for everyone's sake it will be a short stay."

Eadric bowed and went to find Thorkell. He needed to determine what they could bring with them. Obviously, the horses would have to be left behind, so he would arrange to sell them, and then tell his men the bad news. He would send a messenger to his estate to tell Ingrith and their son that he would be accompanying the king's family for a time, and that he would send word when he could return home again. Then he would visit his separated wife, and perhaps the pretty Brita as well.

The voyage across the sea to Normandie was a fairly short one. He traveled with Thorkell, and was disappointed that the light winds were not favorable for using the ship's massive woolen sail. The Dane's warriors reluctantly plied the long oars and rowed with precision through the calm seas. There was nothing of the sensation of speed that Eadric knew this ship was capable of creating.

While waiting at the ducal estate to be given a place to sleep that was worthy of his status, he sat outside in the sunshine on some stone steps. He had time to think about the king's weak responses to the invasion of Sweyn and the Vikings. He was a king, yes, and he was a wolf, like his father had explained to him. But there was nothing fierce, nothing aggressive about him. He looked to appease. He looked to placate his adversaries and merely defend his situation. Aethelred was likely not the answer he had wanted for almost a dozen years to the question of Thorunn's death.

Duke Richard was a congenial and a generous host, but nobody who had come over to Normandie with Aethelred's family could feel entirely comfortable on foreign soil. Of course, Queen Emma was among her own people. There was a different language, different foods, different manners and customs. Within weeks the king himself arrived, and kept a sullen look on his thin face for his entire stay. Kings do not like being chased from their own country after having every personal whim satisfied.

Christmas came and went, and the visitors pretty much kept to themselves. Some of the Normans spoke passable English, but communicating with most of them was a struggle, and sometimes Eadric actually believed that they enjoyed making their guests look silly or stupid. Finally, everyone knew that Normandie had a good relationship with the Danes, and the Danish king in particular, so there was an unspoken limit to the duke's generosity, and to the likely duration of their stay.

Eadric spent a good deal of his time walking alone along the beach, even in the constant wind and cold that were common during the winter in Normandie. Sometimes snow covered the sand, and he felt his separation from his family even more powerfully looking at the stark and lifeless expanse before him. However, Eadric's loneliness felt like a trivial thing when he thought of the people he loved. His son was developing without a father, and his woman probably brought her bedding out to the hearth in the evening to keep warm without him. There seemed to be no end in sight for this exile.

Chapter Twenty
Home Again

Early in February 1013, a messenger arrived from England to inform the exiles that Sweyn Forkbeard, the acclaimed king of England since Christmas, had suddenly died. After a brief celebration, Aethelred immediately went to church to express his gratitude for God's generosity in ending Sweyn's life. However, shortly after that, he was informed that leaders in the Danelaw, as well as the warriors in the late king's fleet, announced their support for Cnut as the next king of England. Where was he to find support for a return to the throne?

To almost everyone's surprise, a group of English leaders from the witan appeared at the court of Duke Richard in Normandie, and conferred with Aethelred. Although Eadric was not a part of the discussions, it was rumored afterwards that they had agreed to support the king's return if the king made some governing concessions, and agreed to forgive all those who had previously given allegiance to the Danish king. There were a great many thegns who had been willing to transfer their loyalty from an English king to a Viking, and each understood the dangers of having a king who feels betrayed by his oath-sworn followers.

Eadric didn't really care what the basis was for the return of Aethelred to England. He was worried about what might have unfolded in Mercia while he was attending to the family of the king. He understood that when a powerful individual leaves a domain, others would look for the opportunities to become more powerful themselves.

Also, he really missed Ingrith and their son. Despite much time apart, they had gotten closer in recent years. They had shared her family's tragedy, they'd grown up together, and their son was very special to both of them. The charms of Brita were considerable, but he didn't have the depth of feeling for her that he had for his Dane, and he'd left her alone. There were also a couple of pretty Norman women who had been interested in sharing his bed while he was in exile, as there had been other women before that, but he ignored their considerable appeal, always wanting to return to Ingrith.

By the end of April, King Aethelred had been invited to return as the English king, having given the thegns the necessary assurances, and Thorkell transported everyone back to London. A large army determined to throw Cnut and his Danes out of England was assembled, and led by the king himself. It quickly moved northward from London towards Lincolnshire and, without a single battle, the Viking army, unprepared to fight, boarded their ships and fled to Denmark.

Before leaving, Cnut cut off the hands and ears and noses of many hostages that his father had taken earlier, and abandoned his allies in the Danelaw to terrible retribution from Aethelred's army. Although the mutilations were customary, his leaving all of his English supporters behind was not. Many steads were robbed and burned to the ground by the king's soldiers, and some men killed. The Dane had shown how ruthless he could be, and in his turn Aethelred earned the enduring hatred of many in the Danelaw for his harsh punishment for disloyalty. Both men were the deserving targets for Viking curses from the Danes in Lincolnshire.

Eadric was finally able to travel to his home in Mercia, and happily reunite with his family. The grateful king had allowed his ealdorman to return and remain at home after the short exile, and he was able to reassert his authority in Mercia without incident. He visited a number of steads that he thought might have been vulnerable to the bishop's acquisitiveness, and assured the owners that he had returned, and was back in command. His domain had been unaffected by the temporary assumption of power by Sweyn, and Eadric hoped that the tranquility of the recent past could continue.

Once again he found ample time to spend with Ingrith and their son. She was as attractive and loving as ever, and he frequently found himself staying in bed with her long after the sun came up, and after his brothers broke their fast in the morning. He often took young Thorunn to the river to fish, and the boy revealed a newfound ability to catch some impressively large fish. He was almost seven, and already growing into an intelligent and observant child. Eadric found him much more interesting now than he had before his stay in Normandy.

One brief conversation broke open an old wound. "Father, where did my name come from? I do not know anybody named Thorunn."

Eadric paused for a moment. " Didn't your mother tell you anything about this?"

The boy smiled. "She told me that I should ask you about it. I was surprised, because she is always willing to tell me what I want to know. But not this time."

Eadric felt obliged to explain what had happened to the father and son in Oxenford. Although he had no desire to stir up any hatred in the boy, telling the truth was the important thing. The child needed to understand that there was good and evil in both Danes and the English.

In the early spring of 1014, Thorkell the Tall unexpectedly came to visit Eadric. The Dane looked extremely unhappy when he arrived, but he was introduced to Ingrith and their son, and quickly warmed to the meeting. He looked at Eadric and winked. "I had no idea that you had captured a great Viking beauty like this. She makes my heart beat faster just gazing at her. And this young warrior looks like he belongs in Asgard with the gods, and not among these English animals. You have done well for yourself." And he looked around at the wall hangings and other furnishing inside the family home. "I think you are far richer than I could have imagined. Perhaps I should take you all prisoner and ransom you?"

Ingrith blushed, and then beamed with pride at Thorkell's

praise for her son. "You are welcome in our home, and invited to stay for some days if you would like."

Thorkell shook his head. "I thank you for your offer, but I am returning to my men shortly. That is what I came to talk with Eadric about." She understood what he was telling her, and she took little Thorunn for a walk in the woods. The two men stood by the open hearth warming their hands for a short time.

Eadric was intrigued by Thorkell's comments. "Well, my friend, what is happening? Where are you going so soon, and why? Are you leaving the king's service?"

The Dane gritted his teeth as he spoke. "Did you ever meet my brother Hemming? He accompanied me when I accepted Aethelred's money and promised to defend the shores of England. He was as worthy of a Danish jarl as anyone alive, and he was a man of his word. Shortly after Cnut fled England, Hemming and a number of his men were ambushed by a large group of English soldiers, and were cut down like dogs. This was no honorable combat. He was helping to defend your country, and he was murdered by men he thought were his allies."

Eadric asked the obvious question: "Did it seem like they were acting on somebody's orders?"

"According to a couple of his men who were able to escape, it was no accident, and there was no provocation from my brother or his men. So the answer is clearly yes."

The Mercian could not think of a response that was worthy of the moment, so he let Thorkell continue. "We have been betrayed, and for no good reason. I am going to slip away quietly and return to Denmark with a few ships, and I intend to offer my sword to Cnut. He and I go back a long way together, and I am sure he can overlook my service to Aethelred."

Eadric was curious. "Tell me about your experiences with Cnut. Very little is known about him, other than his father's successes, and his cruel but predictable mutilation of the hostages at Sandwich before he fled to Denmark. I spent perhaps an hour drinking with you both, and merely saw that he is ambitious. Lots of men are ambitious, and end their days with unsatisfied dreams."

Despite his anger and frustration, Thorkell was more than

willing to talk about Cnut, and with genuine enthusiasm. "I have known Cnut for most of his life. His father Sweyn brought me to him and asked me to give him some guidance, to help him become a warrior and a leader. I did everything that I could."

"From an early age, he showed me that he was a good listener and a canny observer. When I or another older Dane tried to explain something to him that he did not understand, he paid attention, and asked questions. He did not assume that he knew better because he was the son of a king."

Eadric nodded. "Clever people, people who are driven to succeed, know what they do not know, and try to reduce their ignorance using their curiosity and some patience."

"That's a perfect statement about young Cnut," Thorkell said. "What is also true about him is that he is able to look at a complicated situation and see what is most important, what needs to be done. I remember explaining to him that there was a conflict in the town of Viborg in Denmark involving two powerful families. Each family included a young man who was accused of killing a member of the rival family, and it looked like the beginning of a feud that could end the lives of many in the town. I asked him what should be done?"

"And what was his answer?" Eadric asked.

"Cnut's answer was immediate: 'Kill both men. The feud must be stopped while it is young.'"

"But what if one of the men is not guilty of the killing?"

Thorkell smiled grimly. "I asked, and Cnut said that he did not care. He said that a leader must restore order, and sometimes the innocent must pay the price for it."

There was a brief silence, and then Eadric muttered to himself: "Perhaps the most vicious wolf will get the prize."

Thorkell looked confused. "What is that? Is there a wolf in the area? They are clever, and difficult to catch!"

"It's nothing--I meant nothing by it. Just something my father talked about long ago. If Cnut accepts you back, what do you expect will happen with him?"

Thorkell snorted. "You mean, if he does not have me killed before I can offer him my sword? Bluntly, I expect him to return with a larger army than before, and take England as his father did.

If he has decided that this country should belong to him, he will do whatever is necessary to accomplish that. He will encourage men to join him with promises of huge wealth and large estates: Danes, Norwegians, even Swedes. England is a rich country, and the soil is good for farming here. I hope when we return with a great army that you can join us. Your support, and that of Mercia, would be most welcome."

"My friend," Eadric replied, "I remain sworn to serve Aethelred, and at this point I do not have any real justification, as you certainly have, for abandoning my vow. Things change, and I may yet become an ally in battle, but that time is not now. Please give my greetings to Cnut when you see him, and tell him that I remember the conversation we had in Canterbury years ago. We will see what the Fates have in store for us."

"Is there nothing I can say to change your mind? I swore to serve the king after he paid my warriors and me for our loyalty. But the killing of my brother changes everything, and I have no hesitation about returning to Cnut's service."

The ealdorman shook his head. "I do not judge you harshly for this at all. If I were in your place, I would probably do the same thing. However, my honor is related to my circumstances, not yours. Go with my good wishes."

Thorkell got up to leave, and looked at Eadric. "Whatever comes, I hope that we can meet again in Valhalla, and drink and fight and wench together."

Eadric smiled. "Who can say?" He realized that he was no authority on the next life, and left the theorizing to others.

In June of 1014, Aethelstan, the eldest surviving son of the king, died after a short illness, leaving Edmund as the atheling and heir to the throne. In his will, he left his most prized possession to Edmund, a sword that reputedly had belonged to King Offa, a powerful ruler from England's misty past. He also bequeathed to him a number of other weapons, perhaps in recognition that there would be many battles ahead for his brother. Among the many important people attending Aethelstan's funeral were Sigeferth and Morcar, two prominent Danish thegns from the northern

Danelaw who had been very close friends of the dead prince.

Eadric had watched as four royal brothers had died, four legitimate heirs, leaving Edmund a single heartbeat away from the throne. He hoped that King Aethelred could outlast this current heir like he'd outlived the others. For the sake of England's future, that needed to happen.

Chapter Twenty-One
Royal Chaos

In the spring of 1015, a witan was called to meet in Oxenford, and an unusually large gathering of thegns and other prominent men arrived. Both the Danelaw and the rest of England were represented, and everyone expected that King Aethelred would discuss the improvements in governance that he had apparently promised when he was negotiating his return to England during his exile in Normandie. Eadric and his two surviving brothers attended, and the ealdorman politely welcomed his quiet adversary Bishop Wulfstan to the assembly. The bishop merely nodded to him and walked past without a word.

Quite unexpectedly, Edmund, now the king's eldest son, was there as well. He seldom attended these gatherings, reportedly because they bored him. The prince had aged somewhat since Eadric had had his first unpleasant meeting with him, his beard already turning gray, but his surliness and hostility towards Eadric were unchanged. He clearly believed that he had nothing to gain from civility to the ealdorman of Mercia, so he either ignored him, or he spoke to him as though he were a servant. Finally the heir to the throne, he walked around wearing chain mail as though he was already a warrior king.

The first day of the gathering was uneventful. In fact, the king seemed to be waiting for somebody else to introduce the subject of governance changes. However, the next morning, things looked very different.

Eadric awoke to two or three loud voices outside of his sleeping room, which he'd shared with some other thegns, including his friend Wenric. He could easily understand what was being said.

"Dead. Both of them. Blood everywhere."

"Are there any signs of a struggle?"

"None. Their throats were cut, so it was either done while they were asleep, or they were held down and any cries for help muffled."

"That means that more than one killer must have been involved."

"Of course. Are there any suspects? Did the brothers have any known enemies?"

"Who knows? They were Danes."

A different voice joined the conversation. "Has anybody seen the atheling Edmund this morning? Could he be in danger?"

"It appears that the heir to the throne left before sunrise, along with four of his personal guards."

Suddenly the conversation became whispers, except for one clear comment. "Let that alone."

Eadric discovered that the murder victims were Sigeferth and Morcar, the thegns from the Danelaw who had been close to the deceased prince Aethelstan. He suspected that the murders and Edmund's quiet departure were related, but nothing could be easily proven. And Edmund's new status as the heir tied many hands.

Although the witan continued after that discovery, the murders had cast a deep pall over the proceedings, and no agreements were reached. Shortly after returning home, Eadric was told that King Aethelred had formally taken possession of the estates in the north of the two slain brothers, and ordered that Sigeferth's widow be detained. Obviously, this raised some serious questions about the possible role of the royal family in the killings. However, there were even stranger developments to come.

Within the month, Wenric, who lived a short ride away from the ealdorman's now-impressive estate, came to update Eadric. There was much for him to share. He bowed slightly, and then blurted out the news. "My lord, I just received a message from a friend in York. It seems that Edmund Atheling, who now calls himself 'Ironside,' has seized the estates of those two Danes murdered while attending the witan, and which the king had claimed for himself. Not only that, he has taken the widow of the one dead thegn and married her! You may recall that Aethelred had ordered that she be taken into custody. Well, Edmund Ironside has ignored the king on both counts."

Eadric frowned. "Are you sure about this? That is not legal. Not only is a widow under the protection of the king, but there is a law prohibiting a widow marrying until a year has gone by."

Wenric shook his head. "Also, Edmund has managed to gather local support, in part because of that marriage, and he is now acclaimed to be the lord of the entire Daneland. The king made no friends there when he had his army ravage the countryside after Cnut had sailed away, and the atheling's rebellion has put him in the good graces of the Danes. I remember seeing the wife of Sigeferth, and she is a real beauty, but Edmund is dancing on the edge of a knife. No woman is worth my head, I can tell you that. The fool!"

Eadric wondered aloud about the extent of Edmund's audacity. "Has the son challenged the father and declared himself king? I know he has been impatient to wear the crown for years, but surely he still acknowledges Aethelred as his lord."

"Thus far, he has not challenged the king, but nobody knows where this may end."

Eadric couldn't resist. "If Edmund's head ends up stuck on a spike, some people might be happy about it. At the very least he is thoroughly arrogant, and maybe much worse."

"Then we will see, lord, how events unfold." Wenric shook his head again, mounted his horse, and rode in the direction of home.

What Eadric saw in store for England was widespread disorder and unpredictable danger. Who could ride out the storm was anybody's guess.

Chapter Twenty-Two
Changes and Choices

Thorkell the Tall's prediction about Cnut's return with another army was accurate. In the mid-summer of 1015, a large fleet of Viking ships appeared off the eastern coast of England. The Danish prince had returned, and with an even larger army than his father had led two years earlier.

He stopped at Sandwich, but he was told that many Danes were angry about his sudden retreat the previous year, which had left them open to destruction by Aethelred's army. Instead of beginning his invasion there, he brought his fleet to the south at Dorset, and began to attack forces loyal to the king in Wessex.

On the direct orders of Aethelred, both Eadric and Edmund began to assemble armies to respond to the attacks by Cnut. They were told to meet near Portsmouth at Cosham, where the king was sick in bed, and to prepare to battle the forces of Cnut not far to the west from them. However, things did not go as any of them had intended.

In early autumn, with the Mercian fyrd assembled, Eadric and his army arrived at the meeting place first. He went to visit the ailing king at one of the royal estates on the coast, and didn't like what he saw. Aethelred lay in his bed bent almost double, clearly in great pain. He didn't look like he would survive for long. Of course, that meant that Edmund would become king, and that was a disturbing possibility for Eadric.

"How do you feel, lord king? What do your healers say?"

"Ah, how does it look, son Eadric? Do I resemble a mighty king right now? My physicians tell me that I have a canker inside, and I am not long for this world. A king doesn't think about death until it is necessary for him to concern himself about his everlasting soul, but I am already considering the best location for my tomb. I may have a few months."

"That is very sad news, lord king. Is there anything I can do to make your remaining time more comfortable?"

Aethelred made a slight groan, and then spoke. "You know that Cnut, that misbegotten son of the usurper Sweyn, has returned with his barbarians. They have begun looting and burning, and aim to take over the country again. But he is an invader, and we are the lawful owners of this island, so we have the advantage." He winced in pain, and then continued. "We know the land, and we know the people. The only thing preventing us from throwing Cnut out again is the possibility of disunity among the leaders."

He paused. Eadric knew what was coming next.

"I know that you and Edmund do not get along. In fact, that is a gentle way of putting it. Although you are brothers by marriage, your dislike for each other is obvious. In all honesty, I believe that the blame is primarily on Edmund's shoulders, not yours. He is a proud and stiff-necked man who listens to nobody but himself, and you have been an innocent target of his hostility. Nevertheless, the two of you must get along if England is to survive."

Eadric lifted his arms out to the side with his hands upraised. "And how can that happen, lord king?"

"I have already talked to Edmund about this. He was not eager to treat with you, but I made it clear that his future would probably depend on your relationship. A king with no country to rule is a ghost, and he does not want to be a ghost. When my son arrives, I want the two of you to eat and drink together, discuss the military situation, and come to an understanding.

Eadric smiled. "As you wish, lord king." He had trouble believing that the meeting would go well, but, as the king said, something had to be done. The future of England could be at stake.

The next afternoon, Edmund and his army arrived. He strode into the hall wearing his now-familiar chain mail, looked around, and demanded a cup of ale from a waiting thrall. His thick graying beard made him look much older than he actually was.

Then he glanced over at Eadric.

"So, young ealdorman, we are to have dinner together this evening. Good. Hopefully you can come to see my position on things, and that will prevent trouble in the future." It was a very discouraging beginning, although the ealdorman refused to accept the challenge to quarrel so early in the meeting.

Eadric had hoped that the king would be well enough to have dinner with them, or at least sit there while the discussion took place, but Aethelred was feeling no better than he had earlier, so it would be just the two of them. He was tempted to bring his sword to the meeting, but knew better than to go armed given their hostility to each other.

The food that was served was delicious. Aethelred had brought with him from Normandie a Frankish cook who had worked for the Norman duke and in other noble houses, and the man was able to offer dishes that Eadric had difficulty identifying, but he relished every spoonful. There was beef, and a variety of wild birds in different sauces, and an interesting pot of bean stew.

There were also bottles of something called wine, which he had only sampled once when he was in exile with the king's family. He was told by the cook while he was serving the food that their Normandie hosts typically kept that beverage for themselves, and provided ale to guests they thought to have less sophisticated tastes.

The two men finished a large bottle of the wine before they said a word to each other, and by that time they were both more relaxed. Edmund suddenly spoke. "You know that the Danes supporting me in the Danelaw are mindless fools."

"Why is that, my lord?"

"Because I hate them. I hate their pagan souls, their mindless cruelty, and their immorality. The ones who have come to live on our island as farmers and traders are as bad as the rest of the Vikings. You can train a wild animal to behave for a moment, but if you turn your back on him, he will attack you. By the grace of God, when I am king, we will destroy these Vikings living among us: all, including women and children. The fry can grow up to be as bad as the adults."

Eadric was stunned, but he kept his voice calm and his

words unrevealing of his true feelings. "Are you serious, lord?"

Edmund was quick to reply. "Of course I am. Do you remember a dozen years ago when my father sent out an order to kill all the Danes on St. Brice's Day? Who do you think demanded that he send it? My father would never have acted if I hadn't bullied him into it. It was just disappointing that the spilling of Danish blood was so limited that day. I had hoped for so much more. English men can behave like such soft women."

"Some years ago, I was directed by the king to help defend the people of Kent against Viking raiders. While I was there I saw the dead bodies of English men, women, and children who didn't pay those savages fast enough, or they didn't have enough silver. I had friends who went into battle with me, who fought with me, and whose guts lay on the field before their unseeing dead eyes. They speak to me from the grave. All Danes are Vikings, and all Vikings deserve to die a slow death. What English man could disagree with that?"

Eadric was careful with his response. "Did you know that I have Danish friends? I consider Thorkell the Tall a friend, among others."

The atheling had a crooked smile on his face. "Then perhaps you need to find new friends. It is simple: either you are with us, and with the true Church, or you are against us. There is no middle way." He started to laugh.

"What is funny, lord?"

"These Danes in the five counties who are supporting me now don't even realize that I demanded that my father have his army wreak havoc on Lindsey and the rest of Lincolnshire for their support of Sweyn and Cnut. He wanted to be conciliatory and forgiving. However, I knew that I had been provided with a good excuse for that destruction in the heathen Daneland, and I took advantage of it. Surely it was God's will. And I even ordered the killing of some Viking mercenaries fighting for us after Cnut fled. We had no more need of them."

Edmund started drinking again, not noticing that Eadric had kept completely silent after he had shared that last information. He finished off a second bottle of that wine all by himself, and when he finally looked around, he was alone. He shrugged his shoulders and quickly fell asleep.

Eadric was staggered by Edmund's proud admissions. Unable to sleep after hearing what the atheling had to say, he thought intently about the implications of it. What Edmund had confessed to exceeded Eadric's worst expectations about him. He was at a crossroad, and he knew it.

I have been in the dark for more than a dozen years. For as long as I can remember, I have kept one eye on my own advancement, and the other on the king.

Aethelred raised me up, above my father's station in life, and above every other thegn in Mercia. However, I was prepared to use the power that he gave me to act against him if the opportunity appeared and some damning evidence was revealed.

Now the man for whom I have the least respect in the kingdom has, from his own lips, testified about his responsibility for multiple crimes. He instigated the massacres on St. Brice's Day. Thorunn and his father and many other good people were murdered on that day.

He has confirmed that he influenced the king to ravage much of Lincolnshire after Cnut fled England, using the excuse of punishing disloyalty to justify burning settlements and executing Danes.

And he has confessed to having Thorkell the Tall's brother Hemming killed in an ambush, along with other Danish warriors who thought themselves allied with the English.

All of this must be added to the killing of the two thegns from the Daneland so that he could steal a dead man's wife and create a domain for himself.

I have sworn an oath of loyalty to Aethelred, my father through marriage, but he is near death, and I have sworn nothing to Edmund. Nor will I ever give him my fealty. Edmund hates all Danes, and is using his religion to justify that hatred. He cannot rule England.

Can I do this? Can I side with a Dane against my own kind? I am English and I have no wish to harm other English men. I can stay here, ignore what I was told, and fight for my dying king. It would be easier, and it would be simpler. If I can just go to sleep, I will make a decision in the morning. Let me close my eyes.

Eadric lay in his bedding for a long time. Sleep did not come as a friend to save him from a decision. He imagined the burning church when his friend was killed. He remembered Thorkell's pain when he talked about the death of his brother. And he thought about the expression of delight on Edmund's face when he enumerated his many outrages against the Danes. It seemed his mind and his heart were as one as he made his decision.

I cannot be a part of making England a graveyard for every Dane in the realm. It must be a place where families, both English and Dane, can live without fear, and it begins with the king. I may have the power to influence what happens, and I choose to use it. My only good option is to ride west and join Cnut.

The Viking army was rumored to be camped near Horton, just north of where they had anchored their ships on the south coast, and Eadric believed he'd have little trouble finding Cnut: he could just follow the trail of destruction from Poole northward.

Chapter Twenty-Three
An Oath And A Visit

At first light, Eadric woke up Wenric, now his second in command, and ordered him to prepare the army to move out, and to do so as soon as possible--certainly before noon. He would ride ahead and meet with Cnut. He didn't want the Vikings to confuse the Mercian army for an enemy when it arrived.

Within two hours he was outside of the Viking camp. Although he was challenged by two drowsy perimeter guards, he was obviously no threat to anyone. He was alone, and his dress and his decorated sword marked him as a man of wealth and position, not an assassin. He was quickly brought to the tent of Cnut, who looked almost stunned to see him.

Eadric thought he looked a little older and more mature since their last meeting at Canterbury. His reddish blond beard was thicker, and he looked more substantial physically as well. His thin nose remained his only unimpressive feature. Resplendent in shiny chain mail and a scarlet cloak with writhing gold dragons sewn on the edges, he looked the part of a royal warrior.

"Lord Eadric, you surprise me. What brings you to this collection of thieves and cutthroats? I had expected to be meeting you and Edmund Ironside before too long, but on the other side of a shield wall. You're welcome, of course, no matter what the reason."

The ealdorman was determined to be direct. "Things have changed, my lord. Some of what I guessed about Edmund has been confirmed, and other things just as bad." Eadric quickly explained what he had learned the previous evening from the atheling. That Edmund was deep in his cups at the time made the self-righteous confession even more convincing.

"So Edmund was behind the massacre a dozen years ago that killed my aunt and her family, and your best friend. And he had Thorkell's brother and some of his warriors cut down as well." Cnut looked at him intently, his eyes glittering in anticipation. He understood the importance of this moment, and was impatient to hear from the ealdorman what he believed was inevitable. "What then are you going to do?"

Eadric looked at Cnut without any expression on his face for some moments. He was reluctant to say the words that were on the tip of his tongue. "Obviously, I have no choice. The king is dying, whether now or in a few months, and Edmund is a horror. He would willingly kill every Dane in England, and think it the wish of the Christian God: my woman, probably my son, every Dane that has settled in England to peacefully make a life for himself, and my Viking friends. We need a king who will respect the English and the Danes, Christians and Odin-worshippers alike. And that is not Edmund. I am hoping that it may be you."

He slowly pulled his sword, his favorite Ulfberht sword, slowly from its scabbard, and held it parallel to the ground with both hands. "I offer you my sword and my loyalty. I swear to be your man, and I offer the support of the fyrd of Mercia as well. Some of the men are inexperienced, but they will fight with heart and fire for me."

Cnut started laughing in pure pleasure, and began to shout: "This is the best news that I have had since my father was acclaimed king of England almost two years ago. You won't regret your decision!" And then he turned serious. "I accept your allegiance and your support with all of my heart. We will do good things for ourselves and for England together--"

Eadric had to interrupt him. "Pardon, lord. Before we go any further, you must know that my soldiers are but a few hours behind me, and will be joining us before too long. They are sworn to me, but they will not yet know that I am your ally, and oath-sworn to you. It would not do for allies to begin fighting against each other when there is so much for us to do."

He paused. "I must confess that I abandon my oath to

Aethelred reluctantly. He has been a weak king, certainly, and he has allowed himself to be influenced by his Dane-hating son, but he has been most generous to me, and allowed Mercia to become stronger. Oaths cannot be given and then denied casually. How those who tell about our actions in the future will present us no living man can know." They shook hands, and the deed was done.

As Eadric started to leave the tent, Cnut called him back. "My lord ealdorman, a moment please." He pulled a large twisted gold armring from a number of gold and silver ones decorating his arms, and handed it to Eadric. "This is merely a small token of my gratitude for what you are doing here today; it was the first armring that my father gave me years ago. When I am king, I will not forget your invaluable role in getting me to the highest place in the land. By Odin, I swear it."

Cnut quickly sent word to his battle captains that they should expect English allies before the sun went down, and they should treat those reinforcements with friendship and cooperation. And he ordered four of his men to forage nearby for as many barrels of ale as they could find. They would celebrate, and then they would march on Wessex.

Shortly after that meeting, Eadric sought out Thorkell the Tall, who had joined Cnut a few months earlier. He found the greybearded jarl sitting in a tent looking immensely bored. His feet were propped up on his sea chest, and he was almost asleep.

Thorkell liked doing, moving, working, and fighting, and he'd had long periods of waiting for something interesting to happen when he was in Kent, watching over the unfortunate archbishop whose capture and ransoming ended so badly. Now he was waiting again for Cnut to begin his war in earnest against the king and his son. Eadric had a plan to get him interested and involved again.

"My friend Thorkell, you look like you have some thick moss growing on your north-facing side. Can I interest you in a little adventure?"

The Dane leaped off of his stool and put an arm around Eadric's neck. "By the gods, Eadric, I am glad to see you. I had heard a rumor that you were seen with Cnut earlier in the day, and I leaped to the conclusion that you and some warriors were joining us. Do I have that right?"

"You do, you ugly Dane. However, I've got a plan to strengthen our forces with a little daring. Would you care to ride with me to London and meet with some old friends?"

Thorkell needed no persuading. Eadric explained that they were going to find some of the warriors and crews that Thorkell had left behind when he returned to Denmark, and attempt to get them away from the English so they could join the Viking army. Thorkell estimated that there were crews for roughly forty ships that were languishing in the city without a leader or something to do. And the ships were sitting idle at Benfleet at the mouth of the Thames as well.

They had to get to London without delay. Although nobody outside of Cnut and Thorkell would know for sure that Eadric was supporting the Danes, the fact that the Mercian forces had left Cosham and gone west may have already raised the suspicions of Edmund and Aethelred, assuming the king was even aware of what was going on around him. However, word would not get back to London for some days, perhaps a week or more.

Eadric and Thorkell met Cnut, who was delighted with their proposition, and received his permission to try to bring the rest of Thorkell's fleet to Poole, where the majority of Cnut's ships had landed. They chose two of the finest mounts that they could find from the mass of tethered horses of the Viking army, and Thorkell paid the owner of each some silver for the loss of his horse. One way or another, they would probably not be returning by horseback.

It took the men almost three full days to reach London. They had brought neither their shields nor helmets, and had wrapped their swords behind their saddles so that they looked like normal, if fairly wealthy, travelers. When they got to the city, it took little time for them to locate some of Thorkell's former warriors drinking in an alehouse and looking, like Thorkell had been at Horton, profoundly bored.

One, a large man with arms covered in ink, started to roar a greeting as he rose from his seat, and Thorkell quickly walked over, covered his mouth, and whispered "Not a word about me, Sitric. I am not here." Sitric stared at him and sat down again.

Thorkell spoke quietly so that only a few people could hear him. "Do you know where you can find some of the ship captains?" Sitric nodded. "I want you to get the word around to all of the crews that we are leaving, but nobody else must know about it. Nobody. We will meet in two days time at Benfleet and take the ships south and west. Tell the men to get there any way they can; I'm certain that they can be resourceful. They should know that if they arrive too late, they'll miss all of the glory and riches to come."

Sitric was excited. "Can we kill some of these boring English after we get to where we're going? We've been keeping track of the insults we've received from these sorry weaklings, and we'd like to pay some of them back."

Thorkell smiled. "Have no fear, old friend. You will see as much fighting as you can stomach before we're done."

The Dane grinned and turned to his two companions, who, after a few words of explanation, got up and left behind what remained of their drinks. Clearly, they understood the urgency of their mission. Sacrificing ale was not done happily by thirsty Vikings.

Thorkell was able to find two more men, including one of the ship captains, and sent them off to find others and convey the same message.

While Thorkell and Eadric were wandering the streets, they tried to look as inconspicuous as possible. It would not do for Eadric to have to explain his presence in London, and there were many in positions of authority who knew that Thorkell had returned to Denmark and probably rejoined Cnut, and was thus an enemy of the king.

They walked in the shadows when they could, and avoided looking anyone in the eye, not an easy thing for men who were accustomed to walking proudly wherever they went, and enjoying the feeling of being noticed. Eadric tried to count how many people likely to be in London could recognize him, and he stopped counting at thirty.

As the two men were about to give up looking for other

Danes to recruit, they heard a voice behind them: "Lord Eadric, how long has it been?" Both whirled around, and saw a pretty blond-haired woman carrying a basket.

Eadric knew her immediately; her large green eyes gave her away. It was Brita, his wife's handmaiden and his occasional bedmate. The two men looked around the quiet street and guessed than no one else had heard her words.

Eadric walked quickly over to her and spoke quietly. "How nice to see you again. How long has it been, six months or more?" Then he whispered. "Brita, we are here in secret, and no one must know about our presence. Not my wife, and nobody else in the family. Am I being clear?" He put two silver coins into her hand and gave it a little squeeze. "And I look forward to seeing you again soon."

She initially looked a little confused, but her face brightened when he gave her the money. She would be able to buy some pretty things for herself, and she certainly had no interest in talking about Eadric with her mistress, or anybody else. Leaving without another word, Brita was mentally already spending the money for some new clothes.

Eadric and Thorkell looked at each other, and both rolled their eyes. Eadric sighed. "That was an unwelcome encounter! Let's get out of London before we meet anybody else we know." They returned to their horses, trusting that nobody else had recognized them, and rode towards Benfleet and the ships.

Chapter Twenty-Four
A War Council

They rode their horses hard, and arrived at the ships at anchor before nightfall. There were already dozens of Danes waiting for them, and they all looked relieved to finally have someone to follow again. They glanced at Eadric with curiosity, but there were moments of great celebration as individual warriors met with Thorkell and hugged each other with a violence that amazed the Mercian.

Obviously, they had been friends for years, and had fought together many times. And sitting around in London, these men had been completely ignored by the king's army, and treated with quiet hostility by shopkeepers and tradesmen. They needed a drastic change in their situation. Thorkell and his English friend brought exactly the change they needed.

After providing considerable business that evening to the ale houses and for some men the single brothel in Benfleet, Thorkell, Eadric, and the early arrivals returned to the ships the next morning to find over a hundred more warriors waiting for them. By the end of that day, almost three hundred of Thorkell's men were ready to join Cnut's army in Dorset. And no one among the English knew enough to try and stop them.

After selling their horses locally for much less than they were worth, Eadric and Thorkell stayed together as everyone boarded their ships. He leaned against the rigging as Waverunner, which he had been told was the name of the drakkar they were on, was rowed away from its mooring. The square sail was efficiently unfurled, the oars were stowed, and the sail quickly caught the wind and started to drive the ship through the water.

He had never learned much about the skills involved in handling a ship like this one, but he couldn't resist grinning as the powerful sensation of speed enveloped him. He remembered his first sailing adventure to Ireland with Thorunn. This large ship was much faster. On this full-sized fighting ship the hull seemed to wiggle smoothly through the water like a sea snake.

Watching him from the other side of the ship, Thorkell yelled over to him. "You look like the great Ragnar Lodbrok, standing there. It's obvious that you love the sailing, the little slither of the hull in the surging sea. Only a real Viking ship can give that feeling. It's not great fun pulling on an oar for hours at a time, but when the sail takes over the ship, there is almost nothing better in the world. Almost nothing." He winked. Thorkell was a man with fairly simple needs. Women, drink, and a good fight were his very favorite things, and sailing competed with fighting for the third spot.

They arrived without incident at Poole, on the south coast, where the rest of the fleet was anchored or beached. When they finally arrived at Horton, Cnut and his Viking army were waiting for them. What surprised Eadric was not that Danes made up the majority of the fighters, but that there was a large number of Norwegians and even some Swedes.

All of Scandinavia would be represented in the war to take England, a country that had proven that it was very rich, and one that had also shown that it might give up that wealth without much of a fight. Wessex, the southernmost kingdom of England, was readily acknowledged by all to be the richest part of the country, and Cnut would want to take it first.

The young Danish leader held a council of war next to his tent while a light drizzle fell. It included Eadric, Thorkell, and about a dozen of the leaders of the biggest warrior bands. The man standing next to Eadric, a fairly young man with long pale hair tied at the back and a short pale beard, introduced himself as Ulfketil.

"Your clothing gives you away as English. Are you here to get riches like a lot of men here, or are you looking for more power, like some others?"

Eadric was amused by the bluntness of the Viking's question. "My name is Eadric, and I have no need for more of either. I am ealdorman of Mercia, and I brought over five hundred warriors with me."

"I meant no offense," Ulfketil replied quickly. "This is your country, and becoming an ally of Cnut has its risks. Your reasons are your own business, and you are welcome here."

Eadric smiled. "No offense taken. I have a question for you—"

Cnut began to speak and everyone else abruptly stopped talking. "I know everyone here. Each of you may not know everyone else, but I trust all of you to honor your oaths to me and to do what you say you will do."

He paused for a moment, and then started again. "Some years ago, my renown father's sister and her family were killed, along with other Danes and their families, solely because they were Danes living in England. Murders like these need to be stopped, and the only way to do that is to throw out the leaders responsible: the old king and his dog of a son Edmund. I can do better."

"A few of you may have already met Eadric here." The other men looked at him. "He is an important leader in Mercia, and he has brought men here for the same reason. He had friends and neighbors who were killed."

"There are many in this country who will side with us with little encouragement, especially in parts of the country where Danes have made their homes. Much better allies than enemies-- we should not give them reasons to hate us."

An older warrior with a bushy beard called Freybjorn, whose arms were covered with swirling patterns of ink and many silver armrings, interrupted him. "Let me be clear. My men and I didn't come from Norway to make friends with the English. I'm here for their wealth, and for their women. I'm sure I'm not the only one. Talk to us about that."

Cnut took a deep breath. "I believe, old friend, that you will get what you desire, but you will need some patience. Many of us here have come to bring Viking rule to this country, or at least make it a land where Vikings can live and prosper. To do that, we have to get the people to submit to my authority, as they briefly did to my father. If they bend a knee to me, we will let them live their lives without fire or plunder."

"However." He paused for dramatic effect, and then continued. "Any thegns or free born men who refuse to accept me as their liege and lord we will treat like enemies, and we may take whatever we want from them."

Freybjorn spoke again. "So we should hope for defiant rebels, so we can fill our pockets and sea chests with their silver and make their women groan with pleasure."

"Exactly. Any opposition makes riches for all of us." Cnut held up a piece of thin sheepskin, taken from a local monastery. It showed a crude map drawn by Eadric's second in command Wenric, made while Eadric and Thorkell were retrieving the rest of the Dane's ships and warriors, and picturing the southern part of the country, and the major towns and settlements.

"We will divide our army into three equal groups, and deal directly with everyone in our paths. Either they take an oath to serve me or we take whatever they own. And kill only when necessary, so that we don't make more enemies than we conquer. I expect that we can control all of Wessex within six months."

After Cnut had finished, and the council had ended, Eadric finished his question to Ulfketil. "So explain your name to me. It looks like you are called 'bucket' or 'kettle,' which seems a strange name for a Viking."

Ulfketil laughed. "You English are caught up with misleading appearances. Our names can involve both direct and indirect meanings. 'Ulf' refers to a wolf, a smart and savage beast. However, 'ketil' can mean 'kettle' or 'helmet,' much like a bucket, or even a chieftain wearing a helmet. A helmet is a very rare thing, and an ordinary warrior does not typically have one."

"What about the meaning of 'Cnut?' Eadric asked.

Ulfketil shook his head. "That's a strange one. 'Cnut' means 'knot' like in a rope. Perhaps a knot connects things together, and Jarl Cnut is meant to bind together people who are now separate. Who can say what the fates have in store?"

It was obvious to Eadric that some of the names were adopted as adults, and some came from parents hoping for ferocious or important sons.

Cnut kept Eadric and his men close to him and his most trusted warriors, probably because the Mercian was the leader with whom he had the least experience. There were no serious battles in Wessex, so there was no opportunity for the two leaders to fight together. However, Cnut realized that the presence of the Mercian ealdorman and Mercian fighters made the subjugation of Wessex much easier. English men trusted other English men, and Eadric was an impressive negotiator.

One evening, Cnut shared a meal with Eadric, Thorkell the Tall, and an older Viking warrior from Norway named Erik of Hlathir, who looked as tough and strong as pattern-welded steel. Cnut introduced him to the Mercian, informing him that Erik was perhaps the most famous fighter in all of the Viking lands. Waving off the compliment, the Norwegian shook hands with Eadric and grabbed a piece of meat from the board.

Then Cnut surprised everyone by bringing up a complicated subject: religion. "My lord ealdorman, please pardon my questions. Tell me about your religious beliefs. Are you a Christian?"

Eadric looked at him for a moment before answering. "Lord king, would you like my public answer or my private answer? There is a difference."

"What do you mean?"

"I have two very different answers to that questions, depending on who is asking or listening to my answer."

The other Vikings looked at each other and laughed, and Cnut raised an eyebrow. "Now you have really captured my interest. Why must there be two answers?"

Eadric tried to explain. "I am an English man, and England right now is a Christian country. Church leaders have great power, and everybody who wishes to have the respect of free born men and women must present a Christian face in public. To the people of Mercia, to my father-in-law the king, even to my seldom-seen wife, I am a Christian."

"However, when I was a child, I was attacked by a priest of the Church, and it changed my private view of Christianity. If a man of the Church acts badly, and that man prospers, what does that say about the Church? Surely most Christians are not evil, and do not support evil, but the Church seems to ignore the faults of its priests. Today, I probably take the stories of Odin and Thor and Loki about as seriously as I take the stories of the Christ.".

At that, the other Vikings sitting there roared, and banged their sword pommels or their eating knives in approval.

Cnut looked at him intently. "My father was a practical man. He privately worshipped Odin, but he saw that the Christian religion was becoming popular in Denmark, so he became a public Christian, like you. He gave money to the Church, and made statements supporting the Church—"

Eadric gently interrupted him. "Your father was a very clever man. What then are you? Are you a Christian believer? I see the gold Thor's hammer hanging from your neck."

Cnut chuckled, thought for a moment, and then replied: "No. I still believe in the old gods. However, your comments have confirmed to me that I will need to become a public Christian when I become king, an enthusiastic public Christian. Asking the English people to accept as their liege lord a Danish Viking will be difficult enough. Asking them to accept an Odin-worshipper as well is probably impossible. So I'll say and do what is needed, including removing the hammer and putting it away. And I will privately ask Odin to forgive my deception." He shrugged his shoulders and drank some ale.

Chapter Twenty-Five
Apocalypse

Cnut's estimate was too conservative: the Vikings were in control of Wessex in less than four months. Faced with the overwhelming force of Cnut's army, and with Eadric and his Mercian soldiers as allies, the vast majority of the thegns and other leaders buckled without any resistence, and gave their allegiance to the Dane.

Raiders like Freybjorn were somewhat disappointed with the lack of opposition, but they still found opportunities to quietly plunder some estates and steads. And invariably, some English women found the attention to cleanliness and grooming among Viking men more appealing than the habits of their own English men.

Near the end of 1015, Cnut took his army north, crossing the Thames at Cricklade, and forcing the thegns as far as Warwickshire to bend the knee to him. Being so close to the borders of Mercia, Eadric took the opportunity to spend Christmas with his family at his estate. Ingrith, who was as exciting as ever, lamented that she had had no one to share her bed for months, and the young Thorunn complained that he had missed going fishing for the same period.

Eadric made sure that he made both of them happy. After so long, his woman was like a lion in bed, touching and being touched with great passion, and they arose late every morning when he was there. He took his son to their favorite fishing spot on the river, and once the boy caught a brown fish large enough to feed every family member at the evening meal.

Before returning to Cnut's army, Eadric selected four armed free men to stay with his family and provide protection to them. There had been no hostile armies in Mercia for many years, but he was taking no chances. These were changeable times, and he had taken most of the men who could be counted on in a fight with him when he went to Cosham, and then to join Cnut.

While he and Cnut were near Warwick, using their army to convince local thegns that Cnut was the future of England, and to submit to him, they received a report from the Danelaw that Edmund Ironside had brought together an army there to challenge them, but it dispersed almost immediately. The reasons were unclear. Perhaps the Danes in that region had no stomach for fighting against other Danes. It was also said that they refused to fight because King Aethelred, who remained too ill to do anything, could not lead them.

However, a short time later, Edmund gathered another small army, made up primarily of English men from the Danelaw, although he was also supported by Uhtred, the ealdorman of Northumbria. The atheling brought them quickly west into the area of Mercia where Eadric's estates were located, and began to pillage and burn wherever they went. Although there was a practical military reason for the attacks, making it more difficult for Eadric to resupply his men, this destruction was clearly aimed directly at Eadric himself, and the men of his fyrd.

Cnut ordered his army north when word reached him, but by the time they entered Mercia, Edmund and Uhtred had fled, Edmund back to London and Uhtred to York. Unexpectedly, Eadric's brother Aelfric met Cnut's army camped outside of Worcestre, and found Eadric sitting with Cnut. With a downcast expression on his face, he first bowed to the Dane.

"Your majesty, forgive my informality, but I have sad news to share with my brother." Eadric looked at him, and a deep chill ran through him. "Here is the bitter truth. Ingrith is dead. Her sister Inga and her husband are dead. Some of our estate is in ashes, and a few other properties have been burned as well. Your son is safe, but there is little other good news to tell you."

Eadric held up his hand and stopped him. "Stay here," he muttered. He walked a short distance from the camp, and slumped down on the ground, hands on his head. The pain and the sense of desolation were almost unbearable. He blamed himself for the deaths. Edmund had wanted to punish him for joining Cnut, and raiding Mercia was the easiest way to do it. On that score, Edmund outdid himself. Eadric sat alone in the woods for some time, not knowing for how long. When he returned, his brother and Cnut were waiting for him.

"Tell me," he whispered.

Aelfric was reluctant to speak, and he began slowly. "When you left recently, Ingrith was as happy as I had seen her in a while. She walked around humming some Danish-sounding song, and was looking forward to seeing you again when your efforts with King Cnut had made a temporary peace."

"There was no warning when we were attacked; our stead was one of the first to be put to the sword. It happened so quickly that the bell in the bell tower was never sounded. I do not know if Edmund knew that the estate was yours, or if the attack was random, but it made no difference. The four men you left to protect us fought as hard as they could, but we were outnumbered twenty to one or more, and they died quickly."

"I fought, as did two of our brothers, and the last time I saw Ingrith alive she was wielding a seax blade like a ferocious shield maiden. Almost surrounded, I got to Thorunn and then some horses, and we barely escaped with our lives. I left the boy with Anlaf and his family, who were fortunate enough to escape the destruction somehow. Almost everybody in our area who looked like a Dane was killed."

"When I returned the next day, there was considerable damage on our estate. The great hall survived, but many of the out buildings were destroyed, and several homes of free men were burned down. We found the bodies of the four men, our old aunt, and even those of three thralls, who apparently had tried to defend the family."

"Then I found Ingrith, lying next to the front door. Other than a little blood on her shift, she looked as though she had just gone to sleep, and her hand still held the seax. We buried all of them separately, but we took special care to place some of her favorite items with her when we laid her in the earth. I will take you to her grave when you come home again."

There was only silence for what seemed like a very long time. Cnut was the first to speak: "Edmund Ironside and Uhtred are dead men. I vow that it will be so. There will be no peace until they are both howling in their Christian hell."

Eadric was beyond any consolation. He spoke very quietly. "I owe Edmund a debt for two precious lives, and even more than that. I intend to pay him for them somehow, and I don't care what it may cost me. I will be patient, and watch for my chance. That's all I will say."

The next day, Cnut's army headed east and north, across Mercia, and into the areas of southern Northumbria controlled by ealdorman Uhtred. The warriors had seen some of what Edmund and Uhtred had done in Mercia, and so they were unforgiving of any who even hesitated to accept the authority of Cnut, and did some pillaging and burning of their own.

As the army approached York, Cnut received a messenger from Uhtred, who now declared that the ealdorman accepted Cnut as his king, and that he would be the king's loyal servant from that day forward. After discussing the situation with Eadric, Thorkell, and Jarl Erik, Cnut sent back a message. Uhtred and up to forty of his men must travel to the settlement called Wiheal just south of York, and there he would in person pledge his fealty to Cnut. The Dane swore that Uhtred and his men would travel under safe passage to that meeting place, and return safely as well.

After the messenger departed, Cnut told Thorkell and Erik to organize a large war party to accompany him to the meeting. He told Eadric to remain and reinforce the guards around the camp while he was away. Within an hour, Cnut and the mounted warriors were gone.

The next day, Cnut and his men returned. Eadric noticed that Erik was not among the group, and he waited while Cnut and Thorkell dealt with their horses. He could tell by the behavior of the other men that something other than a peaceful meeting had taken place, but he hoped that Cnut would explain. And after drinking down a cup of ale, the Dane described the previous day's events.

"I made certain that we arrived at the hall where the meeting would take place before the ealdorman would get there. In fact, I was able to arrange for a servant of the ealdorman to delay their arrival for a time, and for Thurbrand, an old enemy of his, to set the scene. When Uhtred did arrive, with forty of his men, they were asked to remove their swords before entering the hall. Kings do not allow swords in their presence except for their guards."

"After they entered the hall, and Uhtred began to approach me to kneel as he should, a large curtain running down the side of the hall was thrown back, and one hundred of my best fighters rushed forward and cut down Uhtred's men. The ealdorman was the last to die, and Erik had the honor of removing his head. That number will not be disturbing the peace of Mercia again."

Eadric grimaced. "That's one of them. And where is Erik?"

"I have named him the next jarl of York and also southern Northumbria, and he is already at work replacing Uhtred's people with his own: Viking instead of English. I want a strong leader in the north in the coming days, as I expect Edmund to fight us with the fierceness and cleverness of a wild boar. He is a very different opponent than his father. Lord Eadric, I hope this provides at least a little relief for your sorrow."

It didn't. He wouldn't admit it to Cnut, but his sadness over the loss of Ingrith was untouched by the recent killings. The violent deaths of forty English men did nothing to make up for the death of the only woman he had ever loved. It was unlikely that Uhtred had been directly involved in the raid on his estate.

It was also unlikely that one of the other men who had been killed had ended the life of his woman. However, he realized that even if Ingrith's killer had died in that bloodbath, that man's death could not salve the loss of another's life. He felt like there was a hole in his heart, and he didn't think it would go away.

Was the death of Ingrith a punishment from the Christian God for his actions, for his rebellion against Aethelred and Edmund--for his taking the side of the Vikings over his own

English people? This question tugged at his heart, but his head knew that he'd had no good choice but the one he took. And he needed to try looking forward somehow. There would be time enough to try to make sense of his losses after the last battle had been fought.

Chapter Twenty-Six
A Bleak Return

Having strengthened his hold on the north of the Daneland, Cnut concluded that the next military move would be an assault on London, which could best be served by a return to his fleet at Poole Harbor, and then a quick sail to the Thames River. Eadric agreed that the stronghold of the king and his son Edmund was the key to the kingdom, and they would have to gain control of it if Cnut was to become the true king of England. So the army was marched quickly back to the ships, and prepared to depart by sea.

On April 23, 1016, King Athelred died. A few days later, a messenger from one of Eadric's friends in London arrived as he was breaking his fast for the morning, and he immediately went to Cnut's tent with the messenger following closely behind him. The young man, who seemed anxious about being surrounded by a large number of Vikings, had lived near Poole when he was younger, which was why he had been selected to ride with the news. He informed the two men of the death of the old king, which did not surprise Eadric in the least, and that a small witan of London thegns and clerics had already chosen Edmund Ironside as their next king.

Eadric quickly dismissed the messenger, and turned to Cnut. "Lord king, it is clear what we need to do immediately. I will send out multiple riders to find every thegn and prelate that we have dealt with in Wessex, and who has bowed the knee to you. As the ealdorman of Mercia, I will inform them that I am speaking for you, and am requiring their attendance at a witan in Southampton within two days."

Cnut blinked and looked at him closely. "Is that really the

best thing for us to do? I have already gotten the allegiance of each of them."

"You have gotten their support, yes, but you now need to have each of them approve of you specifically becoming the king. Formalities can be very important to the English, and it would be well for you to have a larger, more impressive assembly of leaders supporting you than Edmund was able to muster."

"What of the fleet?" Cnut asked. "Before this news, we were planning on sailing within the next day or so. Shall I wait for your meeting, or can you represent me to these English people?"

"Sail with the ships to the Thames, lord king. The men attending this witan will know who I am, and my support will be added to their oaths of fealty. We can be certain that the witan will vote for you. After the vote, I will ride north to visit my son Thorunn, who I have not seen since he lost his mother in the destruction by Edmund's raiders. Then I will ride east and south to meet you at the river."

Cnut nodded. "I will do as you suggest, and please tell your son of my sorrow about his mother. Again, I'm indebted to you for your support and counsel, and I will remember this after I finally receive the crown."

Most of Eadric's soldiers had already left for home. Like every fyrd, almost every warrior was a farmer during the growing times, and they needed to return to their steads to sow the seed and cultivate the plants so that, when winter came again, they and their families wouldn't starve. The cycle of life did not stop because war happening somewhere else, and spring meant green sprouts and newborn lambs. The fyrd would regain its full complement of fighters after the harvest. And the remaining men would follow Wenric aboard the waiting ships.

The fleet left at midday as planned, and the following day Eadric met with a large group of the most important men in Wessex. His conversations before the witan began made it clear that Cnut would be voted king by acclamation, largely because everyone was convinced that, inevitably, Cnut was going to be the military victor against Edmund. Cnut controlled southern Northumbria and most of the Danelaw and Wessex, and he had the support of Mercia. What other conclusion was possible?

After a brief discussion took place, with only one subject at issue, the vote was virtually unanimous in support of Cnut. There was no great enthusiasm for the Dane, but these men were realists, and protecting their own positions and holdings required a vote for Cnut. Eadric thanked each thegn and religious leader in person, and he left the witan expecting that Wessex would remain with the Dane for the duration of the conflict.

As Eadric rode northward towards Mercia, he had time to reflect upon the death of Aethelred. The king had always been generous to him. He had lifted Eadric up by naming him ealdorman, and made his authority more legitimate by arranging the marriage to his daughter. The fact that the husband and wife seldom saw each other, and had never shared a bed after the first night, did not detract from the political benefits to Eadric of that union.

He had come to understand that Aethelred was a weak man, and he had let his son Edmund exert a terrible influence upon him. However, Eadric was grateful for his support, and was sorry that the king probably never forgave his son-in-law for joining Cnut against his son.

He rode through the night, and by the next evening he began to see familiar landmarks. He found the Severn River, and followed it up until he saw the path that he had always taken when he was returning from fishing. As he approached the family estate, he saw that work had been almost completed on the smaller buildings and free men's homes that had been burned to the ground.

In fact, there was almost no visible trace of the destruction in the front of his house. Eadric was greeted by his brothers Aelfric and Aethelwine, who welcomed him home like he had come back from the dead. However, there was no loving Danish beauty to greet him, and the great hall was silent. Aelfric showed him where Ingrith had been buried, and he stood there alone for a while.

Later, Eadric walked over to where Ingrith's family home used to be. It was gone, plants already growing up through the charred remains of the long house. He put his head down and kept walking, knowing where he was going without thinking about it.

After what seemed like hours, he got to Anlaf's stead, and looked around. He saw the long house, exactly like the one that had belonged to Ingrith's family, but he noticed, as he really hadn't before, that it was surrounded by massive yew trees. Unless a raider was looking for the house, and knew exactly where to look, it would be remain invisible. The trees probably saved the house, and the people inside.

As he approached the doorway to the long house, he was surprised to glimpse a familiar face. He saw Ilsith, the mother of Ingrith, emerge from the shadows and walk towards him. Aelfric hadn't mentioned her when he had met Eadric and talked about who survived and who had been lost, so Eadric assumed that she had died under a sword like her daughter. She had lost some of her energy and most of her youth, but who couldn't understand that after all of the loved ones she had buried? She was obviously still grieving. He hugged her, and they stood there together in silence.

He tried to think of some good news. "Did you hear that one of the two leaders of that attack is already dead? Cnut made short work of him and many of his raiders as well. And Edmund will receive his reward in due time."

She looked up at him. "My two daughters and one son-in-law have joined my only son in the earth. The deaths of other men will not change that. I think that what has saved me from applying a sharp blade to my wrists because of my sorrows is your son Thorunn, my beloved grandson. Anlaf has allowed me since the boy lost his mother to care for him as though he was my own. I hope that I have been able to fill some of the emptiness in his life."

However, she had something to add. "When I hear that Edmund Ironside has finally been beaten by Cnut, or even better if I hear that he has died a bitter death, I will make a grateful offering to Odin."

Eadric found his son fishing at the river with a Danish friend, exactly where they fished the last time he and the boy were together. Bigger than he remembered, the boy now more clearly resembled his mother. As soon as he saw his father, he ran to him, and they put their arms around each other.

Thorunn didn't cry, probably because the other boy was

present, but he was close to tears, and Eadric could tell that the pain of loss was still there. He noted that his son wore a small wooden Thor's hammer pendant on a leather thong around his neck, and Eadric made no comment about it.

He only stayed a day, knowing that he needed to meet Cnut at the Thames near London, so he kept Thorunn with him, letting him ride behind on his horse while he visited two of his other estates near Shrewsbury. One had been raided earlier, but the buildings were still standing, and the other had not been attacked at all. So it could have been much worse for the family fortunes than it was.

After he gave some silver to Ilsith, telling her that she was free to spend all of it on herself and Thorunn, he had a difficult goodbye with the boy. Eadric reassured him that he would return as soon as the fighting was over, and he promised to take the boy sailing down the Severn with Anlaf as he had done as a boy. Then he rode quickly away, needing to go before his emotions took hold of him.

Chapter Twenty-Seven
Marching Westward

During the several days that it took him to reach the mouth of the Thames, there were many times when he'd wished he could have sailed with the fleet instead of riding his horse, but he was glad to have been able to see his son, and he was relieved to know that Thorunn was being cared for by his grandmother. He hadn't expected to see her alive, so the visit was doubly gratifying for him.

As he got closer to London, he stopped at the market town of Wantage, and found feed and water for his mount. He shared a cup of ale with a thegn named Aelfwine, with whom he had developed a friendship during some of the witans they had attended together. The man was ambitious, but he had no great love for Edmund Ironside, having dealt with the man's arrogance on more than one occasion. In fact, he had disturbing news.

"My lord, I have been told that the pretend king rode just south of here a day or two ago, accompanied by about fifty armed men. The story being told is that he has come back to Wessex to gather as much support and as many fighting men as he can to defend his claim to be the king."

Eadric was shocked. "Is that possible? The witan, attended by almost every important leader and prelate in Wessex, bent the knee to Cnut. I was there. I presided over the assembly, and there seemed to be no hesitation over the decision."

"Lord, I was there as well, but things can change. There are many men in this kingdom who would prefer any English man over any Dane. I hear that sentiment from many in this place, where King Alfred the Great, who saved our country from the

Vikings, was born. With Cnut going east with his huge fleet, some oaths can apparently be blown away by a gentle breeze."

Eadric tilted his head and frowned. "Aelfwine, surely vows are not treated so lightly in Wessex?"

"Let me tell you what many here would say: 'What does a vow mean when given to a Dane? They are pagans, and we need not honor any pledge made to them.' I will send word to you about what happens in the coming days."

The ealdorman thanked him for his ale and for his comments. After leaving the thegn, he picked up the horse's pace from the earlier part of the journey, knowing that he needed to reach the ships without delay and update Cnut about the wavering support in Wessex.

Two days later, he found the fleet at Greenwich, with men still unloading supplies from the hundreds of ships that were either beached or floating in the wide Thames. The town had surrendered immediately, and they were only a few miles from the edge of London, but getting that city to accept the authority of Cnut would be difficult. The leaders and many residents had been resolute supporters of Aethelred, and were equally behind Edmund Ironside.

He found Cnut meeting with Thorkell, his second in command Wenric, and a number of other leaders from the army. All seemed to be in a good humor when they greeted Eadric, but their mood didn't last long.

Eadric shared the bad news: " It would appear that Wessex is turning its back on the oaths given to this king, and many leaders are beginning to support Edmund. We may not be able to count on Wessex warriors or provisions when we might need them. I expect to hear more in a few days."

Cnut reacted calmly, as though he was not surprised at all. "Did anyone here think that this would be an easy thing, and that the English would simply accept a Dane as their king? My father forced them to accept him, and we will have to do the same thing. London is one of the keys to the throne. We can win without making London bend the knee, but it would be more difficult. There is actually some good in what Eadric told us."

Thorkell looked mystified. "What have we learned that

179

should make us smile?"

Cnut's explanation was simple: "Edmund is not here if he is in Wessex. We can begin our siege of London without any interference from him. Then some of us can turn to the west and fight him on Wessex soil. Let us see how those who would betray their oaths will like battles between two great armies where they live. Every horse and all of the food that can be found will be taken from those in the paths of each army."

"Now, to the siege. First, we will surround the walls of London and cut off supplies from reaching it. Let us see how long this city can survive without the river and large amounts of food from the land around it. We need to control the Thames on both sides of the large bridge, so we will have men drag some ships through the shallow water south of the English fortification at one end of the bridge. For now, we will control everything on the river but the bridge itself. Then we can turn to Edmund and the Wessex oath-breakers."

None of the Vikings at that meeting were enthusiastic about a blockage of the city. There would be no battles in which they could win glory or riches, and a siege would require that some of their warriors would be thinly arrayed in a circle around the walls, and vulnerable to serious attacks from outside or from within. In addition, a large number of warriors would need to guard against an attack from the burh at Southwark, which prevented a direct assault on the city using the bridge. However, Eadric and Wenric both agreed that a waiting game made more sense that a frontal assault, and the other Vikings had no choice but to agree with them and with Cnut.

Within two weeks, a large force had encircled the walls, and a place where ships could be dragged had been found so that Viking ships could pass singly to the south of the bridge while avoiding the arrows from the burh defending the bridge. Over two dozen vessels were already upriver enforcing the siege from that side. Finally, Cnut was ready to take a strong war band to Wessex to confront Edmund. Eadric and what temporarily remained of his fyrd would accompany him, along with Thorkell and hundreds of Viking warriors. The ealdorman and most of his men would see real warfare for the first time.

While they were riding westward together, near the front of the long line of the advancing army, Thorkell tried to explain to Eadric the realities of the shield wall. The Mercian had already told the Dane about his childhood rehearsals in the meadow near his home, and Thorkell had started laughing.

"Lord Eadric, there is nothing wrong with some war play when a child is young, but you need to be prepared for what you will really face on a shield wall, and what comes after."

"All right, my friend," Eadric said. "Sing me a song of shield walls." And he chuckled, trying to hide his nervousness.

Thorkell sighed. "Yet another infant I need to instruct." They both laughed.

"As you know, shield walls begin with men lining up next to each other, with shields overlapping. At the beginning, after the walls collide, there is nowhere to go forward easily, and if you run, you will expose your fellow warriors to a quick death because of the gap you have created in the wall. You must look to stop any weapons aimed at the men next to you, and they must do the same for you."

"There will be warriors behind you who may be able to attack with swords or spears, but you will only be able to use a sword over the top. At first, an axe or a seax or other shorter bladed weapon will serve you better, so you can get to the enemy's legs or crotch or feet. However, keep in mind that a shield wall only lasts for a time. Sooner or later it will break up into individual battles, and then a longer weapon like your sword will become your best option."

Eadric glanced over at his friend on the horse next to him. "That is all I will need to remember?"

Thorkell gave him an amused look. "Everyone on a shield wall is afraid, or drunk and afraid, or berserk. You will get close enough to your foe to know what he ate or drank last, to smell his dirty body, or his shit and piss if he has fouled himself because of the fear. And then you will smell blood, and the opened guts of men. If you are fated to survive the day, you may also feel the great excitement of being fully alive, of killing worthy enemies, and of winning a great battle. Or you will be dead."

All of the men who were marching nearby, and Eadric himself, were silent after that until they stopped for their evening meal.

Thorkell, being the most battle-experienced of Cnut's jarls, urgently recommended sending out scouts to locate Edmund's army, telling them to fan out west and south, and if they found nothing after a half day, to return to them and do the same the next day. The scouts did that for several days, and Cnut's army continued to march west.

One evening, Cnut and Eadric were eating a fairly sparse meal by themselves; the foragers hadn't had much luck that day finding Wessex cattle or pigs. Cnut casually mentioned to Eadric that he had gotten married three years before.

The ealdorman was shocked--the subject had never come up. "I had heard nothing about it. Tell me about her."

Cnut spoke quietly. "My father was planning to invade England, and he arranged for a marriage which would strengthen our family ties with the northern Danelaw. It was a traditional Danish handfast marriage--not something in a Christian church, but a true marriage nonetheless."

Eadric was mystified. "Please explain the handfast meaning."

"I know there is nothing like this among the English. We have a ceremony that involves the tying of a cord around the right hand of both the bride and groom. Sometimes this is just for the length of the ceremony. Sometimes the hands are tied until the bride is bedded. In this case, the bride was the daughter of a prominent thegn from the Danelaw."

The ealdorman couldn't imagine who it could be. "And her name?"

"It is a pretty woman named Aelfgifu."

"What? The daughter of Elfham, the man who was murdered before me in the woods near my home?"

"The same."

For some moments, Eadric was lost in his thoughts. "I assume you are serious about this. She blamed me for her father's death, even though it would have made no sense for me to have him killed under those circumstances. The evidence seemed to say that her two brothers were blinded by the king, or perhaps his son, so the royal family was probably involved in her father's death as well. I hope that she has given up thinking that I was responsible."

Cnut shook his head. "She still blames you. She would like you dead. I know the story, and I have tried to talk her out of her desire for revenge, but nothing has worked. I simply change the subject whenever she speaks of you."

"My hand was not in this murder. What did I have to gain? The king replaced her father with Uhtred, who was as bad as Edmund, and who ultimately allied with him to savage my lands in Mercia. You had him killed. Should I fear her hunger for vengeance?"

Cnut looked at Eadric. "No. I need your help and support more than I need peace with a woman right now. You are my most important ally. She is safe and guarded by trusted men in Denmark, and is no threat there to you or me."

Eadric gave a slight bow. "I am glad of it. I don't want to keep looking over my shoulder." However, he was not happy about this confirmed enemy in Cnut's family. In fact, he had to admit that his voice of optimism was a very false note. That woman had not only kept her hatred alive for over a decade, but she had probably cultivated it and watched it grow.

Further, he was very aware of how much power a woman can have over her husband and his view of the world. He remembered Ingrith's mother making a comment when he was disagreeing with Ingrith about some small matter: "Happiness for your wife will give you happiness for your life." Of course, he had never actually married her, but he always thought of that as a mere formality.

As he tried to fall asleep after the sun went down, he thought about personal power. "We have the swords, we have the chains and emblems of office, we have lives that allow us to see the world. But we are sometimes like puppets in the hands of our women." He knew this: Aelfgifu could be very dangerous, even at a distance. He slept little that night, and awoke the next morning with a sour feeling in his stomach. Although he resisted the temptation to begin looking at every armed man as a potential assassin, he did find himself wearing his chainmail more frequently than he had before the conversation about Cnut's wife, even when a battle was not on the horizon. A measure of caution would be a good thing for the foreseeable future.

Chapter Twenty-Eight
Bluster and Blood

Finally, one scout returned at midday with news. He found Edmund's army near the settlement at Penselwood, not far from Southampton. As Eadric was familiar with the area, he suggested that the army get closer before they halt for the day, and after a few more hours, he told Cnut they should stop and prepare for tomorrow's battle.

That evening, as some men sharpened their spears or knives or axes, the campfires of Edmund's army were plainly visible on a slight rise of the otherwise flat landscape, dotting the darkness with glittering points of light. Surely the nearby campfires of Cnut's army were visible to Edmund as well, so surprise would not be an advantage for either side.

This was all new to Eadric, who had learned about swordplay from Anlaf, and had played at shield wall tactics as a boy, but who had never been required to defend his life against someone wanting to take it away. He wished that Anlaf were with him now to remind him of the battlefield tricks he had been taught.

His Ulfbehrt sword was in perfect condition, he had just bought a long sharp seax from a Dane from across the sea, and his chain mail had been polished with sand before he had left Greenwich. He refused to wear a helmet. Thorkell had suggested some time ago that Eadric would be better off without one because it took some time to get used to, and he'd probably be dead long before he could become accustomed to wearing it. All that remained was the fighting.

The next morning, some of the Viking warriors were

already drinking ale, a few barrels of which had been seized at a local farm stead. There was a jittery excitement among the men around Eadric, and he was both nervous about the coming encounter and curious to see how he would react to combat for the first time. He knew that bravado was a familiar theme among these Vikings, but he also knew that in a moment of immediate danger, men can do unexpected things. He needed to act with courage, as there would be many eyes watching him, including Cnut's.

When the leaders of the Viking forces met, it was agreed that Eadric, Wenric, and the reduced fyrd would all be on foot, placed in the center of the shield wall. However, despite his protests, Eadric was to position himself behind the first line, out of respect for his inexperience. His responsibility would be to watch for attacks on the men in front of him, to help keep them alive, and to avoid getting gutted by long spear thrusts through and past any small gaps in the shield wall. Perhaps he might even be able to use his sword, being far enough away from the first line for that to be possible.

As the two armies approached each other, Wenric and Eadric gave their mounts to a young thrall to keep safe, and the more experienced thegn, who had battled in a shield wall at least once before, explained something about them that Thorkell had neglected to mention.

"My lord, there are two ways to break a shield wall. First, if you have a larger army, you can wrap around the enemy so that the ends of your wall get behind the ends of theirs, and an attack from the front and behind will end things fairly quickly. Today, it looks like the two forces are of a similar size."

"Second, a wall can be broken somewhere in the middle, because of a mistake or because of a great individual warrior gashing through. Sometimes, one side will organize a group of fighters in the shape of a boar's tusk, and with one or two powerful fighters at the point of the formation, attempting to pierce the shield wall and raising havoc from behind. Sometimes it works, and sometimes the leaders at the front die and the attack fails."

Within five minutes, two lines of men formed, over a long

spear's throw away from each other, and then quickly every shield overlapped its neighbors with a huge din of wooden thumps. A few men from each side threw insults at the enemy line, hoping to provoke someone into single combat, abandoning their positions and creating dangerous gaps in the wall. On this occasion, nobody took the bait. To Eadric, it seemed like both armies were acting out a familiar ritual: the preparation, the formations, and the individual provocations. So far, everyone was comfortable with his role. That was likely to change quickly after the shield walls met.

As the warriors on the two lines gathered their courage to attack, Eadric looked across at Edmund's shield wall. He did not see anybody he recognized, but he was sure that there were English men he'd had discussions with at witans, men with whom he had shared a drink or two. He was not happy to be fighting fellow English men, but he knew that they were fighting for Edmund, and that man needed to be defeated.

A horn sounded, which Cnut had indicated would be the signal to advance, and his shield wall advanced slowly towards the other. At almost at the same time, Edmund's line started to move forwards. Each was careful to keep the shields overlapping each other. When the two lines collided, every man in the front was shaken by the impact, as well as the next two or three men behind the front line. The thundering crash from the collision was deafening, but everyone initially maintained his place in line.

Warriors were yelling and screaming, and everyone was lunging at each other across the double barrier of the shields. The boundary line where the two sides had met swayed and flexed slightly as one side would exert a small push in a small area, and then there would be other small pushes elsewhere. It was like the muscles of a slowly moving snake.

Spears were thrust over the shields, and men tried to cut under the shields with short blades, but little blood was spilled. The smell of caution seemed to fill the air: no one was very eager to expose himself to great risk. There was no charge through either army shaped like a boar's tusk. Eadric deflected an ax from hacking into the shoulder of the Viking in front of him and to the left, and he made an overhand cut with his sword which bloodied the arm of a man trying to use a short spear to stab at Wenric's head, so he prevented any injury to his comrades. However, there were very few casualties.

Within a short time, both lines slowly withdrew from the fray. Despite the lunging and the wild swings and spear thrusts, Eadric could see not a single body left on the field, and very few soldiers with significant wounds. He was shocked. The shield walls remained intact, and there was no individual heroism or battlefield folly, no mindless berserkers. This was nothing like what had been described to him--or what he had imagined. His conclusion was simple: these two armies were not ready to fight each other.

Cnut, having watched this encounter from behind on horseback, surrounded by his personal guards, was shaking his head as he walked into the tent where his leaders had assembled again. To a man they looked like defeated warriors. Half were sitting slumped over on stools with their heads in their hands, and the others had arms folded.

Cnut spoke first. "I accept the blame for this sad effort. There was no fire in the bellies of our men. What else can I say? They fought like little girls, like the English, not like Vikings. Lord Eadric, no offense intended."

Eadric nodded, dismissing the words with a slight wave of his hand. This was no time to be personally offended.

For a brief time, nobody said anything. Then Thorkell stood up. "Lord king, I have seen moments like this before, and I believe that you need to do nothing, and you need to say nothing to these men. Give them a few days to rest, and to think about what just happened. They will be embarrassed by it, and the next time they face that army, they will fight like they are immortal. Just do not wait too long. This shame should be fresh in their memories."

The other Viking leaders, all experienced fighters, grunted or nodded in agreement with Thorkell. Eadric looked at Wenric, who tilted his head slightly to indicate that he had never seen something like this before, and neither Mercian said anything. They knew what they didn't know, and let the seasoned veterans speak for them.

Cnut and his jarls watched the next day as Edmund took his small army to the north, probably to recruit more men to his cause. Two Danes rode after them at a safe distance, and the Viking army prepared to follow as well. Before they left, Cnut shared some information with Eadric.

"You should understand that I am trying to defeat Edmund before he is able to gather enough fighters to be able to defeat us. These are your English people, not mine, so Edmund has the opportunity to enlist much larger numbers than I can. If we do not vanquish him soon, the odds of winning may begin to turn in his favor. Wessex, particularly the western regions, is full of potential fighters for him. I think that one trained Viking is worth two or three English farmers in battle, but if the numbers become four or five to one?"

Eadric smiled. He had an encouraging answer. "Remember, lord king, that after the harvest the fyrd of Mercia will be replenished, and we will be in the hundreds once again, not the few dozen fighters that we have now."

"We will need them," Cnut said. "One way or another, they may be the difference in this war."

Cnut's army caught up to the English army before the small settlement of Sherston, near the widening of the Severn River. As the two sides prepared to meet again, Thorkell pulled his horse next to Eadric's. He needed to explain that the ealdorman's role would be different this time.

"Lord Eadric, we intend to use the horses that we have, instead of leaving them at the camp. You, Wenric, I, and the other fighters with mounts are going to attempt to attack Edmund's line at either of the ends. Understand that horses will not charge into a solid shield wall. It cannot be done. However, we can look for openings, or else force their wall to curl back upon itself, and then they will have nowhere to run. Our swords will be of better use from our horses, and we will leave the shield on shield battle to the others. Cnut suggested it, and I agreed with him."

Eadric was relieved. He had felt like a newborn calf during the first skirmish, trying to fight without knowing what he was doing. Fighting on a horse against men on foot was something he could understand.

"That is the best idea I have heard today. But what warnings can you give me? What should I understand about our role in the battle?"

Thorkell was ready for the question. "A horse is not simply a platform above the fighting which will make it easier to kill. It provides mobility. Use it. When you stay too long in one place surrounded by your enemies, you can be pulled off your horse to the ground and gutted. Dart in, dart out, and keep looking for foes that are exposed and may not know it."

"Also, watch out for long spears. Stay away from them. An enemy with a spear can either wound your horse and defeat you that way, or run you through, even with your chain mail, without getting close enough for you to kill."

Eadric smirked. "Stay moving and watch for long spears. That is all?"

Thorkell started laughing. "Yes, my friend, that is all you need to remember, other than staying on your horse, and making sure you don't strike a sword blade with your blade and risk it snapping, and being careful to avoid killing a friend or ally." He paused. "Follow me. Begin by doing what I do, and perhaps you will still be alive this evening."

"Fair enough," Eadric replied. "We will drink to that after the fight is over."

The first moments of the battle revealed that it was going to be a very different encounter than Penselwood. There were the usual insults from both sides, but they seemed to be more intense, nastier. As Eadric and Thorkell and others watched from a distance on their horses, the two shield walls collided with a earth-shattering roar, and men tried to cut each other down around their shields. Eadric could already see some men fall in the front lines, and they were quickly replaced by warriors behind them. Thorkell spurred his horse forward with his prick spurs and, after a momentary hesitation, Eadric followed.

With a few other horsemen, they galloped towards the one end of the two shield walls, looking for an opening to attack, but being alert for and staying away from the scattering of long spears, which were a part of the English line. Thorkell rode back and forth, and at one point suddenly urged his horse forward and hacked down with his sword in a momentary gap in the shield wall when an English fighter was distracted by an axe-wielding Dane, and forgot to maintain shield contact with his neighbors. He paid for that error with his life.

Thorkell quickly wheeled the horse around and got some distance away from the fighting, looking for another chance. Eadric understood the nature of the game, and tried to find his own opportunity. Keeping his horse moving, he saw another English man stumble over the body of another fighter, and he bolted forward suddenly. Swinging his sword with a fully extended arm, he drove it into the neck of a panicking man and then quickly withdrew to a safe distance.

Slowly, the ferocity of the battle cut into the discipline of both shield walls, and men began to fight as individuals, not as a long, wavy unit. There were now many groaning or silent bodies on the field. The riders still needed to be wary of the long spears, but there seemed to be fewer of them now, and Eadric and the others found vulnerable foes everywhere. They could ride through clumps of fighters, recognizing who was a friend and who a foe, and slash down at heads or shoulders as they passed.

Eadric rode down one man and severed his head from his body. There was no one else close by at that moment, so he looked down, and was startled to see that the dead man's face bore an uncanny resemblance to the face of Edmund Ironside. It was clear from his clothing that the man had been a humble soldier, but Eadric had a sudden inspiration. He dismounted, grabbed the severed head by the hair, and rode back towards the heaviest fighting. Then he held the head up, and began to yell at the top of his voice, hoping to be heard above the din of the battle.

"Men of Wessex, your leader is dead. Edmund's head is here before you, and you are fighting for an empty cause. Flee while you can."

He could see that men nearby had heard him, and that his words were being spread to others. There was confusion, and hesitation, and some of the English army began to back away. There was nothing to be gained by risking your life for a dead leader. It appeared that the tide was beginning to turn in favor of the Viking cause. Eadric dropped the bloody head and looked around for Thorkell.

Then it was as if the tide changed again. He saw some of the English fighters return to the fighting, and he thought he heard some saying "The king lives, the king lives" and the battle resumed as though nothing unusual had happened. It would seem that Edmund had been able to show his face to the men around him, and draw attention to his presence with his polished helmet and chain mail, so the deception only lasted for a short time.

Eadric was a conspicuous target for English fighters because of his fine clothing and his own chain mail, but he was able to wound or kill a number of foes without a scratch on him. Certainly, some of it was luck, but the rest reflected his keen sense of what was a good opportunity to inflict damage on the enemy, and when the risk to his limbs and to his horse was too great.

The battle lasted for hours, until both sides were too weary and bloodied to continue. Then, as though a signal had been given, the two sides stopped fighting and separated. There were bodies piled all over the field, and each side collected its dead to bury. If either side had gained an advantage as a result of the carnage, it was not immediately obvious.

When the leaders of Cnut's army assembled to judge the current situation, there were a few who were missing. Among them was Ulfketil, the Dane who had talked with Eadric about Viking names when the Mercian was first introduced. A witness to his death said that he had been sent to Valhalla by one of those long spears that Thorkell had been warning about. Another jarl whose name escaped Eadric, but who had made it clear that he did not approve of English soldiers in Cnut's army, was nowhere to be seen as well. Eadric's Mercian friend Wenric had received a minor wound to one arm, but he attended the meeting anyway.

Cnut waited until everyone sitting was able to catch his breath, and then spoke quietly. "That was a bloody encounter. Both sides remembered the folly of Penselwood, and fought bravely. Edmund is going to have to withdraw and look for more men, and we should return to the siege around London and resupply ourselves before the two armies meet again. It is close to nightfall. Bury our dead as quickly as you can while treating them as honored warriors, and then let us depart without delay."

The large shallow grave took hours to dig, fill with the fallen warriors, and cover with earth. Nobody grumbled about the work, but the entire army was eager to leave that killing place.

The next morning, as they began their long ride back to London, Thorkell felt compelled to ask Eadric about the severed head. "What were you doing there? I couldn't hear anything, and there seemed to be a strange pause in the fighting."

"It was an impulsive thing, nothing more."

Thorkell, being a curious sort, would not let it go. "You tried to gain an advantage. What was it?"

"I took a chance with no risk in it," Eadric said. "I held aloft a head that looked like Edmund, and told the English their cause was dead like their leader. The effect was sudden and clear, but short-lived. Not far away, Edmund pulled off his helmet before some of his men, they sent the message out to the others, and the deception failed. Certainly, the attempt will be forgotten by tomorrow."

Thorkell snorted. He enjoyed being sarcastic sometimes. "What about the question of honor in war?"

Eadric smiled and shook his head. "We both know there is no honor in war. We try to trick our opponents into thinking we are in one place instead of another. They pretend that their main attack is here when it is actually there. Sometimes a Viking leader will mutilate a dead body to make his enemy believe that a living man was tortured, and create a bigger fear. People talk about the agony of the legendary Blood Eagle as if it is real. There is no fairness, I have learned, in either war or in the gentle warfare between men and women."

Thorkell gave him an exaggerated salute. "Of course, you're right. Think about this. Other than Vikings having the advantage of armies made up of trained fighters instead of farmers, whose hands are hard from plowing and not from wielding weapons, our biggest edge is our dragon ships. We do not announce where we will strike, warning our prey so they will be prepared for us. We slip into shallow water, attack, and then leave before any defense can be mounted. The only problem with your attempt at deception at Sherston was that it did not work. "

Eadric became serious. "As for honor, when I was a child I lost a great friend, and then my beloved woman not so long ago." Eadric gazed at the horizon. "Neither of their deaths was honorable."

The Dane looked at him. "Sometimes the gods laugh at us. I hope we entertain them."

Eadric sighed. "Someone is laughing, for certain. At the moment, it is definitely not me."

They had a long ride back to London.

Chapter Twenty-Nine
Up the River

When Cnut's primary force returned to London, it reinforced the siege around the city. Some food and other supplies had made it into the city with most of the army going westward but, with more warriors now blocking entry, the Vikings hoped that before too long the residents would give in to their hunger and surrender the city to Cnut.

Within a few days, the men in Cnut's army, who thrived on action and the thrill of adventure, were already bored with their current responsibilities: blockading supplies from reaching the English, and remaining vigilant against an attack from Edmund's forces coming from any direction. A siege was designed to drain a city of resources, but it also required a huge amount of food for the surrounding army, which was already growing short.

A week after their return to the siege, Eadric was finishing his morning meal when a stocky red-bearded Dane named Halfdane, whom he had met at Sherston, showed up at his tent.

"My lord, a pretty young woman slipped through one of the town gates before we realized anything was happening, and told the first man she encountered that she wished to speak to you. A few of us were tempted to take her into an alley and show her how a Viking can make a woman happy, but we weren't sure that you'd approve, so I brought her here. She is nearby, guarded by one of my friends. I would suggest that you meet with her very soon, as she is a very tempting morsel, and a lot of our men have been without a woman for a long time."

Eadric smiled. "I think I know who she is. And yes, I would have been very disappointed if she had been abused."

As soon as he caught a glimpse of her, he knew it was Brita, his occasional bed partner. She seemed even more appealing than she had been when he last saw her, although he strongly suspected that his long abstinence had something to do with that. She was wearing an attractive green gown, which called attention to those startling green eyes of hers.

"Lord Eadric, I thought I would find you here with these—people. Queen Emma and your wife are not happy with you, but that is not why I was told to try to see you."

"How can I be of service, Brita?"

"I will be honest with you. The food in the royal household is getting low, and the two ladies I mentioned would ask that you might consider sending me back with some provisions for them. They hope that you don't want them to start eating rats and mice."

"And the reason why my beloved wife didn't try to see me herself?"

She pursed her lips together. " How many reasons would you like? As the daughter of the dead king she might be a logical choice for ransoming. She also thought that you might rather see me. And bluntly, if something went wrong, my violation or death would be of no importance to anyone but me."

"Brita, you undervalue yourself. And I certainly care what happens to you."

"Then why, my lord, have I not seen you for several months?"

Eadric gave her a long look. "I have been very busy."

She spoke almost in a whisper. "And you lost your Danish woman. We knew about her."

Eadric thought about that for a moment, and stood up. "Did Edmund know? If he did, then her killing may have been deliberate."

She shook her head. "I am sorry. I am not certain, but it is likely that he knew of her. The king certainly knew, and for a long time."

He sat down again and covered his face with his hands. He had run out of tears for Ingrith, but he still did not want to show his private pain to Brita. There were no words to say to each other for some time. She knew that she should wait for him to break the silence.

He spoke quietly. "I will do what I can. I will bring a sack of salted pork and some fish and some bread as close to the gate where you appeared as I can. I will make sure that you are not left unescorted, so no harm will come to you on this side of the walls."

"The family will be grateful." She paused for a moment, and then winked. "May I return after I have delivered the provisions? I would like a little change in my life right now."

He assured her that she would be most welcome, and after the food was conveyed to the city later that day, Halfdane brought her back to him. Walking into his tent, she pretended to be angry with him. "Am I forcing myself on you? I was the one to suggest that I come back here, and you simply seemed to agree."

"Forgive me, Brita. Women have been just a memory for me recently, and when battles are at the center of my mind, beauty and softness get pushed aside. And so I felt awkward asking you for anything. I would very much like you to stay with me."

She stopped pouting. "I did not know if I would be welcome. People change." She smiled. "Where can I put some clean clothes of mine?"

She stayed with him for a week. Fortunately, he had his own tent, so there was some privacy available for them, and they needed it. Eadric had forgotten how delightful her body looked with her clothes removed, She was soft and hard at the same time--feminine and yet muscular. He was quickly reminded about how joyful she was as they moved together. Their passion was amazing. It was as though he had been without a partner in bed for years.

They both were careful that they made very little noise, remembering that there were scores of lusty men sleeping around them, and they didn't want to flaunt their pleasure, and provoke Vikings who did not take kindly to someone else having what they wanted, and didn't have. At the moment he was bedding a pretty woman, and they were not. And that could be a dangerous situation for him and for her.

What ended Brita's visit with Eadric was not a dispute or disagreement between them, but rather a shocking morning attack by Edmund's army against Cnut's siege perimeter not far from Eadric's location. The sound of fighting was unmistakable, and men were running around, locating weapons and any hardened leather armor or chain mail. Eadric threw off his blanket, got to his feet, and looked around for his clothing. Brita did the same, although with a little more panic in her movements.

His reaction was swift. "Gather whatever clothes and belongings you have here and return to the gate where you had free access some days ago. Things are going to become really dangerous very soon, and you need to be away from here." They kissed quickly, he said he hoped to see her again soon, and then she was gone. Suddenly, with warriors scrambling around like it was Ragnarok, the Viking end of the world, it was as though she had never been there.

There was no battle formation because Cnut's army was in a ring around the city of London, and with all of the barricades and cover for the warriors involved in the siege facing the city, and nothing protecting their back, the Viking forces were suddenly in trouble. Everyone on that side of the river was in peril. Eadric couldn't locate either Thorkell or Erik, the two leaders he trusted the most, so he needed to make a quick decision.

An immediate withdrawal of the men north of the river to the available ships was imperative, so he sent one of his men away from the fighting to the east, and gave him one message to spread: "Get to the river west of the bridge. We will board the drakkars and assemble upriver."

He sent another messenger west to the river to let the rest of the army know about the attack from Edmund's army. And then he ordered every Viking who would listen to him to take only what supplies he could easily carry, and get to the river. A few men were sprawled on the ground in the sunlight, looking too drunk to listen to anything, and he guessed that they would be dead long before they had a chance to get sober.

He found his horse, saddled up, and rode slowly enough so that he could move men in the direction he wanted them to go, and realized soon enough that Cnut and his jarls were already aware of the attack. Meeting Eadric on board a ship in the river,

Cnut realized that if the men north of the river were not removed, they would be slaughtered. Reluctantly, he ordered Thorkell and the ealdorman to abandon the siege, and take the ships and all the men who could board them upriver from the bridge.

They were told to find the closest place in the river where men could wade across on foot when the water was low, called Brentford, and try to prevent Edmund's men from crossing there and attacking the main Viking forces from somewhere south of the river. Although Cnut had been careful to keep watch on all main roads coming from the west, Edmund's army had avoided using those roads, and surprised the widely dispersed Viking army by attacking from the north. Cnut did not want to be surprised again.

Very few of the ships in the fleet were big enough to take horses on board. There were only four knarrs, merchant vessels capable of carrying them, in Cnut's entire fleet, and none of them were west of the bridge, so Eadric and Thorkell would have to leave their mounts behind. Everyone boarding one of the ships would have to walk until they found another animal worth taking from its owner.

As the Viking ships were gliding up the Thames, the rowers were fortunate, because the tidal waters at that time were moving in the same direction, so they did not need to work hard at all to drive the vessels forward. They were soon at the small settlement at Brentford, and they beached their ships on the south side of the river, next to water deep enough even at the lowest tide to permit rowing back down the river within minutes.

For almost two days, the men worked to make any fording by Edmund's army as difficult as possible. Thorkell identified the shallowest part of the river, which fortunately was a small area that fewer than fifty men might defend. The softly sloping riverbank on the far side was left undisturbed, but the near side, which was somewhat steeper, was made much more challenging.

When the river tide was low, hundreds of sharpened sticks were pounded into the soft earth at the bottom, so that beginning a climb up the bank would be perilous. The simple wooden walkway and steps that had been in place at this popular crossing were pried up and removed. All dead branches and other debris were taken away from the bank, so there was nothing a hand could easily grasp.

A number of men spent time splashing river water on the bank above the high water line, using kettles and anything else available, making the slope into a mud slide. Finally, some modestly sized trees were felled, stripped of their branches, and dragged to the top of the slope, creating a rough wall as a final protection for the Viking defenders.

After all of the work had been completed, except for the continued wetting of the already-sodden bank, Thorkell stood at the top of the bank and turned to Eadric.

He spoke with a grim smile. "This is a killing place. Although the approaching English army is probably much larger than our forces here, they will have great difficulty in moving us off of the top of this riverbank. If Edmund wants this ford, he can take it, but it will cost him dearly. And we have our ships as a ready escape."

Eadric thought for a moment. "I do not think I would want to have a try at climbing that bank. Death is waiting at the top."

"My friend, you're far off the mark. Men will be dying long before they reach the top of the riverbank." Thorkell the Tall spoke from vast battle experience: he had seen situations like this before.

Later that afternoon, the advance scouts for Edmund's army reached the Brentford crossing, and rode back the way they came to report, giving the Vikings time to make final preparations for their defense. The river crossing was about as shallow as it was likely to get, with the tidal water at low ebb. A man on foot would get water up to his waist; a man on horseback might be able to avoid getting his feet wet. However, the river would slowly change as the tide turned, and a man wearing waterlogged clothing and leather armor could easily drown. A man wearing chain mail would have no chance at all.

Thorkell took charge of the array of the warriors at the crossing. In the front of his line was a shield wall and men with battle axes at the end of long handles, or with swords, or with short handled spears. Eadric was among that group. Right behind them were many spearmen with the long shafted spears that could gut a man from several feet away. The shield wall resembled a porcupine with the myriad of spears jutting out at the front. Then behind them were men with light throwing spears; those would be the first weapons to create chaos in the enemy's front line.

As the Viking battle line was completed, a mass of English soldiers started to emerge from a clump of trees not far from the river. There were many hundreds of them, and they were carrying every type of weapon imaginable. Several banners fluttered in a light breeze, all of them featuring a red Christian cross.

In the vanguard of the army that was surging forward was a warrior on horseback with glittering chain mail and a burnished helmet, and a purple cloak trailing behind. Surely that was Edmund Ironside, who would always try to lead an attack from the front. He was bellowing and waving his sword about, urging the army forward.

The men led by Thorkell and Eadric were outnumbered several times over. Edmund had many men, perhaps a thousand or more. Even he did not know how many. The Vikings had two days of preparation, a somewhat steep hill, and mud. They also had a river filled with water which ebbed and flowed in very predictable ways, but which could not be halted or slowed by anyone.

The men on Edmund's front line saw the width of the Viking shield wall and correctly concluded that the realistic crossing area was no more than that width, and they reacted without any planning or discussion. No one wanted to drown at the beginning of a battle, so men at the center advanced toward the water and others on the outside stood still. The English army adopted the shape of a funnel, and men in the narrow part began to wade into the warm water of the Thames. The riverbed there was firm and unobstructed from so many men having walked there for unknown centuries, so nobody stumbled. The men at the very front got halfway across the river before the situation quickly changed.

Thorkell yelled "Now!" and dozens of spears were thrown, as far as the Vikings could throw them. A few landed in deep water, and some fell short and stuck in the river bottom, sticking up like dry reeds. However, most fell among the wading Englishmen. Standing hip deep in water, the chances of avoiding a spear thrown at you were very small, and several soldiers were knocked off their feet, disappearing under the water, with blood from their bodies coloring the river red. More sticks looking like dry reeds dotted the crossing, and there were now dead men lying on the bottom. Other soldiers were screaming in pain. Suddenly, there were obstacles in the water.

The English front line kept on advancing, in large part compelled to do so by the mass of men behind them who were also moving forwards. A few men on either side ventured out wider than the shallow crossing, and began struggling to keep their heads above water. In the middle, warriors were stumbling over bodies and moving around spears stuck in the riverbed. More spears were thrown, but far fewer this time, and the front kept advancing.

Then the first men began to climb up the riverbank, trying to get close enough to actually fight the Viking enemy. After a few steps, each man slid back down into the water, and into the man behind him. A few creative fighters slung their shields over their backs, kept one hand on their weapons, and tried to use a knife to stretch forward and get a firm anchor in the mud of the hill. They pulled themselves close to their knives, stretched out again and planted their knives in the mud.

After seven or eight of those exhausting efforts, they approached the top of the hill, close enough for the spearmen who, having waited for their chance, lifted the butt ends of the spears up over their head, slanted the spearheads downwards, and stabbed the first attackers. There were multiple screams made at almost the same instant, and mortally wounded or dead men slid down the bank and into the river. One had his throat ripped open, another gutted by a spear to the stomach, and a third got a thrust right through his eye.

The dead and the dying were beginning to pile up at the bottom of the riverbank, and others used them to crawl closer to the Vikings at the top. There were starting to be too many English fighters for the long spears, so they were withdrawn. It was time for the shield wall and the downed trees to slow down the English advance.

Knowing that the serious battle was about to begin, and also knowing that his small force would be overwhelmed sooner or later, Thorkell sent two score men back to the ships and the skeleton crews that were left with them. They were told to make the ships as ready to sail as they could without having a full crew. They would need to be prepared for a very quick departure.

As Eadric readied himself for the fight, he noticed two things. First, Edmund Ironside was climbing near the top of the slope on the side away from him, having abandoned his horse as useless in this fight. Somebody would have the opportunity to end this war by putting an end to Edmund. Second, the tidal waters were slowly returning to the crossing, and the river was inching its way up to the shoulder height of most soldiers. Within a relatively short time, those same soldiers would drown. So the longer the Viking forces delayed the English, the more damage could be done to Edmund's army.

The first man Eadric had to face was armed with a reaping hook, so he was a farmer, probably from Wessex. His coarse clothing was dripping as he swung wildly at Eadric's chest and legs. The fact that he had to try to balance himself on the body of a dead fellow soldier made it impossible for him to follow through, and Eadric kept stepping back from every swing until the man swung too hard, stumbled forward, and Eadric slashed diagonally across his chest. The man went down without a sound.

He looked over to where he had seen Edmund, and he glimpsed him battling a big bearded Danish jarl with glittering silver inlay on his sword. Suddenly, another fighter came at Eadric with a long seax blade, and the Viking next to him swung a battle ax and cut deep into the man's neck. That ended the man's fight. Eadric caught his breath for a moment, and when he looked over again, Edmund was gone. There was no sign of him or his burnished helmet.

The ealdorman didn't have much time to think about it before another English man came at him with a short spear. The man made the mistake of stepping towards Eadric, who blocked the spear with his shield, and cut the man open with a straight thrust of his sword. His screaming did not last for long. Only with a major effort was Eadric able to withdraw his sword from the man's body, and then he looked for the next threat.

Suddenly, there was nobody to fight. He looked down at the river, and the rising tidal waters had forced the English soldiers who had been in the river to withdraw to the far bank, and the men who had been laboring to get up the slope were trapped between high water and the Viking shield wall. Thorkell, Eadric, and two Viking jarls were urging the warriors in the shield wall to work slowly down toward the water, forcing the English soldiers to choose between fighting a fierce enemy coming downhill, and trying to swim to safety on the other side. Most chose the water, and many of them drowned, dragged down by their equipment and clothes. The rest were quickly slaughtered.

A large army remained on the other side of the still rising river, but there was nothing for those soldiers to do except wait for the river to recede again. They exchanged insults with the Vikings, who actually seemed to be more effective at ridicule and offering challenges about the parentage of their adversaries. However, the English army had suffered major losses, both from attempting to fight uphill against ferocious opposition and from the battle with the Thames, which no adversary wins. On the other hand, the Viking losses were modest.

It would be several hours until the waters receded enough for the English to attack again, and then they surely would overwhelm the small Viking force. Standing at the top of the river bank, Thorkell suggested to Eadric that it was time for them to return to London and strengthen Cnut's siege, and the Mercian agreed.

As they informed the other jarls of the plan, the Dane who Eadric had seen fighting Edmund spoke up. "My name is Thorketill, and anyone will tell you that I am a great fighter. Cnut says that I am one of the best alive. As some might have seen, I fought that swine Edmund sword to sword, and I opened him up, a wound that could easily lead to his death. His men took him away after I gave him a big gash in his side, cutting through his chain mail with a great swing of my sword. If he dies, I expect a story stone to be carved for me, and for my sons and their sons to talk of me with family pride."

There was nothing more for the Viking forces to do there, so they quickly buried their dead above the river, boarded the ships, and then rowed down toward London. Going against the tide, the effort was much more difficult, but the rowers were feeling good about their battle, so they didn't mind the work.

On their return to the city, Thorkell and Eadric told their story to Cnut, and with as little exaggeration as they could manage. Cnut was delighted, both about their diminishing the size of Edmund's army and the news about the significant injury to Edmund himself. If Ironside died, the game would be over. Cnut made sure that he found the warrior who wounded the leader of the English, and awarded him an elaborate silver armring.

They learned some days later that Edmund had only been wounded, and still survived in a weakened state, but his return to Wessex to recruit more men for his depleted army was also a necessary time for him to try to heal himself. He was in no condition to lead an army anywhere.

Chapter Thirty
Setbacks

With the withdrawal of the English army to Wessex, and the return of the ships from Brentford, the Vikings strengthened their siege of London. However, it had already become clear to Cnut, after his return with Thorkell and Eadric, that their army was very close to running out of food, almost as quickly as the residents of London. If Cnut really wanted to take the city, he would have to do it with a direct attack, and soon. Otherwise, he would have to find an area elsewhere in which his men could forage and replenish their supplies.

Ancient Roman walls surrounded the city of London, and those walls had been strongly reinforced for over a hundred years. In addition to the bridge crossing the Thames River, there were seven other roads that allowed entrance into the city. However, all were now blocked by massive gates. Probably the best chance of getting inside the city was by assaulting the fortification or burh at Southwark, which was at the south end of the large bridge across the Thames.

Nobody among the Viking leadership was happy about the prospect of frontal assaults on fortifications involving thick walls. Not Cnut himself, nor Thorkell, nor Eadric, nor Erik of Hlathir, who had come down from York to assist in the taking of London. They all knew that such attacks would be both costly in terms of casualties and unlikely to be successful, but they would have to attempt it.

The burh at the bridge was the primary target. The wall was shorter and not as monumental as the city walls, but it was defended by trained soldiers. There was a deep ditch in front of the wall, as deep as a man was tall, and the frequent rain made the bottom of the ditch a sea of mud. Getting through that would be the first problem. Then the wall would have to be dealt with. Long ladders were made from oak and other hardwood saplings, and a number of grappling hooks were fashioned from iron by a few warriors who had also been skilled blacksmiths in Denmark or Norway.

Thorkell was in charge of the attack on the Southwerk burh, but he had strict orders from Cnut for him and Eadric to remain at a safe distance from the actual fighting. They stayed behind as hundreds of men began the assault. They first screamed the expected insults, waving their weapons about, shaking their round shields, and working themselves into a frenzy. Then they started to run into the ditch, the first few rows taking some steps, and then stopping as their feet sank into the muck, all the way up to their knees.

Nobody could wade across the swamp that lay ahead of them. Some men brought ladders and laid them on top of the mud. Men started to crawl forward using the tops of the ladders, slowly making their way towards the wall, and then the arrows began to fly. Scores of them filled the air. Within moments a number of bodies covered the ladders, making advancing to the wall even more difficult.

Two dozen men were killed trying to get through the ditch, and those that succeeded then had the wall to deal with, and there were enough fighters inside the burh to shove the several ladders that were raised against the walls down to the ground. Every time a grappling hook secured a possible way to the top the rope was cut--even before a soldier could begin to climb. Many Viking warriors were killed by spears and arrows loosed from the battlements at the top of the walls. The attack on the Southwark burh was a complete failure.

Another attack on a gate near the river was equally futile. The ladders that had been made were barely tall enough to reach the top of the city gate, and more men were needlessly killed by arrows, and by large rocks thrown down on them from above. Although there were a few men who were able to reach the tops of the ladders, they were outnumbered by the English defenders, and none of them survived. Thirty men died there, and probably three hundred more could have died without having any more success. London was not going to be taken by anything less than a massive army, and Cnut didn't have one.

The meeting that Cnut had with his jarls and Eadric after the failure of both assaults was a short one. His next move was obvious. He needed to get food and other supplies for his army, and that wasn't going to happen while they were surrounding London. Eadric, who knew England better than the rest of them, was the first to speak.

"Lord king, I would suggest that we use the biggest advantage we have, our ships, to go just north to the Orwell River, find what we need upriver, and then return. I would also suggest that we deal gently with the people we need to get supplies from. When you become king, you do not want people to hate you, and burning and killing tend to create enemies. Also, we are going to the Danelaw, so we could be hurting likely allies--never a good idea."

Cnut and the jarls were generally in agreement, although Freybjorn, the grizzled Dane with ink dragons covering his arms, was not happy. "Once again we are told that we need to keep our swords in their scabbards and our purses empty. I support the son of Sweyn in his desire for the crown of England, but I am no richer now that I was when our invasion began. When can we begin to squeeze these overfed English so that we can have treasure to share with our men?"

His complaint was openly ridiculed by the other Viking leaders. However, many of the most vocal among them were privately unhappy for the same reason, and they hoped that they might have opportunities for glory and silver before the war was over.

Cnut ordered everyone onto the ships, left many of the mounts they had, and they sailed up the coast to the Orwell River. Going inland, they encountered many Danes who were sympathetic to their side, and other locals who realized the futility of resisting. As a result, the army acquired ample provisions at Ipswich and elsewhere along the waterway, through purchase or seizure, and sailed down again to the mouth of the Thames. Going down the Medway River, and into Kent, they thought they were finally prepared to deal with Edmund.

As they soon discovered, they were wrong. Edmund had returned with a larger army than he'd had at any time earlier in the war. More men from Wessex joined him, as well as contingents from other parts of England. There were even a large number of Welsh fighters now in his ranks, who surprisingly saw the Vikings as a bigger threat to them than the English. He had scouts following the fleet, and when the Vikings left their ships at Aylesford and went west a few miles to Otford, he met them with this larger army.

Although Cnut and his Viking army were not actually surprised by the presence of Edmund's army, as his scouts had found it and returned to report, they were shocked by the size of the force arrayed against them. Not only were there more men available for the shield wall, but the English had many more mounted fighters as well. Cnut's army had very few horses as a result of their travels aboard their ships. And that could make things difficult for the Vikings when the shield walls broke down, as they always did sooner or later.

The battle at Otford was brief, but fairly one-sided. Vikings typically did not relish fighting when they were outnumbered, and that was the situation that day in Kent. The two sides began to form their shield walls, and Edmund's forces had both a slightly longer wall and a considerably deeper one as well. There were the usual insults and family slurs from both sides, and then both lines moved forward and met with a crash that could be heard for miles.

Eadric was one of the few mounted fighters on the Viking side, and with his aristocratic apparel, decorated sword and scabbard, and shiny chain mail, he attracted the attention of two mounted English soldiers. They charged directly toward him, intent on taking his head. Fortunately for him, Erik saw them approaching, and sent his horse at a gallop in between the two English fighters. Within moments, the first horseman was on the ground groaning in agony, holding his shoulder where his arm has previously been, and the other rider--no fool--jerked on his reins and wheeled his horse around, quickly returning to the safety of his own side of the line.

Eadric laughed and made a quick salute to Erik, who waved and looked around for another enemy to deal with. He was an older Viking warrior of great renown who had certainly been an even better fighter when he was younger, but he was still capable of demonstrating very quickly to any opponent that he continued to be a skilled and deadly enemy.

Within a few minutes, the English line began to assert itself. Rather than stretch his shield wall and begin to wrap around the ends of the Viking wall, Edmund had decided to maintain a much deeper formation, so the strength of his line slowly began to drive the Vikings back. Rather than allowing the English to control the battle, Cnut signaled for his line to withdraw, so they separated from the fight while still facing the English line. The English front line was both relieved that so few men had been wounded or killed, and also confused with the Viking retreat so soon after the battle had begun.

By the time Edmund was able to summon his captains and to make clear to them that he wanted the Vikings pursued, and how he wanted that done, Cnut's army was halfway back to their ships. He was furious, having wanted so desperately to strike a fatal blow against his enemy, and knowing that a great opportunity had been lost.

He'd had almost every advantage: a bigger army, many more mounted men, and the beginnings of battlefield momentum. He struck two of his thegns in frustration, and almost slew a third for asking an unwelcome question, but none of that changed the situation. He would have to find another place to fight a battle that could end the war.

What the Vikings did was completely predictable. They returned in their ships to the Isle of Sheppey, on the edge of the wide mouth of the Thames, where many Vikings before them had gone to over-winter or to find refuge, and where they knew they could leave on short notice. Cnut realized that he was slowly losing the fight while Edmund continued to grow his army, and something more creative would have to be tried.

Chapter Thirty-One
Things Change

Eadric and Wenric and the small number of fellow Mercians who had remained with Cnut's army after the fyrd had gone home in the spring did not sail with Cnut and the rest of his warriors. They stayed at Aylesford in Kent after the fleet left, and waited in the center of town for Edmund to arrive with his pursuing army. It was a short wait, with the first English scouts entering the town not long after the last ship's departure.

Eadric sat on an overturned basket that he had found, and had his sword in its scabbard lying at his feet. Each of the other two score Mercians had disarmed as well, all of their weapons on the ground in front of them. That raised some confusion when the first men from Edmund's Wessex army came into the town, so the newcomers waited for someone in authority to give them their orders. Reacting to an unexpected situation was not a strong suit for any of them.

Edmund Ironside rode in shortly after that, slumped over in the saddle and looking like he was in agony with every step that his horse took. He made no sound, which was a testament to his will, but he was a hair's breadth from groaning because of the pain.

When he saw Eadric, his facial expression changed, and he sat up straight. He approached, slowly got off of his horse, and walked with some difficulty to within a man's height of the ealdorman.

Standing up as Edmund approached, Eadric began things with a slight bow. "My lord. You have fared well against the Vikings. In fact, you have surprised them with your leadership.

They admire your tenacity and toughness."

Edmund had his hand on the leather grip of his sword, but he made no move to draw it. With a grim look on his face, he almost spit his response to Eadric's greeting. "I did not think I would see you alive again. Why have you stayed behind and let your Danish pretender run away to his ships without you?"

"Clearly, my lord, I have made a grievous error. No explanation can justify what I have done, no words can make up for the damage that has resulted. However, I am ready to swear a solemn oath to you--I have not done that before. There are some important things which I can pledge to you, on my honor."

Edmund leaned on his sword for support. "Go on. I am listening."

The ealdorman spoke very slowly, making sure that the words were carefully chosen. "First, I swear that I will support your claim to be a king. You are worthy of that."

Edmund stared at him. "If you hadn't begun with that, I probably would have had you killed immediately. In fact, I am still not certain that I should let you live."

Eadric gave a slight bow before he spoke again."Hear me out before you do something you might regret afterwards. You can always kill me after I have finished, as I am at your mercy here."

"Second, when the harvesting in Mercia is completed in a month or so, I swear that I will bring the fyrd to whatever meeting place you will name."

The English leader thought about that briefly. 'That is a well-timed promise for you to make. It is a good reason to keep you alive."

"Third, I will swear that I will never take up arms against you in the future."

Edmund sighed, and sat down on a folding stool that one of his guards had brought for him. "I would much prefer to have you slowly killed in front of me, but I may need to forgo that pleasure for now. The substance of these oaths will make it easier for me to defeat the Dane and his heathen bastards in one great battle."

"So you will accept my oaths, and accept me as an ally?"

Edmund Ironside sat there for some moments before answering. "Kingdoms are won and lost by decisions like this. Reluctantly, yes. What other choice do I have? I want this war ended, and you can help me to achieve that. Now swear to those three things, and be clear about it." And Eadric did.

This was an alliance of convenience, and the ealdorman had no illusions that Edmund would allow him to live if the Wessex army was able to defeat Cnut, and he was acclaimed as king of the entire country. Once Eadric was no longer needed, the newly crowned king would have him executed without a moment's hesitation.

Edmund made no effort to introduce Eadric to other leaders of his army, he asked for no counsel from the ealdorman, and Eadric and Wenric and the other Mercians kept to themselves for a few weeks. They were treated like servants but were given no duties whatsoever. With nothing else to do, Eadric taught Wenric how to play the game of hnefatafl. Although a quick learner at the game, the student had only modest success in that tactical game against the teacher.

Because Ironside expected Cnut's forces to once again cross the mouth of the Thames in his ships and look for supplies in East Anglia, the Wessex army was marched to Brentford where it could cross the Thames and then north and east to meet the Viking forces. Several scouts were sent out to watch the coastline and track the Vikings after they landed somewhere in Essex.

Edmund summoned Eadric to his tent, and curtly explained the reason for this unwelcome conversation. "The autumn harvest has already begun, and should be completed shortly. You are ordered to return to Mercia, and gather the fyrd as you swore to do weeks ago. I will expect you to meet us somewhere west of Essex in three weeks' time, which should mean the middle of October. There we will combine our forces and end this conflict with a final battle, and I will be recognized by a complete witan shortly thereafter. Then I will deal with your situation."

It was once again plain to Eadric that there was no real question about his fate as far as Edmund was concerned, other than the precise manner of his execution, but he was told that he was going home, so he nodded his head, bowed slightly, and left the royal presence as quickly as he could without saying something that would offend Edmund. He found Wenric, they located two mounts worth taking, and they left the camp with a profound sense of relief.

They were near Eadric's home in Mercia within a few days, and Wenric was instructed to select a handful of men to scatter throughout the kingdom and notify every healthy man that he was required "on full penalty" to appear armed and ready to fight on behalf of Mercia. Anyone who refused would be subject to a substantial fine. Eadric needed a large and impressive fyrd to accompany him to Essex and the meeting with Edmund's army.

He spent the next ten days with his son Thorunn, who he noticed had visibly grown since their last time together. He remembered that he had promised the boy that he would take him on Anlaf's boat when they next saw each other, and he was as good as his word. Although the now older Viking trader was not quite ready to sail down river and cross the sea to Ireland with a full load of goods, Eadric gave him some silver as incentive to change his planning. They soon found themselves watching the riverbank fly by, and then they were out in the Irish salt sea.

He found himself looking at the boy and seeing a smaller version of himself. They seemed to share a love of sailing, and Thorunn was clearly delighted by the sense of speed, and the rush of the boat's prow through the water. The boy stood near the bow with his head up, taking in the sensation that they were flying. Eadric had devoted too little time to his son up until now, and he wanted to remember these moments spent together. He was hoping that his son would as well.

Since Anlaf didn't have his normal allotment of items to sell, they didn't spend much time in Waterford. Eadric helped to unload some bolts of cloth, and even Thorunn tried to help, but there was little opportunity for Thorunn to see whatever the town now had to offer, and little time for Eadric to notice any changes in the steadily growing settlement. There were no successors to the two young women who had so generously offered themselves years before, and he also thought that there were more Irish doing business there.

While they were waiting by themselves near the dock for Anlaf to return and for them to sail back to Mercia, Eadric looked over at the boy, and it was obvious that he was crying. Walking over to him, Eadric realized that he had not seen Thorunn weeping for some years.

He hugged the boy close to him, and the only words out of his son's mouth were "I miss my mother." It was the first time that he had seen Thorunn openly grieve for the woman who had been everything to him.

And Eadric said, "I miss her too, very much." He looked out over the water. "Did you know that she believed that you were the best thing she had ever done in her life?"

"Did she really say that?"

"She told me that many times. In fact, she said that to me the last time I saw her alive. She had looked at you when you were asleep the night before, and said to me that you were perfect. She whispered that she loved you more than sunsets, more than deer running through the woods."

Thorunn hesitated. "Do you think she loved me more than you?"

"She loved us differently." Eadric smiled. "She loved you as her son, as a piece of her. She loved me as her man. And I was lucky for that. We both were very lucky for a little while."

They spent most of the time during the sail back to their home with his arm around the boy's shoulders.

Chapter Thirty-Two
Assandun

Gathering the men of the fyrd together was a complicated matter, and Eadric let Wenric work out the details. His friend and second in command gathered the men from the northern areas of Mercia, and together they went south with several wagons loaded with food and other supplies, meeting additional men as they marched. Many met them at Worcestre.

Eadric was delighted: there were several hundred armed men, most with real weapons instead of merely farm implements with sharp edges. Some of the thegns had swords, though none were the equal of his Ulfberht. Most men had spears or axes, although a number had a long blade that looked like a battle seax, and many had good round shields with a raised metal boss. He was one of only a dozen or so mounted warriors, but they would be enough to cause problems for the enemy if a shield wall collapsed.

From Worcestre they went south briefly and then turned due east. They would follow the morning sun until they met Edmund's army. As the fyrd traveled, families fled with their livestock from anywhere near the path of the oncoming army. Whether those people supported Cnut or they favored Edmund, they knew that a force of this size would take all of the cattle and sheep and chickens and horses that could be found. And whether families lived or died during the coming winter months would depend on them keeping their animals for themselves, and away from Eadric's army.

Finding the location of Edmund's forces required no tracking ability at all for Eadric's advance scouts. They found the

Thames and followed it to Brentford, and then it was easy to walk on the wide trampled swath of land that the men of the English army had left in their wake as they marched north. Within a few hours after they wheeled about they caught up to the rear guard of Edmund's main force.

Eadric passed the word that they would stop and set up camp for the evening ahead, choosing a hill covered with leafless ash trees above where he expected the battle would take place. No one could surprise them there. He knew that Edmund would have been told of their arrival, and he would order his thegns to set up camp nearby.

A short time later, Edmund surprised the ealdorman. Instead of sending a messenger to summon Eadric, he rode into view, coming up the hill with three personal guards. Still struggling to stay in the saddle, he stopped his horse next to Eadric, so he could look down at the standing thegn. Then his gaze shifted, looking over the fyrd that had come from Mercia to stand along with his men.

Edmund's eyes widened a little as he scanned these late arrivals, and then he made a fist, which he raised and shook. "You have done well. This is a much larger number than I could have hoped for from you. My scouts tell me that the Viking army is just ahead of us. I expect that we will meet the heathens and the pretender tomorrow, and I hope for all our sakes that he does not survive the day."

Lowering his head for a moment as a gesture of agreement, Eadric then looked calmly at Edmund. "I hope that tomorrow will be a great day."

Edmund wasn't finished. "We will rise early tomorrow, and hope to begin the fight before midday. I will send for you, and give you final instructions. Tomorrow then." He didn't wait for a response, and directed his horse back to his own camp with a light prick of his spurs.

The next morning, Eadric woke up very early, gnawed on a piece of dried meat and a chunk of brown bread brought by one of his soldiers, and sent Wenric to get the rest of his men awake and alert. That they assembled so quickly indicated that many of them had not slept much, obviously in anticipation of a battle. It was crisp autumn weather, with not a cloud in the sky, but the men were looking to their weapons rather than the heavens.

Wenric made a comment about the unhappiness of the men to be fighting alongside fighters who may have raided in Mercia itself, and suggested that the ealdorman tell some of them a joke.

Eadric hesitated for a moment, considering whether he should respond at all. Then he spoke quietly, so only his deputy could hear him: "None of us want to be here. Even Edmund Ironside really doesn't want me--or us--to be here. He only accepted another alliance with me because he needed to. He does not trust me any more than I trust him, but without the warriors from Mercia he will likely lose this fight, and probably the crown. And he knows it."

Then he walked a short distance way, sat on a fallen tree trunk, and thought about both the past and the day ahead as he waited to be summoned by Edmund.

A nervous soldier rode up and requested that Eadric to follow him to the king. He hastened to comply, and they arrived at the biggest tent within a few minutes. Edmund was pacing back and forth, and when he saw Eadric, he sat down on an elaborate folding stool and motioned him forward.

"My scouts have reported that the Viking army has seen us as well, and they have foolishly turned to face us. They are foolish because we have more fighters than they do, and we should be able to kill them like cattle. I want you to set up your fyrd on the left flank of our line, and you and your mounted warriors will harry that end of the Viking shield wall."

"When your men hear two blasts of a horn, they must begin to advance against the enemy. We will meet again when the pretender has finally been beaten. Good hunting today. Assandun will be long remembered as the place where the righteous overcame the wicked."

Eadric made a slight bow, turned, and was leaving the tent when he heard Edmund call after him.

"My brother-in-law, do not forget the oaths that you gave when I accepted you back. Only one has been fulfilled thus far. You have much to answer for, and you will have a chance today to make up for some of your sins. Christ Jesus holds you to those promises, and the Lord will punish any who forswear their honor-bound commitments. I will say no more."

Eadric was smiling as he mounted his horse and returned to the fyrd. He was clear about the oaths that he took. And perhaps the Fates were smiling as well.

He quickly found Wenric, and explained to him exactly what Edmund expected from their fighters. Then he carefully gave him some additional instructions--very specific orders--and waited for him to respond with any questions.

Wenric looked at him hard, and tilted his head to one side. "Say that again slowly."

Eadric repeated the instructions, using exactly the same words, and asked if anything was unclear.

Almost in a whisper, Wenric answered. "No, my lord. You have been very clear. I will do as you order."

"Make sure that your man with a horn understands his role. Share with every individual thegn in the fyrd what he needs to know, and the same with every mounted soldier. Miss nobody. They will be essential to our success."

"I will spread the word immediately, my lord. There will be no confusion in the fyrd today."

Eadric felt like he needed to say this one more time. "Remember, my friend, there will be three blasts of the horn." Wenric nodded.

The two men parted, Eadric to begin leading the fyrd down the hill, and Wenric to share his information with the other thegns from Mercia scattered among the fyrd.

Edmund's scouts had been correct. Cnut's army was slowly approaching, dust billowing in its wake. Eadric's forces left the rise in order to join the rest of Edmund's army, and together they narrowed the distance between the English and the Viking forces. Cnut's warriors were already yelling and chanting about their coming bravery and glory, and some of Edmund's soldiers were shouting religious slogans.

Within a short time they approached to twice the range of the mightiest spear thrower, and looked at each other. Each line started to overlap shields, wood striking wood, and men prepared

219

themselves for a terrible struggle. Many of the Vikings were beating on their limewood shields with their sword hilts or seax handles. English flag-bearers were waving their flags with bright red crosses. It would not be a sorry skirmish like the Penselwood encounter in Wessex.

What surprised Edmund was that he clearly had superior numbers, and yet the Viking army, despite that reality, acted like it held the advantage. That wasn't like them. Vikings typically did not choose to fight when they were outnumbered--or even when they had only an equal chance of success. They were cold realists. So Edmund was faced with an important mystery, and he really wanted to try to solve that mystery. However, he had a war to win, so he would save the question until after the victory was his.

Similar to what he had done in earlier battles, Eadric joined other mounted fighters near the end of the left flank, threatening the end of the Viking shield wall. As Edmund had ordered, the men of his fyrd were at the left end of the shield wall, and their shields were overlapping like the rest. They had the look of an impressive fighting force. What was unusual was that there was very little noise or shouting from the Mercians. They were simply standing in place, and obviously waiting for a signal to move. Edmund paid no attention to that, but then he was too preoccupied with other concerns anyway.

Two blasts from a horn in the middle of the English shield wall startled the assembled hosts of both armies. With that, Edmund's line began to move slowly towards the line of the Vikings. It appeared to be significantly longer than that of Cnut, and it looked unstoppable. In response, the Viking line began to move forward at the same careful pace. It was like a long-practiced dance of death.

Suddenly a horn sounded from the Mercian fyrd, three times in quick succession. And, quite abruptly, Eadric and the other riders with him turned their horses, and started to ride at a slow pace away from the English army. Those with swords openly slid them back into their scabbards. Clearly and unmistakably, they were withdrawing from the fight. Other men on foot started to follow them as well: first a few, and then larger and larger numbers. Men looked at each other, looked around, shrugged their shoulders, and left the field. Some were walking, some were running, but they were all leaving in the same direction. The fyrd of Mercia would not fight at Assandun that day.

Eadric refused to look behind him at the melee that was sure to follow immediately after his withdrawl. And it didn't take long for the tide of the fighting to show itself. He had been in enough battles to recognize the sounds of one army beginning to assert its will against another, and the echoes of panic filling the air. He would take all of the men who chose to follow him north for perhaps a mile, leaving an escape route for the survivors from Edmund's army.

The remaining left side of the English shield wall was disappearing, exposing the rest of the formation to attack from the front, from the side, and from the rear as well. Very quickly the entire army was in disarray. Men from Wessex and other parts of the country were frantically looking around for some way to safety, but with a huge part of their formation exposed, there was none. They were being attacked from all directions. In fact, a substantial number of soldiers from Wessex followed the Mercians, realizing that their army was doomed, and simply wanting to return to their homes and wives. The Vikings wisely chose to ignore anyone who appeared to be leaving the field.

There was no time for Edmund or his thegns to adjust to the situation. Already the Vikings who had been facing Eadric's men were attacking what had been the center of the shield wall from all sides, and there was no stopping them. What had looked like certain victory had suddenly become a debacle.

The slaughter was immense. English fighters were battling against multiple Viking warriors they were facing, and were cut down by a battle ax or a sword from behind. An unexpected and unseen spear thrust killed many. Most of the men of Wessex fought bravely, but the sudden loss of the Mercian fyrd doomed them. Thegns were pulled from their horses and killed. Viking axes and spears and swords flashed and men were hacked apart.

Still tormented by an earlier battle injury, Edmund was wounded in his left arm, but he was able to wield his sword with his right, so he kept on fighting. Two Vikings fell before his sword in quick succession, and that renewed his hope. He had been convinced all along that God was truly on his side, and he doggedly told himself that if he and his army continued to battle against the heathens, some miracle from Him would show itself, and they would triumph. In fact, he was certain of it.

He wanted to believe that the shocking betrayal of Eadric was merely a test of their religious mettle, and the day would still be theirs. However, it didn't take long for reality to assert itself: the English army was being crushed. As the situation deteriorated, Edmund's guards physically restrained him from continuing to fight, because otherwise he would have done so until he was killed.

The day was not theirs--it clearly belonged to Cnut and his army. Many of the men who had come to that place to ensure that Edmund Ironside would become the next king of all England lay dead or wounded. Decimated by the one-sided battle, what remained of the English army had to withdraw. Those who survived came together and went west, leaving all of their provisions behind, and hoping to reach the heartland of Wessex and somehow rebuild the army.

Cnut realized that he needed to prevent Edmund from reconstituting his forces, which might prolong the struggle for months, if not years. He intended to follow up on his army's success at Assandun and pursue the greatly reduced forces of Edmund until the English could not possibly win. They must not be allowed the opportunity to enlist another army. However, first, he would meet Eadric and the Mercian fyrd, and thank the ealdorman personally for their victory.

Very soon, the crown and throne of England would belong to him and his line. Even the normally skeptical Cnut could see that now.

Chapter Thirty-Three
Two Months Earlier

When the Viking army had returned to their ships at Aylesford, they had just been driven from the field at Otford by the English army. The men from Wessex had been joined by fighters from other parts of the country, men who for various reasons were loyal to Edmund and his family. The English now seemed to have the upper hand, and something needed to change if Cnut was going to regain the advantage that he seemed to have held earlier.

He called together his jarls and Eadric to quickly consider their options. There was little time before the English reached them. Erik of Hlathir, still absent from his domain at York to help lead the army, offered the first suggestion.

"We are having problems because Edmund is able to recruit additional fighters from the south and west, and our numbers have been steady, other than the dead men we have buried. It seems to me that if we turned northward in the Daneland, maybe as far as York itself, we could match the English recruiting with our own. Any Dane worth his salt should be willing to find a weapon and join us. Let us grow our numbers to match the English army."

Cnut already had an answer for that. "I understand your desire to return to the north, but I believe that if we do as you propose, Edmund will follow close upon us, and deny us the ability to recruit new fighters. Acquiring new men takes some time, and I am not sure that the English will be willing to give us that time."

Thorkell offered another proposal. "Perhaps we should

consider loading our ships with the army and returning to Denmark, where we will find more warriors, and come again to England with a much larger force. Surely there are more men eager for fame, or for silver, or perhaps even some good rich farmland that isn't frozen for most of the year. In a year or two we will be ready again."

Cnut sighed and spoke very slowly. "Thorkell, my old teacher, I do not have the patience for that. We could both be dead in a year or two."

Another Dane named Goric, who had knotwork designs in ink on his neck, arms, and probably other places, muttered something, and Cnut asked him to repeat what he had said. "Perhaps our best chance is to raid whatever lands that we can before the English arrive, and take the spoils back to our own countries. Why not make ourselves rich and be gone from this cursed place?"

Cnut's response was quick and angry. "I want what my father had for a brief time: the crown of England. We have not done all of this for some trinkets. I certainly haven't."

There was silence for a few moments. Perhaps there were no other options. And then Eadric spoke up. "What about using some clever deception to get what you want?"

Cnut looked at him closely. "I don't understand, and I think nobody else here does either. What are you talking about? Good soldiers welcome trickery when it serves their side, but I have no idea how it can help us now. Explain."

The ealdorman explained. "As all of you know, I lost most of my soldiers in the spring because they are farmers and breeders of animals when they are living their normal lives, and they returned to their steads to start what they needed to do to live through the next winter. It has always been so. They are not trained warriors like all of you and your men."

"In under two months time, the harvest will be finished, and the fyrd of Mercia will be available once again. Edmund would be very eager to add those men to his army, with the prospect of eliminating your claim to the throne forever. Perhaps we should allow him to have those soldiers."

Thorkell had a look of confusion on his face. He snorted.

"Maybe I am missing something. Will you offer your fyrd to Edmund? In truth, he might have you killed before you get five words out of your mouth. And, more important, if you do what you suggest, won't you be signing our death warrants?"

Eadric smiled at his friend. "You could be right. Edmund could have me slain as soon as he sees me. But I do not think so. He certainly knows about the cycles of a fyrd, and he may believe that having several hundred additional men could strongly swing a final battle in his favor. Perhaps he will want to be king more than to watch me die right away."

Cnut followed up Thorkell's last question. "Go on. Where is the benefit to us? What haven't you told us yet?"

Eadric went on, calmly and clearly. "When Edmund next faces you in battle, he will have the fyrd of Mercia in his shield wall. Right before the fighting begins, I will take my men and leave the field--all of them, and all at once. That will leave a huge hole in the battle array, and your warriors should have little trouble defeating the English army."

The seated Viking leaders looked at each wide-eyed in astonishment, Thorkell started laughing, and then the rest began laughing as well. They had never heard anything like it.

Erik, catching his breath, could not help himself. "Behold, the spirit of Loki the trickster is among us! He offers us great surprises!"

Cnut brought them all back to earth. "Lord Eadric, that is certainly an interesting suggestion, and it might even work. Let's consider this. I am not suspicious of you myself, but let me ask you something for sake of the others here. Why should we trust you? You are an English lord, an ealdorman. Why would you not willingly trick us now instead of tricking your own people later?"

Eadric stood up, and looked for a moment at each of the other leaders. "Is hatred a good enough reason? Or vengeance? I swore an oath to a friend when I was young, and he was taken from me. I loved a woman, she was taken from me, and I swore that justice would be served. Both were Danes, and Edmund Ironside had a hand in their deaths. He uses his Christian religion, which I have strong reasons to despise, to act with hate instead of fairness and justice. He cannot be king. I will honor my oath to

225

you, and I'll do what I say I will do."

The assembled jarls looked around at each other. Some of them already knew about Eadric's enmity towards Edmund. Cnut had mentioned the story months earlier, and Thorkell had shared the stories over cups of ale with a number of them. Others heard it for the first time, and the telling had the ring of truth to it. What other chance of victory did they have? They all nodded in agreement with Eadric's plan.

Standing up, Cnut spoke for all of them. "Then we plan to see you when the harvest has been completed. May your courage and daring help us win a final victory."

The other men stood, and each jarl earnestly wished Eadric good fortune with his plan. Then they left, and the fleet soon departed with wind-filled sails.

Between the time when the meeting was ended and Edmund's forces began to arrive in Aylesford, Eadric had some time to reflect on how his situation had just changed in unanticipated ways. He'd had no intention of suggesting the deception that he had offered. However, none of the jarls had another good path forward to suggest, and he knew that none of them could have the impact on the next battle like he could.

So it is up to me now. I must assume that Edmund will not kill me as soon as he sees me, that he will listen to me, and accept me into his service. I am certain that my fyrd will follow me and leave the field if I order it. And I would think that Edmund's army will be soundly defeated if a large number of his men refuse to fight for him. Some very good warriors from Wessex will die on that day, certainly some that I have broken bread with. I deeply regret that, but they have chosen to support an evil man who must not be supported. Further, many of them pledged their fealty to Cnut and then sided with Edmund.

What choices did I have this morning before the meeting of the jarls? If Edmund defeats Cnut, and either drives him back to Denmark or kills him, I am a dead man. Not only I, but also Ilsith and my son Thorunn will die. My two surviving brothers will die. Surely he would murder everyone connected with me, and then he would attempt to kill every Dane living in England.

I could leave England now, taking my son with me, but where could we go? I don't speak another language, I would be giving up my authority as ealdorman, and we would have to start a completely new life. However, the biggest problem is that I would have betrayed my oath to my childhood friend, betrayed my love for my murdered woman, and I would have left the struggle before the war was finished.

If Edmund died tomorrow, that would change everything. If England was finally rid of this wretched example of a human being, I could leave the field and look to find a safe place where I could live out my days. But while he breathes, I must stay in the fight until he is defeated. If this effort costs me my life, I can accept that. And if defeating Edmund requires my death, I will give it willingly.

Our lives are so very short--the blink of an eye. My father was a man of some importance, and he never saw forty years. My mother never saw twenty-five. I began with six brothers and a sister, and only two remain above the ground. I am around twenty-six years of age, and who knows if I will reach thirty? I believe we must act while we can, and we cannot be too afraid of the consequences. Other men who follow will have their own decisions to make.

As for this deception, I shrug my shoulders about it. This is a war, and wars are, at their best, a terrible thing. I have never gotten used to the daily terrors and atrocities of battle that have become a part of my life. The glory and the nobility are thin smoke made by the storytellers. Wars are won and lost because of the seeming certainties that have no substance, the tricks that succeed and the deceits that fail.

I know this. I will not swear an oath to serve him without any conditions, and be his man. If I can't find a way to avoid committing myself to him, I will simply not make a vow of fealty. And he will do whatever he chooses to do. What promises can I make that will not interfere with my plans or violate my honor? What can I offer him that will be like a mirage on a dry and barren field-- looking like water and merely tricking the eye. I have a short time to think about that before Edmund arrives with a sword in his hand. And I will need to be careful with my words.

Eadric told Wenric to gather his two score Mercians

together in the center square in Aylesford, and explained to them that they were waiting for Edmund's forces to arrive. More, he told them that he was going to ask Edmund to accept them into the English army, and that in good time his reasons would become clear. He then instructed them to remove their swords or other weapons, and place them on the ground in front of them. He wanted no misunderstanding from Edmund's men about their immediate intentions.

Chapter Thirty-Four
After Assandun

The rout of Edmund's army at Assandun had ended some hours before. Eadric's scouts had watched from a distance as the remnants of the English army traveled west. While he waited for the rest of Cnut's army, Eadric and Wenric watched and listened to the comments of the soldiers as they prepared for the evening.

Almost to a man, they were mightily relieved that the battle had gone on without them. Very few of these men knew anybody from Wessex. Their stead or their settlement was their whole life. They understood that they might need to fight and even die, but they identified with the kingdom of Mercia, and with the ealdorman who had authority over them. Distant kings were a whisper among the clouds.

As sunset neared, Eadric saw a small group of riders approaching, and quickly realized that it was Cnut and some personal guards. They dismounted, and the Dane approached and embraced Eadric. His spirits were high, but he spoke quietly.

"Lord Eadric, I salute you. Our journey is almost over, thanks to you. I held my breath when the battle was about to begin, waiting to see if Mercia would stay with Edmund, and then the second horn sounded. I knew then that we would win the day. Some men from other places left with your fyrd as well, so we were able to batter their line with little trouble. The carrion birds are already feasting on the English dead, and a small number of our warriors are already on their way to Valhalla."

Eadric's reply was subdued. "My heart was torn. Many good men died today. Sometimes our lives are fashioned by what we choose not to do. I know that the English will see what I did as a betrayal, but I believe it was necessary. Surely it will be forgotten in the mists of time."

"And the deception worked perfectly." Cnut motioned for his horse. "Tomorrow we will follow the remainder of Edmund's army, and try to end this business quickly. However, I may yet have need of your help to placate Edmund and avoid further fighting. Stay close to me."

He mounted his horse and turned to Eadric. "You know that I will owe you my crown when this is over." He straightened in the saddle, looked at the ealdorman for a moment with narrowed eyes, and then pricked his horse into startled movement.

The Viking army, once again reinforced by the Mercian fyrd, hotly pursued Edmund westward for several days, through the upper reaches of Wessex, making it impossible for him to gather more men to himself. Of course, everywhere the Vikings went, they took livestock and provisions from steads owned by many of the men who had reneged on their support for Cnut as the next king. Cnut thought that was mild retribution for their disloyalty, and he particularly enjoyed watching his men eating food that had been involuntarily supplied by the people of Wessex.

As Edmund's diminished forces approached the mouth of the Severn, they may have hoped that they might find ships available to take them away from their pursuers, but there was nothing there to provide an escape. They turned to the north following the river beyond Gloucestre, and past the border of Mercia, and it was there that Cnut's army caught up with them.

Eadric knew this river in great detail, having sailed up and down it a good number of times, and the land they had passed through was already starting to feel like home. Some of his soldiers lived nearby, and he allowed a small number to return to their homes and families. There was a village called Deerhurst nearby, and Edmund had set up camp there.

Cnut and Eadric had been riding close by each other, and the Dane brought his mount next to Eadric's. "I've thought about this. I would like you to meet with Edmund during a truce, and take the measure of his condition, and his willingness to settle our conflict without more deaths. Keep in mind that we are now in your domain, and more fighting will bring suffering to your people."

"Why choose me, lord king? Surely he must hate me more than any other man alive."

"You are his brother-in-law, and you know him better than anyone here. Further, given what is left of his army, he is in no position to anger me by maiming or killing my chosen representative. And a fair settlement will serve him well, given his other choices. Go and speak for me."

Eadric shrugged his shoulders. "As you wish." He was certainly not looking forward to this meeting.

When the two armies were able to see each other, Cnut halted the advance of his men, and nodded to Eadric to keep riding. After breaking off a branch from a nearby pine tree, Eadric went ahead with Wenric and another thegn, who he told to hold the branch high in the air to signify that they approached in peace. After a few moments, four riders emerged from the English camp, one of them clearly having trouble staying on his horse. It was Edmund, and as the two parties approached each other, he could not hide the pain that he was experiencing.

However, he summoned the strength to ride right up to Eadric and begin shouting. "Judas! You are a disgrace to your blood, and you are a disgrace to your English heritage. You are foresworn and therefore cursed by God."

Eadric had expected that outrage from Edmund, and he was determined to remain calm. He would not be baited into becoming angry himself. "If you are unwilling to treat with me, there are Vikings who you can address, although they may not have my tolerance for your insults."

Suddenly acting much less furious, Edmund asked about the purpose of this meeting.

Eadric thought about his words before he began. "Cnut is interested in an end to the fighting. After years of war, England needs peace. Perhaps you and he can reach a conclusion to it all." He paused for a moment. "However, I did not break an oath to you."

Edmund could not help himself, and began shouting again. "What? What outrageous denial did you just offer to me?"

Eadric waited for calm to return. "I did not break an oath I made to you. I swore that I would bring the fyrd to you, and I swore that I would not fight against you. I have been true to my word. Finally, I swore that I would support your claim to be a king, and I abide by that statement. However, that possibility is now up to you and your talk with Cnut. There is an island nearby that is called Olney, in the middle of the Severn, and there the two of you can discuss what needs to be settled. Will you meet there with Cnut?"

Edmund grunted. "Do I have a choice? Of course." With that, he glared at his enemy, turned his horse, and with difficulty rode back towards his camp.

While Eadric had been having that exchange with Edmund, he realized that the man's wounds were far more serious than he had suspected. There was the unmistakable odor of sloughing, the slow dying of a part of the body. Whether it was his gut or his arm, or both, Eadric knew that he did not have long to live.

When he returned to report to Cnut, the first information he wanted to share concerned Edmund's health. "Lord King, I have encouraging news for you. Edmund's body is rotting from the wounds he has suffered. You could offer him a part of the country, knowing that he would be a king of it for a very short time. He has perhaps a few weeks to live, and at the outside a month or so. You could offer him the whole world, and it would slip through his fingers like sand." Eadric realized that by making that suggestion about giving Edmund a kingdom, he was fulfilling his last oath to Edmund, and he was relieved to know that.

"Let me think on it," Cnut said. "You have done well, and I will not forget it."

The next day, the leaders of the two armies met on the island, brought there by men with boats who had just been released from any further fighting by Eadric, and who were glad to help bring peace to their kingdom. Cnut and Edmund were only together for an hour, and, upon his return, he called his jarls and Eadric together.

"It is finished. We have agreed that Edmund will be king of Wessex, and I will be king of Mercia and the other places north of there, and London will be a part of our portion. As long as we both shall live, that division will stand." He glanced for a moment at Eadric. "Fighting will stop now, and will not begin again. England will pay seventy-two thousand pounds as the gafol payment to our Viking army. London will have to pay its own gafol, which will be decided later. Finally, whichever of us outlives the other will become the king of the entire country. Remember those last words in the coming days."

With that, Cnut ordered the Viking army back to London, where the payment amount would be decided. Eadric released the remainder of the fyrd and they returned to their homes and families. Before Cnut himself departed, he told Eadric that he would remain the leader of Mercia, but that his domain would be greatly expanded and he would be called an earl, like the jarls of Scandinavia. He would now also control the Danelaw counties which had traditionally been a part of Mercia. Cnut would reserve control of Wessex for himself when Edmund expired, Thorkell would be in charge of East Anglia, and Erik of Hlathir would control York and the north. Eadric was relieved to hear that Cnut was including him in his future for England.

Within a month of the peace agreement, Edmund Ironside was dead. His wounds had devastated his body beyond any attempts at healing. There was much public lamentation for a man who always wanted to be a warrior king, and who finally became one for a brief time, but Eadric privately felt only relief.

Ignoring the man's surly and arrogant disposition, he remained a small man who refused to distinguish between farmers and traders who had invested in a peaceful life in England, and raiders who wanted to enrich themselves at the expense of everyone except their allies. His hatred and self-righteousness made him unworthy to be a king of England, a country that had become, by the beginning of the new millennium, a mix of two different peoples.

The Danes that he had known in Mercia wanted nothing

more than to live in peace with their neighbors. If some of their ancestors had arrived as invaders, that time was long past. Outsiders had become part of the country, and their eagerness to explore and find a new home had brought a different energy to England.

Chapter Thirty-Five
Adjustments

Eadric had lived with a desire for revenge for many years, and he had thought that desire had been renewed and strengthened by the killing of Ingrith. However, he now realized that his decisions over the last two years had been governed primarily by his certainty that Cnut would be a much better monarch than Edmund. So there was no feeling of triumph or even consolation to be had.

It was good to be home again. Physically, the estate was as it had been before the devastation. It had become a large compound in recent years, and it had been restored to its former impressive state: a worthy home for the new earl of Greater Mercia. When the peace had been concluded, he had been tempted to ask Ilsith to bring his son to him, but when he first talked with her after his return, her eyes begged him to allow the boy to stay with her.

She had little else to care about, and Eadric did not know how much his new responsibilities would require of his time. Better that the boy should stay with her, and have the comfort of a grandmother's love. He could see Thorunn every day if he wished. Perhaps he might even ask Ilsith and his son to join him on the estate. Of course, there was also the question of Brita.

It didn't take Eadric more than a few days to realize that his home was a very quiet place now. There were no children there, and his difficult aunt had died in the raid almost two years before. Other than an overseer of the estate, he and his surviving brothers Aelfric and Aethelwine and a small number of thralls were the only residents in the house. There were no women to provide a softer element to his life, and he had to admit that he missed that. In fact, having been among only men, and many of them particularly brutal ones for so long, made him appreciate even more the company of women.

Cnut had called for a witan in London to confirm his accession to the throne, so Eadric saw this as a perfect opportunity to meet with Eadgyth, and ask her permission to invite Brita to join him at his home in Mercia. He had not seen his wife for two years, and bedding her was no longer even a consideration, so he hoped there would be no objection. However, he wondered if, given the choice of staying in London or going to live in the woodlands of the Mercian countryside, Brita might choose the busy and crowded streets of England's biggest city. The long ride to London gave him the time to worry about how he should ask her, and what she might say.

His concerns were unfounded. Before the witan, he visited his wife at the royal estate where they had first met. Eadgyth, still an attractive woman, was both cordial and understanding. Given the current family circumstances, she was quite willing to give up one of her servants, and was delighted that Eadric might have the companionship of such a pleasant woman.

Then she apologized for neglecting to thank her husband for providing some welcome provisions during Cnut's first siege of London. She told him that he had saved her from having to eat some really unpleasant things--she couldn't bear to be any more specific.

Summoned from her work elsewhere in the house, Brita acted surprised to see Eadric again. Eadgyth politely excused herself, and they were left standing alone.

"Lord Eadric, I was not informed that you were alive, let alone in London, and under very different circumstances than when you were last visiting the city." Her green eyes flashed with amusement. "And you asked to see me, which honors me." Having shared every intimacy with him, she had never been formal with him when they were alone, and she now hoped for a joking response. Was he still the same man that she had known?

He grinned. "Hello. My name is Eadric of Mercia. You may arise, my lady." She continued standing as he strode over and embraced her. "I have a important question to ask you."

She pretended to be angry. "After a half year of my hearing nothing from you, you now have a question for me?"

He raised an eyebrow. "I was busy. We were all busy. Perhaps you heard?"

She gave up the pretense and smiled. "Please proceed with your important question. I know your marriage to my mistress remains intact, so I am certainly not waiting for a proposal. Do you need a free born servant? I think that my time here may be growing short."

Eadric smiled as well. "Since I have no intention of murdering my legal wife, and an annulment from the church at this late date seems most unlikely, despite the physical barrenness of our union, another marriage appears to be out of the question." He paused. "However, I am a lonely man on a very large estate, and I do care for you. I certainly need not remind you of the pleasure in our mating. I would ask you to join me in Mercia, live with me in our home as an equal, and we can share our lives with each other. I swear that you will be provided for if anything happens to me."

She said nothing for some moments, and stared out a nearby window. Then she turned and looked at him. " Hmm, this is a difficult choice that you give me. I can either continue to be a handmaiden in a house which has been an adversary to the coming king of England, or the companion of a young and powerful man, living in his grand home, and enjoying life in the country. You may not know this about me--I have not lived my whole life in a busy place like this, and I know I will not miss the stench and noise of the city. Yes, I will. I'll come with you, and share whatever life has to offer us in the future."

He embraced her again, this time pressing her against him. "I'm delighted. We will have the time for you to tell me about your childhood, and anything else you want to share which will allow me to know you better."

She had a question for him. "Have you any thoughts about more children? I know you have one son."

His answer was immediate. "I will accept what comes. God, or the Norse gods, or the Fates will decide."

She nodded. "I feel the same way. Time will take care of that question."

Eadric then attended the witan, where the important men of the realm, including the clerics, quickly accepted the agreement that Cnut had made with Edmund, and then they overwhelmingly voted him king. The coronation and the great accompanying celebration would be planned for the Christmas of 1017 and, as the gathering ended, everyone who had participated felt like a huge burden had been lifted off of their shoulders.

Privately, many of the thegns remained uncomfortable about Cnut ruling England, but they were war-weary. After all of the fighting and raiding, there would be one strong ruler, and he would defend both English and Danes. Peace and stability were slowly returning to the nation. And Eadric and Brita rode to Mercia together.

Chapter Thirty-Six
Consolidations

He had not been with a woman since Brita had found him outside of the walls of London a half year ago. Eadric had never found the charms of a paid woman appealing, so when other Vikings availed themselves of the services of whores who followed the camp, he had ignored the opportunity and busied himself with preparations for another day of a blockade, or the next battle. He still remembered the two young women in Waterford who were so willing to give themselves for something small, probably a scrap of silver, and he found that a forlorn memory.

His first night with Brita in his own home was special. Perhaps because she was no longer a servant, but a woman of means living in a fine house that she shared, her passion was unlike anything he had experienced with her before. After the thralls and Eadric's brothers had gone to sleep, the couple went to Eadric's private area of the house. Normally Brita liked to play before they came together, but not this time. They were both on fire, and within a few moments they exploded together.

Eadric felt like a boy again, bedding a woman for the first time, and he had been unable to control himself. However, Brita looked down at him and whispered. "That is just the beginning" and quietly laughed. And that made him laugh as well. They made love long into the night, and slept in each other's arms.

One of the first things that Eadric did upon his return to his estate was to locate the treasure hoard that he and his long-dead friend had discovered as children. He made sure that none of the thralls or his brothers were watching, and he found the small flat rock that the two boys had placed there. Almost all of it was still there, as his need long ago to pay men for their help had been short-lived.

After re-examining the silver and gold, he removed a large number of silver coins, and returned the treasure to its hiding place. Then he put the money in a sack and brought it to Brita, who was supervising the preparation of the evening meal by two female thralls.

He knew that he had to be careful with the money. "Can I have a little time with you, Brita? Let the two girls attend to the cooking."

She smirked as she walked towards him. "Did you want me to just lift my slip?"

He laughed and shook his head. "No, no, no. I need to speak with you. And no distractions right now, please."

She shrugged her shoulders. "As you wish. Perhaps I can speak to you later, and you will be pleased with our discussion."

Brita followed him out the door and he motioned for her to move closer to the house so they would not be seen from the inside. He handed her the sack.

"I told you that I would provide for you whatever happened to me. This is yours. I am also going to provide for my son, so you need to see this as your own shelter if a storm appears. Keep it hidden and in a safe place should that time ever arise."

She shook her head as she looked at her silver. It was more money than she had ever seen, even in the home of the king. She hoped that she would never need it, and she said as much. Eadric was pleased that she was pleased.

The next day, he rode over to Anlaf's long house where Thorunn was still staying with his grandmother, and he brought the boy back to the estate and showed him what remained of the treasure. His son was wide-eyed as he saw the precious pile for the first time.

"My boy, this is yours. This is meant for your future, and for the people you love. Leave it where it lies right now until you are in need. Wealth is unlikely to change your life completely, as I thought it might for mine, but it can be a helpful thing to have."

He also gave the boy a silver Thor's hammer pendant that

240

he had bought for him from a Dane during the London siege, replacing the simple wooden one that he had seen Thorunn wearing. The boy had probably begun wearing one soon after moving to Anlaf's house with his grandmother Ilsith. Eadric himself had no use for religious trinkets, especially Christian ones given his history with priests, but he had no problem with his son having beliefs like the Danes. Beliefs did no harm; it was the hatred that beliefs could create that was so terrible.

"Be careful how you wear that pendant. If it continues to mean something to you, keep it inside your tunic and near your heart. Christ followers will hate you if they see it hanging from your neck, so think of it as a private thing." He hoped his son would remember this advice in the years to come.

The winter and spring months of 1017 seemed to pass very quickly for Eadric and his new woman. Although he frequently needed to travel, especially to the areas of Mercia that were part of the Danelaw, places where he had never previously gone as the highest official in the kingdom, he still had ample time to spend with both Brita and with his son. Fortunately, Thorunn decided that he liked the woman who was now in his father's life, so the two of them could share Eadric's available time at home without any conflicts. The boy had no intention of allowing Brita to take his mother's place in his affections, but nobody expected that of him.

When the weather started to turn warmer, Eadric paid Anlaf some silver to take the three of them sailing down the Severn and out into the sea, and they shared some good food at noontime that Brita had packed. Early on, the weather was quite fine, and they were able to enjoy the speed of the boat gliding through the water. All three stood near the bow of the vessel and gloried in the wind blowing across their faces. Those moments were beyond words.

Later in the day, the waves became very choppy, and the boat heaved up and down as it cleaved its way toward home. Brita became uncomfortable with the motion, and then grew ill. Eadric put his arm around her shoulders and guided her to the gunwale near the stern, and encouraged her to purge herself. After she did, she seemed to feel better as the boat went back up the river.

However, she was very grateful to step off the boat and sit in the grass for some time. The boy went to her and assured her that he had seen experienced sailors become sick just as she had done, and he hoped that she would sail with them again soon. Eadric nodded his approval as Thorunn finished speaking. When the father and son walked to the door of Anlaf's home, Eadric only said "Thank you my boy," and patted him on the back before returning to the horses where Brita was waiting.

In May, Eadric received an invitation to attend the marriage of King Cnut to Emma, Aethelred's widow, and made definite plans to attend. Brita was not invited, and she complained about that briefly, but she knew better than to expect anything different. For Cnut, it was an opportunity to consolidate his authority and give to his reign a sense of continuity with the past. However, Emma remained a very beautiful woman, although ten years older than Cnut, and that was no small thing to her younger fiance.

Emma had no good choices other than marrying Cnut. If she became his mate and queen, she retained her substantial land holdings in England, and would keep her great status in the kingdom. If she returned to her brother in Normandy, she would have nothing, and would be completely dependant on him. More significantly, as rumor had it, by marrying Cnut, her two sons by Aethelred would be permitted to stay alive and remain in Normandy. They were potential claimants to the throne in the future, and thus future threats to Cnut's line, so their lives rested on the sharp edge of a knife.

The wedding itself was a traditional Christian church wedding, which surprised Eadric, since Cnut had been married in the traditional Danish manner to Aelfgifu, the daughter of the slain ealdorman, four years before, and had two sons with her. However, since that first marriage had not taken place in a Christian church, it had no standing with the Church, and the Church could proceed as though it had never happened.

Cnut was the perfect picture of Christian piety and devotion. To no one's surprise, Aelfgifu did not appear at the wedding or the festivities afterwards. Eadric was told that she was furious at being put aside in favor of another bride, but she had no choice. Cnut was laboring to strengthen his English identity, and she was a hindrance to that end.

A good many powerful people attended, but the showing was certain to be dwarfed by another event. It was announced immediately after the wedding that a joint coronation would take place at Christmas. Cnut would be anointed as king, and Emma would be crowned queen for the second time. Every person of importance in the kingdom would be expected to attend, including Eadric, and his distant wife Eadgyth. To be absent from that event would be a dangerous choice, and in the early days of King Cnut's reign, nobody wanted to risk offending him.

At the end of the summer, Eadric learned that Eadwig, the last surviving son from Aethelred's first marriage, and the brother of Edmund ironside, had been killed on Cnut's order. The king had banished him in the previous year, but allowed him to return to England in 1017. It was clear that his permission to come back was done to lure him home, and then murder him. Surprisingly, Eadric could learn nothing about the circumstances of the death. There had been no trial, and no one publicly questioned the killing. A potential heir to the throne from the House of Wessex had been eliminated.

Chapter Thirty-Seven
The Wolf's Den

Three days before Christmas, Eadric celebrated the traditional gift giving, and the Danish Yule season, at home with Brita, his son, and his brothers Aelfric and Aethelwine. He needed to begin the long ride to London, so they planned to have their holiday early. They refrained from making any animal sacrifices as some ancient Nordic customs demanded, but they toasted each other with ale.

Eadric gave his son a beautiful miniature Viking ship in bone that he had commissioned with a local Dane months before, to Brita a glittering gold-embroidered fillet to adorn her forehead and hair, and silver-decorated seax scabbards to his two brothers. Aelfric gave him a piece of amber with an insect trapped inside from far across the sea, and Aethelwine presented him with a small gold medallion, which represented his new position as Earl of Mercia. His son gave him a little wooden animal he had carved himself, which Eadric couldn't recognize, but was delighted with anyway. Brita gave him an amulet intricately woven from lengths of her hair.

"It will keep you safe during your journey," she whispered.

Later that evening, as the two lay next to each other, Brita admitted she was troubled. "I do not know how to explain it, but I am worried about this journey you are taking. I have had no strange dreams fortelling some terrible events, but I have an uncomfortable feeling about the next few days. There are times when we get hints about the future, and I am caught in that place right now."

"Would you have me stay here and offend Cnut by my

absence from his coronation? That could place us both in danger. I have no choice but to attend, and I promise that I will return to you as soon I can depart without angering anyone. We do what the Fates allow us to do."

Brita turned her face away from him. "Then let us lie here in each other's arms, and sleep so until the morning."

He had asked Wenric to accompany him to London to have some company on the long ride, and as they rode they talked about the possible changes that might be coming to England, and to Eadric's own responsibilities in the greatly expanded Mercia.

Wenric, as usual, was most concerned about the immediate future. "I think the next year or so will bring the greatest changes to the country, and to our lives. It is clear from his recent marriage that he is trying to make himself into a liege lord that the English people will be comfortable in serving. He connected himself to the last king and presented himself as a true Christian believer, something those of us who fought with him know to be a performance."

"The killing of Aethelred's son Eadwig shows that he wants no challengers to his sons being kings after him. If Emma had not married him, her two sons with Aethelred would probably be dead by now."

Eadric was interested in the more distant future. "Surely, Cnut is capable of being ruthless, but let us forget about that reality for the moment. I wonder if he will over time keep the four parts of the nation as they currently are, or if he will slowly dissolve that division and give more power to the leaders of each county or shire. That would give the king more power, and more control over the taxes which are collected."

They continued these discussions until they reached London on Christmas Eve, the day before the coronation. Eadric visited his wife Eadgyth, and was invited to share a meal and sleep there that evening. After eating, they talked at length about the upcoming ceremony, even though neither of them had a formal role to play in it.

Then her voice became very quiet. "My lord, I think I should finally tell you something. I have kept this a secret for a very long time, but it has been hidden long enough. And Edmund's death has made my confession a little easier." Then she stopped.

"What is it?" Eadric asked. "We are friends. You can trust me with a secret."

"When we were first married, I know you must have wondered why I showed so little interest in passion with a man, and have avoided you, and every other man, since our wedding night."

"Of course, but I knew that I needed to respect your wishes, and left you alone. Is there something that you wish to share with me now?"

Eadgyth whispered. "I don't know how else to say it. I was damaged. Damaged beyond any healing." She stopped again.

Eadric waited until he couldn't wait any longer. "What are you talking about? What happened to you?"

"My brother happened to me. When I was very young, Edmund, who was some years older than I, secretly touched me in ways that a brother shouldn't, and in ways that nobody should touch a child. He treated me like a toy until I was old enough to understand my shame, and his terrible sin. Ever since, these memories have never been far from my mind."

Eadric slumped down on his stool. "Why didn't you tell someone? This information might have changed everything. Perhaps he could have been arrested, and taken to court. Something might have been done."

"Eadric, it is so easy for you to say these things. You are a man, you have power, and you have had an army. I am merely a woman, and dependant on the good will of the men around me. However, here is why I was silent. First, Edmund ceased his assaults, and at that point the damage had already been done. Second, I have little doubt that my brother would have had me killed if I had tried to sully his name. And last, he became the atheling and then the uncrowned king, and at that point he was beyond the law or justice."

She paused. "My only choice was silence, and I have survived. But I have paid a price for my silence, as has our marriage. Thank you for listening to my sorrow."

He walked over to her, gently put his arms around her

shoulders, and held her briefly. She rested her head on his shoulder, but she shed not a single tear. He had never seen her cry, and he suspected that she hadn't cried in many years.

Later, after many candles had been lit, a messenger arrived from the king, asking that Eadric attend him the next morning. He was told to appear at a hall Cnut had taken possession of near the church where the coronation would take place later in the day.

Early the next morning, Eadric dressed in the fine clothes that he had brought along for the occasion, put on his scabbard and his best sword, and had a thrall fetch his horse. When he arrived at the hall, one of two guards stationed outside asked for his sword before allowing him to enter. For as long as anyone would remember, weapons had not been allowed in the presence of the king, except for his own personal guards, so Eadric was not surprised, and surrendered his Ulfberht blade. He was then permitted inside, but was asked to wait in an outer hall, and was there for quite some time.

When the inner doors were finally opened and he was told to enter, he walked into a large hall with elaborately carved beams overhead, and the doors were closed behind him. He noticed that there were several heavily armed guards posted at intervals around the hall, and two flanking Cnut, who sat in a large chair near the back of the hall. Erik of Hlathir, the grey-bearded warrior recently named Earl of Northumbria and York, stood beside him. Curiously, the renowned fighter stared at the floor after the Mercian entered.

Cnut spoke quietly. "Lord Eadric, please approach."

He walked several steps forward, stopped, and bowed. "Lord king, I am very glad to see you once again. We have seen much together, you and I."

Cnut put his head down, resting it on his hands for a moment. Then he raised it again and looked at Eadric. "I have a problem."

"Is there something I can do to help you with the problem, lord king?"

Cnut sighed, and sat there for a long time before he spoke again. "You are the problem."

Startled by that statement, Eadric did not think he had heard the king correctly. Then he immediately became alert. He looked around, and saw that there was nowhere to run, and he was unarmed. There was only one door into and out of the room, and the guards were in control of that. He would simply have to see where this went.

"Tell me, lord king. I don't understand."

"Eadric, you have been a brave and loyal supporter for more than two years. You fought for me, you have advised me, and you risked your life in returning to Edmund so that the battle at Assandun could be ours. It is not unreasonable to suggest that I owe you my throne. Edmund Ironside might be sitting here now if it weren't for you. And that is part of the problem. I owe you much more than I can possibly pay."

Bowing once again, Eadric protested. "Lord king, you have given me authority over all of Mercia. That is probably more than twice the size of my earlier domain. It is a large reward, and I wish for nothing else from you or anyone."

"It is still not a throne, Eadric. You have led me to mine, and I cannot then give it to you. My debt to you is a dangerous thing."

"Let me be clear. That worry alone would not force me to act. However, there is another problem. My handfast wife, Aelfgifu, was put aside so I could marry Emma in a church, and she was much more than angry. I asked her if I could give her something in return for her public silence, and she immediately said 'Eadric's head.' She has always blamed you for the murder of her father, and nothing I could say to her has been able to change that. Nothing."

Eadric raised his voice a little. "You would let a woman's desire for revenge, directed at a blameless person who has served you well, cost him his life? You are a bigger man than that, lord king!"

"Of course, Eadric. I may have uses for that woman some day, but her blindness and fury do not deserve payment in blood. That reason by itself would not be sufficient."

Cnut stood up and paced back and forth as he spoke. "Finally, there is the problem of Assandun itself. I know what you did for me, and what it meant to my ambitions. However, I am the king of England, and many of the people in my realm are English, not Dane. And they hate you and your name. As I give you full credit for giving me my throne, they blame you completely for losing the battle for the English side, and costing Edmund and his heirs the throne. Simply, they want you dead. Some would like me dead as well, but I am obviously not going to give them that option. And because of their anger, I need you to die. I am sorry, but I have no other choice."

Eadric felt strangely calm while he was listening to Cnut. "Is there nothing I can say or do to change this?"

"Nothing, Lord Eadric." He hesitated before he continued. "This morning, I had three thegns killed in this same room. You probably knew them. I didn't trust them, so they died. Guards held them, and Erik slew them. Like cattle being slaughtered. You are the last on my list to be dealt with, and I did not want to do that to you. Guard, hand him his sword." A guard at Eadric's side moved towards him, and his Ulfberht was given to him.

"If you would like a few moments to pray to the Christian god, you may do so. I never thought that you were a serious believer in the Church, but only you know about the state of your faith, and you deserve a chance to face death on your terms."

"Lord king, I have never felt close to the Christ, and in my youth I was given good reason to dislike priests and monks. I stand here alone, and face my fate with open eyes."

Cnut nodded. "You are going against Erik here and now in fair combat, his sword against yours. I expect him to win, and you to die, but you can end your days with a sword in your hand, and, if my private faith is true, be taken to Valhalla. I hope that we will see you again in the great hall of the gods, and we will drink and eat and fight together! When he comes for you, Eadric, remember to keep a tight hold on your sword."

Eadric thought of the people he loved. "One more thing, lord king. I pray that you would not harm my wife, nor my son and his grandmother living in Mercia. They are harmless and blameless."

Cnut waved his hand, dismissing the concern. "They have nothing to fear from me. My subjects' desire for revenge does not extent to your loved ones. You may rely on my word for their safety." He sat down again.

This felt to Eadric like a chilly nightmare, from which he would soon awaken. Truth to tell, he had expected some sort of honor from Cnut for his service this morning, and he was looking at the face of his death in front of him. He knew that he had no chance against Erik. None at all.

Erik drew his sword, a weapon known to friend and enemy alike as "Death-Whisperer." He slowly approached Eadric, and spoke as though something was caught in his throat. "My lord, we were in battles together--you, me, and Thorkell. I regret that I am required to do this, but he is my king, and I am sworn to do his bidding. I know that Thorkell the Tall will be very angry about what happens here."

Cnut spoke up once again, loudly, making sure that Eadric could hear him. "You will receive an honorable burial, my friend, and your great name will live on. Your sword will lie with you, and be yours when we see each other again."

Almost within reach with his blade, Erik repeated the words of Cnut. "Keep a tight hold on your sword, my lord. Hold it very tight. We will meet again."

The moment seemed so unreal. Eadric gripped the handle tightly, and waited for the killing blow.

The fight ended with one lightning swing of Erik's sword. Eadric was going to try to parry Erik's first effort, but he did not get a chance. The Mercian was no match for Erik's skill and experience, as Cnut had expected, and with a slight feint with the tip of Erik's blade and a slashing attack, it was over quickly.

The warrior wiped his sword, and spoke with a husky voice. "What are we to do with his body and his sword, lord king? His wife will surely be at the church today, and she can be told to deal with the remains after the ceremony has ended. "

Cnut answered curtly. "I have other plans for him. We will dispose of his body without regard for respect or honor, and you will tell the other guards to share a story to anyone willing to listen. They should report that the man was executed for his disloyalty, and his body treated like offal."

"All of this needs to be done for the sake of my crown, and

for my acceptance by my new English subjects. He was hated by the supporters of Edmund's family and their line, and especially those in Wessex. I needed to satisfy their fury over losing to me. I had no choice--they demanded the death of the man who I allowed them to blame."

He straightened his splendid white linen cloak with wonderful gold embroidery, and asked his guards to make sure that there was no spot of blood on it. "These men needed to be put in the past before my coronation. Now I can be washed clean, touched with the Christian holy oil, and start fresh."

He looked over at the Ulfberht sword lying next to Eadric's body, and then he thought for a moment. "And keep that beautiful sword close to you. It has as fine a blade as any amount of silver or even gold can buy, and it will be given to one of my sons some day. You may keep any of the armrings that he was wearing except for that thick gold one. That was given to me by my father, and I want it back."

Chapter Thirty-Eight
In The Shadows

That afternoon, Eadgyth, in a location of the church selected to make her presence and her support of the new monarch obvious to others in attendance, enjoyed the spectacle of both a king and his queen being formally invested. It was the biggest and grandest occasion to take place in London in many years, and everyone fortunate enough to attend the event was dressed in their finest apparel, displaying deep, rich colors in every imaginable hue.

Every item of gold and silver jewelry that people possessed was on display, and glittering jewels flattered the necks and fingers of the women who were there. The fact that much of the jewelry was gilded and not gold, silver coated and not silver was of no concern to the attendees. This was a great spectacle, and a little sleight of hand could be forgiven.

The royal couple was presented to and acclaimed by all those present, and they swore oaths to defend the law and the Church. Then they were both anointed with oil, handed symbols of authority, and crowned. They both looked so vigorous, and so alive--and so proud. At the end of the ceremony, Eadgyth remarked to a friend that she hadn't seen her husband there, and hoped that he had enjoyed the beautiful ceremony. She had never witnessed a coronation before, so it was a special occasion that should not be missed.

Returning home after the grand event, she realized that her conversation with Eadric had begun to allow her to feel less troubled by her memories, about what Edmund had done to her, and her powerful guilt. Perhaps they could speak again soon about her secret, and she might finally begin to find some peace. She had found that she could be honest with her husband, despite their long separation, and she wondered if something of their marriage might possibly be salvaged in time. Eadgyth wept a few tears that evening.

Back in Mercia, Brita sat at her eating table with Ilsith and Thorunn, letting two thralls clean up after the evening meal. She reflected on how wonderful her situation had become since she had begun sharing a home with Eadric. She had her own clothes, her own simple jewelry, and she felt like he respected her suggestions about arranging the house in a certain way.

She loved walking in the woods, especially wandering with him and his son, and she looked forward to enjoying her time in this place for many years. It already felt like home to her, and she had never had that feeling before. Brita sometimes found herself making up songs about little things that she noticed: the beauty of a winter sunrise, the lattice of ice covering the tree branches, the sight of a solitary fox hunting for a meal in the brush.

Brita wondered if she might have a son with the earl, and with luck raise him to be a good and perhaps even a powerful man. He would have the advantages of status and wealth that she had seen up close, but hadn't ever experienced for herself until now. It was a dangerous thing to be hopeful about tomorrow in that fragile world, but she felt positive about the future. She was probably happier than she had ever been in her entire life.

After the sun went down, a strong wind arrived, followed by a heavy rainstorm, pummeling the thatched roof and rattling the glass windows. Water poured down through the hole over the hearth that permitted smoke to escape from the hall. Hissing as it hit the flames, it quickly put out the fire, and left everyone in almost total darkness, except for a few flashes of lightning. Thorunn was shivering in fear at the sudden change, but he refused to cry out, and his grandmother found him in the blackness and held him close to her.

Fortunately, one of the thralls found the flint and steel and was able to start a small fire, so some candles were lit. The boy could see around him again, and he started to breathe easier. A short time later, the rain stopped as suddenly as it had started, another fire was built in the hearth, and the house felt safe once again.

As they sat comfortably, next to each other in the flickering firelight, Thorunn's grandmother began to tell him a powerful Viking story about a hero named Sigurd. She described in considerable detail a great glittering treasure and a gruesome dragon named Fafnir, and the hero's betrayal by people Sigurd had good reason to trust. Two beautiful women, a magical sword, a cursed ring, and one-eyed Odin were involved as well, and Thorunn was delighted by all of it.

Listening to the tale told by his grandmother, he forgot about the storm and his fears. The boy was confused by some of the details of the story--she had included many unfamiliar names and complicated situations--but he enjoyed hearing about the adventures of great people and brave deeds. Perhaps his father might explain some of it to him when he came home.

After the story was ended, and his grandmother bade him goodnight, the boy went to his sleeping area, and the details of the adventure he had heard melted together into a simple feeling of pleasure. He lay down on his straw-filled mattress, drowsiness quickly found him, and he fell into a deep sleep.

He was soon dreaming about sailing on a beautiful little boat on the dark blue sea. The prow was cutting through the water like it was magic. The sea birds were making their music and, in the bright sunlight, the surface of the water was glittering like rare jewels. Thorunn looked across the deck and saw his father, hair in the wind, looking out at the horizon. Then he turned to the boy, and his face lit up. Eadric was smiling at him, and looking very proud.

Epilogue

Eadric of Mercia was twenty-seven years old when he died. After he was killed, his body was thrown over the city wall and left unburied, and his head was placed on a spike high on London Bridge. His two surviving brothers considered asking permission from the king to bury him, but when they discreetly inquired about it in the city, they were told that there was room for more heads on the bridge, and they should probably return to Mercia.

Without a body to bury, Eadric's brothers held a funeral for him anyway on the family estate, and a fine etched gravestone was securely planted not far from the house. They were gratified to see a large number of local people attending, and even some from distant settlements. A pretty young woman who told the brothers that she was a healer came to pay her respects, saying that he had brought real open-eyed justice to places in Mercia which had forgotten what that was like.

Two leaders from Westburh attended as well. There were several people for whom he had done small favors, and they remained grateful. The brothers had to pay a priest an impressive amount of silver for him to say some words of benediction over the empty grave, because no cleric wanted to have anything to do with the informal ceremony for the deceased "ealdorman thief."

Stories were circulated about Eadric being killed because Cnut did not trust him, or because he wouldn't let Cnut win a game of hnefatafl, or perhaps, least likely of all, because he had bragged about having assassinated Edmund Ironside. The first reason was probably the closest to the truth, but the root of any suspicion belonged entirely to Cnut.

In addition to Cnut's multiple killings during the holiday season and on Christmas Day in 1017, there was the murder of

Edmund's brother Eadwig. There were no trials preceding or resulting from any of those deaths. Two sons of Edmund Ironside were more successful in avoiding Cnut's deadly intentions when he sent them to Sweden to be killed. They ultimately found safety beyond his reach in Hungary.

Cnut promoted his image as a devout Christian at every opportunity, having churches rebuilt and restored which, for many years, Viking raiders had ravaged, and he had their coffers filled again. He encouraged a strong ecclesiastic presence at every public ceremony, and his piety was unchallenged. With a Scandinavian on the throne of England, the personal and social differences between Danish settlers and Anglo-Saxon peoples diminished. And for a time Cnut reigned as king of England, Denmark, Norway, and part of Sweden.

Having been named the Earl of East Anglia, Thorkell the Tall was suddenly a man of stature in England. When Erik told him about the death of his friend Eadric, the Dane was furious, and was tempted to draw his sword on Erik, but his survival instincts intervened, and he kept his weapon in its scabbard. He knew that the Norwegian was still a formidable fighter, and his chances of killing him were small. Besides, fighting Erik would not bring back Eadric, and Thorkell had some living yet to enjoy.

At the suggestion of King Cnut, Thorkell offered to marry Eadgyth, the widow of Eadric, and after a year of mourning, she accepted. He liked the idea of replacing his friend as protector of his woman, and also marrying both the daughter and the sister of English kings. She liked being married to another powerful man.

He was surprised that his new wife had no interest in sharing a bed with him, but there were plenty of attractive women in East Anglia, and he became friends with a number of them. Cnut trusted Thorkell enough to have him act as the king's regent when Cnut returned to Denmark for a time. Interestingly, Thorkell had a falling out with Cnut in 1021, and he and his wife were banished, forcing them to move to Denmark. However, Cnut's old mentor was accepted back into the king's good graces within a year, and was named Jarl of Denmark, after which his name disappeared from the records.

Cnut's first wife Aelfgifu, who made no trouble about

Cnut's subsequent marriage to Aethelred's widow Emma, was treated as a queen in York and the north, and was never disavowed or removed as a royal spouse. In fact, in 1030, she and her son Svein were sent by Cnut to rule over Norway, but their harsh governing was so hated that they were driven out of the country after four years. Her family history did not make her a gentle and generous ruler.

Eadric's son Thorunn grew into a fine man who was determined to avoid political entanglements of any kind. He married a pretty, robust Danish woman named Bera, and they had four children, who gave him and his wife much joy. They also stayed clear of public lives, and were never sorry about that. Always somehow having enough silver to obtain whatever he and his family ever needed, Thorunn spent much of his life as a trader, taking local goods down the Severn River on his own lap-straked boat, and sailing across the salt sea to Ireland.

Waterford was bigger than ever, and the fortifications around the settlement were being neglected and falling into ruin. On every trip, there were many moments when he vividly recalled the pleasure of sailing on that same watery path with his father, a man now publicly reviled by many English men who had never known him. Then he would remember his adoring mother and her generous and affectionate nature. And he would smile just like his father had smiled. He still missed them both.

Comment on the History

At their best, historical novels provide us with both a familiar reality and a different world. They certainly highlight the commonality between our time and an earlier one. People's needs and desires have not fundamentally changed, and in fact the best writers from the past have reminded us that we are not very different from our ancestors. Chaucer, Shakespeare, Cervantes, Dostoyevsky and others show us individuals that we recognize in our own lives. Human nature remains what it has always been, and is perhaps our inescapable curse.

However, historical novels can--and hopefully do--present a time when the fabric of peoples' lives was dramatically unlike our own. Peoples' lives were shorter, and they were typically in poorer health, but that is only the beginning of the story. We are allowed to see how people spent their time differently, and the complications resulting from material and cultural and technological differences. We can witness lives dealing with divergent behavioral norms, and the personal risks and problems of a much earlier historical period.

One small example is worth noting. People perceived time differently in the early 11th century. Until clocks became a widespread phenomenon in the 17th and 18th centuries, small units in time were unknown, and hours were only acknowledged during the late Anglo-Saxon period by a select few by using candle clocks--candles divided into segments which each took an hour to burn.

Sundials were extremely rare, generally found at churches, and were too crude to mark the passage of hours precisely. Obviously, they were only useful on sunny days. So punctuality was an unknown concept, and knowing the duration of anything was only an approximation. Seconds, minutes, and hours were phantoms to the Vikings and the Anglo-Saxons. And there are no references to those units of time anywhere in this story.

To any reasonable historian, Eadric, the Ealdorman of Mercia at the time of the Danish Conquest in the early eleventh century, remains a profound mystery. The one roughly contemporary commentator was the writer of the *Anglo-Saxon Chronicle* during this particular period, an English monk who lamented the defeat of the English by Cnut and the Vikings, and who blamed Eadric for that defeat.

His primary contributions to the Eadric story included the ealdorman's involvement in the negotiation for the payment to Thorkell and his men, and the ransoming of the Archbishop of Canterbury, which ended in the cleric's death. He described his taking of some ships and joining the forces of Cnut, and suggested direct involvement by Eadric in the killings of the two Danish thegns.

He indicated that Eadric was behind the killing of Ealdorman Uhtred, which two other sources definitely blamed on a local family enemy. He talked about Edmund's ill-advised acceptance of Eadric's return to the English side. He also provided a brief description of the ealdorman's withdrawing his soldiers from the field at Assandun, resulting in a resounding victory for Cnut. Finally, he indicated that Eadric participated in the final peace accord between Edmund and Cnut, and that Eadric was killed in London, along with a few other English lords.

That the chronicler was outraged by Eadric's withdrawal at Assandun, which presumably did take place, colored his other retrospective statements about the ealdorman. Whether the other events as they occurred were presented accurately by him is open to question. In reality we cannot be certain about what happened to Eadric, and whether the violent end that I reluctantly presented here actually took place.

Eadric became an extremely unpopular ealdorman among churchmen, and particularly among those who held positions in the Worcester diocese. There had been no ealdorman responsible for the English portion of Mercia for over twenty years before

Eadric was appointed by King Aethelred. During that period, the Church had expanded its land holdings and sphere of influence greatly; the bishop had expanded his authority over a large number of properties, and potentially men at arms. As the new ealdorman, Eadric began to recover some of those properties and that authority for himself and the king, particularly in the Worcester diocese and directly south of it. And the Church was extremely unhappy about even the slightest surrender of its prerogatives and its power.

Who else contributed elements of the Eadric story? A monk named Hemming, who lived at the Worcester Priory around fifty years after the death of Eadric, wrote his *Cartulary* summarizing the property losses suffered by his diocese at the hands of powerful people, and included both Eadric and Cnut among the evil takers of Church lands. He may have originated the appellation Eadric "Streona" (the grasper or taker) as he has been named ever since. One should remember that in this document intended to support land claims of the Church, he provided between twenty-five and thirty completely fake land charters to buttress his case.

Another monk from the Worcester Priory, now known as John of Worcester, wrote about Eadric being responsible for the assassination of Ealdorman Aelfham while they were hunting together. He provided this story, as well as other condemning descriptions, approximately one hundred years after the death of Eadric.

William of Malmesbury, a monk living in the early twelfth century at Malmesbury Abbey, from a neighboring diocese which probably also lost property to the ealdorman, railed against Eadric's calumny and deceptions.

In fact, some have suggested that a written saga about Eadric, presumably produced at the Worcester Priory, existed during the eleventh century, but no copy has ever been found. He was predictably reviled by churchmen from that area of England, and the chances that his role in the history of the period would be presented without malice or distortion are pretty small.

A little information about an eminent churchman may be instructive in this regard. The Bishop of Worcester Wulfstan, for much of his life also Archbishop of York, was one of the most highly regarded clerics of his day. He is most famous for his homily entitled *Sermon of the Wolf to the English*, in which he identified the attacks by the Vikings as God's punishment for the lax ways of the English people.

However, he also created from whole cloth two non-existent historical works, *Laws of Edward and Guthrum* and the *Canons of Eadgar* because they were useful to him as precedents from the past. He had points to make, and he had no problem fabricating early writings to support them. I do not believe that he was the only cleric to be "creative" in his writing. In fact, he may have been more honest and reliable than many of his contemporaries, who were more concerned with defending the Church than they were with providing completely factual narratives.

All of these chroniclers were among the very few literate people in England during this period, and their writings help us to tentatively add to what would otherwise be an almost empty slate. We can be grateful for their accounts, no matter how flawed they might be. However, we cannot forget that these churchmen had powerful agendas to further, some ecclesiastical, some political, and some personal.

Much of what we are told remains inexplicable. Welsh annuls make reference to Eadric sacking St. David's monastic settlement in 1012, but there is no explanation for why he did so. We also do not know why Eadric suddenly went from an apparently loyal son-in-law of the king to a full-bore supporter of Cnut.

We have difficulty imagining how Eadric was able to return to the English side for a short time before he caused his Mercian fighters to leave the field at Assandun, dooming Edmund and his army. Finally, we really do not know why Cnut, not long after reaffirming Eadric's status as earl of a much-expanded domain of Mercia, had him killed on Christmas Day, and apparently disposed of his remains in a manner which spoke of personal disgrace. Eadric had proven his loyalty to Cnut, and would have been a reliable administrator in Greater Mercia.

Ultimately, some of the stories about Eadric which have

come down to us are simply implausible. Not long after the death of Edmund Ironside, rumors were circulated that, rather than him dying from a battle wound, he had been murdered. Of course, some would have believed that Eadric must have had some responsibility. One version told long after Edmund's death was that Eadric had a henchman position himself in a garderobe, a drainage chamber underneath a toilet where Edmund was sitting, and shot him from below with a crossbow. Another version, told by a Henry Huntingdon in the early twelfth century, involved Eadric's son stabbing Edmund from beneath the toilet.

The problem with the first version is that crossbows were not in use in Western Europe until approximately the Battle of Hastings in 1066. The problem with the second version is that we have no real historical evidence of Eadric ever having had a child of either gender. The young Thorunn was my own invention, as was his charming mother Ingrith.

It is clear that Edmund Ironside and Eadric, despite being brothers-in-law, were extremely hostile to each other, although we don't know why. Edmund's virtual kidnapping of the widow of a murdered Danish thegn, and then marrying her against his father's wishes, suggests that he had his own agendas, and being a respectful and obedient son and subject wasn't one of them. He was clearly complicit in the killing of the husband and the brother, and the marriage that followed shortly after was patently illegal.

He was certainly an aggressive and probably a charismatic leader, and his willingness to battle the Vikings at every opportunity provides a sharp contrast to his father's willingness to appease them. Most English histories tend to treat him very favorably because he was a fighter, and a fairly successful one. My suggestion that Edmund was behind the St Brice's Day massacres, one of the major follies of Aethelred's reign, is a convenient guess, although Edmund's long-standing hostility to the Vikings is clear.

It is conceivable that a collection of Christian monks were responsible for the same sort of distortions involving Eadric of Mercia as Shakespeare committed in his portrayal of Richard III. The Bard did a wondrous hatchet job merely because he wanted the favor of Queen Elizabeth, whose ancestors were the Tudor adversaries of Richard III, and the House of York. The recent discovery of Richard's remains has confirmed that he was not significantly deformed physically, and it's almost certain that Shakespeare's portrayal was less than accurate in other ways as well.

Ironically, the people who were most hostile toward Eadric of Mercia were the only historians whose accounts have survived. The monks, especially those from the Worcester diocese, saw Eadric as an enemy of the Church and its interests, and we should expect that they savaged him and his reputation in retribution. As someone suggested on a history blog a few years ago, "History is not written by the winners but by those who know how to write." Perhaps they won't--or at least shouldn't--have the last word.

One thousand years after the end of Eadric's story, perhaps the much-maligned Mercian deserves better than what historians have done to his reputation.

David Mullaly
Annapolis, MD
April 2017

Map Appendix

The following maps, drawn by the late Reginald Piggott, and provided by the Department of Anglo-Saxon, Norse, and Celtic of the University of Cambridge, give a clear visual explanation of the history of the Danish Conquests of England from 1013 to 1016 A.D.

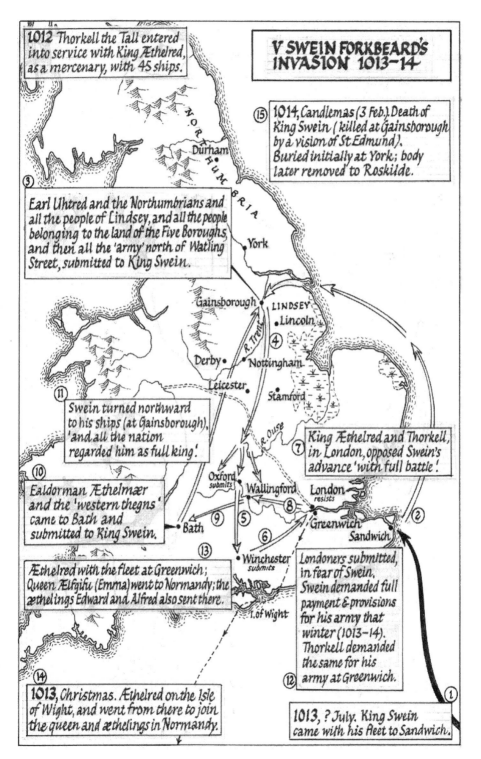

1012 Thorkell the Tall entered into service with King Æthelred, as a mercenary, with 45 ships.

V SWEIN FORKBEARD'S INVASION 1013–14

(15) 1014, Candlemas (3 Feb.). Death of King Swein (killed at Gainsborough by a vision of St Edmund). Buried initially at York; body later removed to Roskilde.

(3) Earl Uhtred and the Northumbrians and all the people of Lindsey, and all the people belonging to the land of the Five Boroughs, and then all the 'army' north of Watling Street, submitted to King Swein.

(11) Swein turned northward to his ships (at Gainsborough), 'and all the nation regarded him as full king'.

(7) King Æthelred and Thorkell, in London, opposed Swein's advance 'with full battle'.

(10) Ealdorman Æthelmær and the 'western thegns' came to Bath and submitted to King Swein.

Æthelred with the fleet at Greenwich; Queen Ælfgifu (Emma) went to Normandy; the æthelings Edward and Alfred also sent there.

(12) Londoners submitted, in fear of Swein. Swein demanded full payment & provisions for his army that winter (1013–14). Thorkell demanded the same for his army at Greenwich.

(14) 1013, Christmas. Æthelred on the Isle of Wight, and went from there to join the queen and æthelings in Normandy.

(1) 1013, ? July. King Swein came with his fleet to Sandwich.

Durham

NORTHUMBRIA

York

Gainsborough
LINDSEY
Lincoln
(4)
Derby
Nottingham
Leicester
Stamford

R. Trent

R. Ouse

Oxford submits
Wallingford
(9) (5) (8)
London resists
(6)
Greenwich
Sandwich (2)
Bath
(13)
Winchester submits
I. of Wight

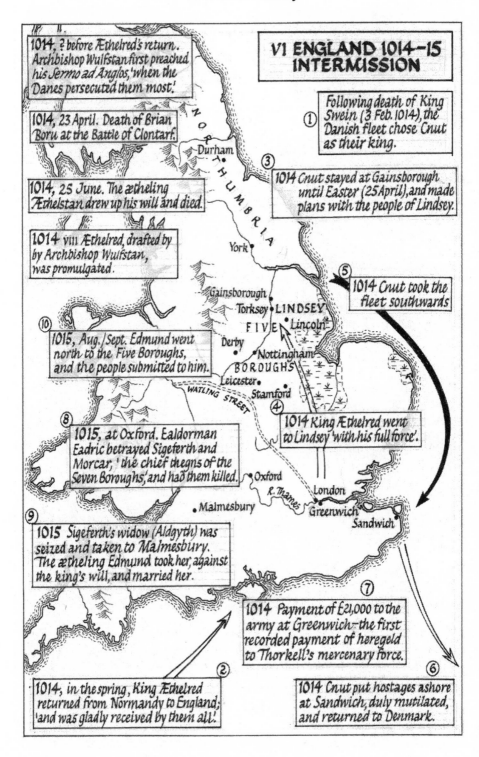

VI ENGLAND 1014–15 INTERMISSION

1014, ? before Æthelred's return. Archbishop Wulfstan first preached his *Sermo ad Anglos,* 'when the Danes persecuted them most.'

1014, 23 April. Death of Brian Boru at the Battle of Clontarf.

1014, 25 June. The ætheling Æthelstan drew up his will and died.

1014 VIII Æthelred, drafted by by Archbishop Wulfstan, was promulgated.

① Following death of King Swein (3 Feb. 1014), the Danish fleet chose Cnut as their king.

③ 1014 Cnut stayed at Gainsborough until Easter (25 April), and made plans with the people of Lindsey.

⑤ 1014 Cnut took the fleet southwards

⑩ 1015, Aug./Sept. Edmund went north to the Five Boroughs, and the people submitted to him.

④ 1014 King Æthelred went to Lindsey 'with his full force'.

⑧ 1015, at Oxford. Ealdorman Eadric betrayed Sigeferth and Morcar, ' the chief thegns of the Seven Boroughs,' and had them killed.

⑨ 1015 Sigeferth's widow (Aldgyth) was seized and taken to Malmesbury. The ætheling Edmund took her, against the king's will, and married her.

⑦ 1014 Payment of £21,000 to the army at Greenwich—the first recorded payment of heregeld to Thorkell's mercenary force.

② 1014, in the spring, King Æthelred returned from Normandy to England, 'and was gladly received by them all.'

⑥ 1014 Cnut put hostages ashore at Sandwich, duly mutilated, and returned to Denmark.

NORTHUMBRIA

Durham

York

Gainsborough
Torksey • LINDSEY
F I V E • Lincoln
Derby •
• Nottingham
BOROUGHS
Leicester •
• Stamford
WATLING STREET

• Oxford
R. Thames
• Malmesbury
London
Greenwich
Sandwich

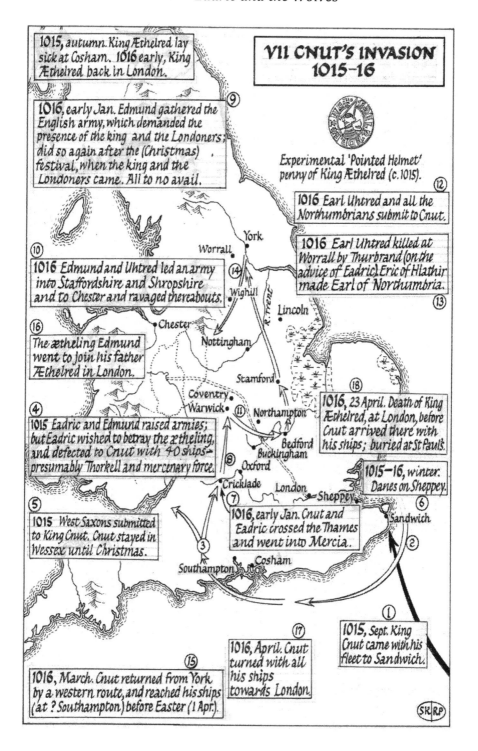

VII CNUT'S INVASION 1015–16

Experimental 'Pointed Helmet' penny of King Æthelred (c.1015).

1015, autumn. King Æthelred lay sick at Cosham. 1016 early, King Æthelred back in London.

⑨ 1016, early Jan. Edmund gathered the English army, which demanded the presence of the king and the Londoners; did so again after the (Christmas) festival, when the king and the Londoners came. All to no avail.

⑩ 1016 Edmund and Uhtred led an army into Staffordshire and Shropshire and to Chester and ravaged thereabouts.

⑯ The ætheling Edmund went to join his father Æthelred in London.

④ 1015 Eadric and Edmund raised armies; but Eadric wished to betray the ætheling, and defected to Cnut with 40 ships – presumably Thorkell and mercenary force.

⑤ 1015 West Saxons submitted to King Cnut. Cnut stayed in Wessex until Christmas.

⑫ 1016 Earl Uhtred and all the Northumbrians submit to Cnut.

1016 Earl Uhtred killed at Worrall by Thurbrand (on the advice of Eadric). Eric of Hlathir made Earl of Northumbria. ⑬

⑱ 1016, 23 April. Death of King Æthelred, at London, before Cnut arrived there with his ships; buried at St Paul's.

1015–16, winter. Danes on Sheppey.

⑦ 1016, early Jan. Cnut and Eadric crossed the Thames and went into Mercia.

① 1015, Sept. King Cnut came with his fleet to Sandwich.

⑰ 1016, April. Cnut turned with all his ships towards London.

⑮ 1016, March. Cnut returned from York by a western route, and reached his ships (at ? Southampton) before Easter (1 Apr.).

York · Worrall · Wighill · Lincoln · Chester · Nottingham · Stamford · Coventry · Warwick · Northampton · Bedford · Buckingham · Oxford · Cricklade · London · Sheppey · Sandwich · Southampton · Cosham

R. Trent

SK RP

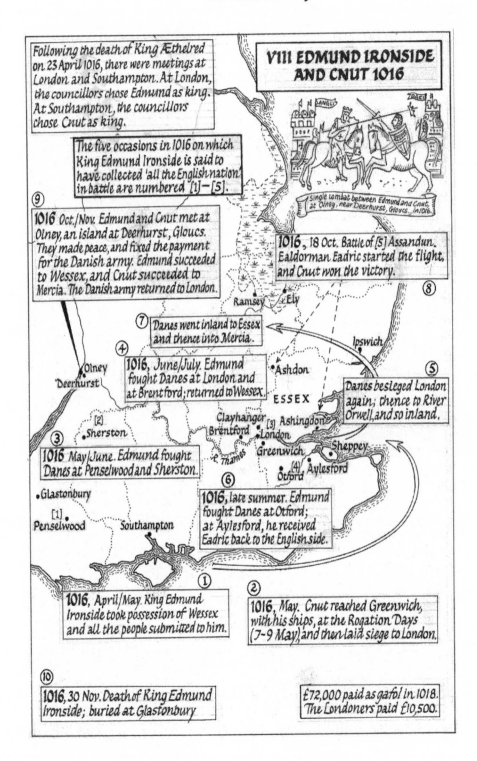

VIII EDMUND IRONSIDE AND CNUT 1016

Following the death of King Æthelred on 23 April 1016, there were meetings at London and Southampton. At London, the councillors chose Edmund as king. At Southampton, the councillors chose Cnut as king.

The five occasions in 1016 on which King Edmund Ironside is said to have collected 'all the English nation' in battle are numbered [1]—[5].

⑨ 1016 Oct./Nov. Edmund and Cnut met at Olney, an island at Deerhurst, Gloucs. They made peace, and fixed the payment for the Danish army. Edmund succeeded to Wessex, and Cnut succeeded to Mercia. The Danish army returned to London.

Single combat between Edmund and Cnut, at Olney, near Deerhurst, Gloucs, in 1016.

1016, 18 Oct. Battle of [5] Assandun. Ealdorman Eadric started the flight, and Cnut won the victory.

⑧

⑦ Danes went inland to Essex and thence into Mercia.

④ 1016, June/July. Edmund fought Danes at London and at Brentford; returned to Wessex.

⑤ Danes besieged London again; thence to River Orwell, and so inland.

③ 1016 May/June. Edmund fought Danes at Penselwood and Sherston.

⑥ 1016, late summer. Edmund fought Danes at Otford; at Aylesford, he received Eadric back to the English side.

① 1016, April/May. King Edmund Ironside took possession of Wessex and all the people submitted to him.

② 1016, May. Cnut reached Greenwich, with his ships, at the Rogation Days (7-9 May) and then laid siege to London.

⑩ 1016, 30 Nov. Death of King Edmund Ironside; buried at Glastonbury

£72,000 paid as gafol in 1018. The Londoners paid £10,500.

Ramsey · Ely · Ipswich · Ashdon · ESSEX · Clayhanger · Brentford · Ashingdon · London · Greenwich · Sheppey · Otford · Aylesford · Thames · Olney · Deerhurst · [2] Sherston · Glastonbury · [1] Penselwood · Southampton

Sources And Acknowledgements

This is not intended to be a scholarly and exhaustive list of any and all substantive works on the period in question, but it tries to give some credit for the historic content that forms the skeleton of this novel.

The most helpful source for information relating to the Viking Conquest involving Sweyn, Cnut, and Eadric is Frank Stenton's old and reliable history, *Anglo-Saxon England*. Last edited about fifty years ago, it remains one of the best texts dealing with this period.

There are a number of recent articles which were extremely helpful. David McDermott's *Edmund Ironside and the Battle of Sherston* on academia.edu is informative.

Also, Tony Sharp's *The Danish Attacks on London and Southwark in '1016'* on academia.edu provides some extremely interesting theories about Cnut's attacks on London.

The Political Writings of Archbishop Wulfstan of York by Andrew Rabin, again available on academia.edu, is an excellent summary of that cleric's works, and in some cases, his imperfections.

A standard reference for clothing during this period is *Dress in Anglo-Saxon England* by Gale R. Owen-Crocker.

I would recommend *The Year 1000: What Life Was Like at the Turn of the First Millennium* by Robert Lacey and Danny Danziger. There is some fascinating information and historical anecdotes.

Julian D. Richards' *Viking Age England* is a recent overview of the two cultures in conflict in England during the period in question.

Another good reference on the Anglo-Saxon side of things is James Campbell's *The Anglo-Saxons*.

The riddle about the onion told by Thorkell the Tall can be found in *The Anglo Saxon World--An Anthology* edited by Kevin Crossley-Holland.

Finally, The Online Medieval & Classical Library provides a modern translation of the *Anglo-Saxon Chronicle*, which is very important as a primary source.

Let me again thank the Department of Anglo-Saxon, Norse, and Celtic of the University of Cambridge for providing high resolution files of the maps drawn by the late Reginald Piggott.

A number of people were extremely valuable resources and editorial contributors for the book. My wife Mardell was an extremely important part of the editorial process. Our two sons Scott and John read and commented on the text and helped me to make important corrections. Tom Valentin, my former department chairman, gave me encouragement when I really needed it. James L. Nelson, author of five volumes of his fictional *Northmen Saga*, took time from his writing to give me some important information and suggestions. I am grateful to him for his high expectations. The illustration for the front and back covers comes from Algol/shutterstock.com. Finally, Rachel Bostwick arranged the covers for the book, formatted the text, and created the map at the beginning of the story.

THE MORE THINGS CHANGE...

England in the year 1000, at the turn of the millennium, was a society divided. The majority of its residents were people of one culture, but a sizeable minority tended to see the world in a very different way. Hate crimes were common, and some religious figures talked about the end of the world. Finally, there were groups of foreigners who intended to wreak havoc on the general population, and some residents were blamed for the violence of those outsiders.

The terrorists were Vikings, and the attacks had been ongoing for two hundred years. The long-established residents were Anglo-Saxon, but many thousands of people with Scandinavian roots had established lives there, some families having had homes in England for over a century.

A young man named Eadric, coming from an insignificant family in the woodlands of Mercia, became a powerful political figure in English society. King Aethelred II named him ealdorman or earl, and he married the king's daughter. However, he ultimately turned against the king and the royal family in favor of a Danish Viking.

This story provides a plausible explanation for an infamous betrayal.

With Eadric And The Wolves, David Mullaly puts his considerable knowledge of all aspects of Viking-age England to good use, crafting a story that is both historically accurate and thoroughly engaging.
~ James L. Nelson, Author of The Northmen Saga

David K. Mullaly received two degrees in English from Penn State, did doctoral work at Northwestern University, and he served for over thirty years as a high school teacher. For more than a decade he bought and sold Viking artifacts, and the required historical research helped to prepare him for this novel. He has published short essays about ancient Viking artifacts on Academia.edu.

ISBN 9781544126531

90000

9 781544 126531